P9-CEU-884

These Vicious Masks

TARUN SHANKER
KELLY ZEKAS

Swoon Reads

SWOON READS | NEW YORK

A Swoon Reads Book
An Imprint of Feiwel and Friends

Our books may be purchased in bulk for promotional, educational, or business use. Please contact your local bookseller or the Macmillan Corporate and Premium Sales Department at (800) 221-7945 ext. 5442 or by e-mail at MacmillanSpecialMarkets@macmillan.com.

Library of Congress Cataloging-in-Publication Data is available.
ISBN 978-1-250-07389-1 (trade paperback) / ISBN 978-1-250-07802-5 (ebook)

Book design by Liz Dresner

First Edition—2016

10 9 8 7 6 5 4 3 2 1

swoonreads.com

One

DEATH. THIS CARRIAGE was taking me straight to my death.

"Rose," I said, turning to my younger sister. "In your esteemed medical opinion, is it possible to die of ennui?"

"I . . . can't recall a documented case."

"What about exhaustion? Monotony?"

"That could lead to madness," Rose offered.

"And drowning in a sea of suitors? After being pushed in by your mother?"

"It would have to be a lot of suitors."

"Evelyn, this is no time to be so morbid," my mother interrupted, simultaneously poking my father awake. "And it is certainly not suitable conversation for dancing. You must enjoy yourself tonight."

"You're ordering me to enjoy myself?"

"Yes, it's a ball, not a funeral."

A funeral might have been preferable. In fact, there was a long list of things I would rather do than attend tonight's monotonous event: thoroughly clean the stables, travel the Continent, have tea with my mother's ten closest friends, travel the Continent, eat my hat, and—oh, yes, of course—travel the Continent. At this moment, my best friend, Catherine Harding, was undoubtedly watching some fabulous new opera in Vienna with an empty seat by her side, meant for me. But when I had modestly, logically suggested to my mother the importance—no, the necessity—of a young woman seeing the world, expanding her mind, and finding her passion, she remained utterly unconvinced.

"Catherine tells me Vienna has grand balls," I put in.

"This isn't the time to discuss that, either," Mother replied.

"But what if tonight, in my sheltered naïveté, I accept a proposal from a pitiless rogue who takes all my money and confines me to an attic?"

"Then better it happens here than on the Continent."

I bit my tongue, for it was quite useless to argue further. Mother would not be swayed to let me leave the country. Instead, she was determined to see me to every ball in England. But what *was* the point of all this? Was anyone truly satisfied with seeing the same people over and over again, mouthing the same false words, feeling nothing, and saying less? Even my London season felt like I was in a prison, trapped in the same routine of balls, dinners, theaters, and concerts that all seemed to blend together, just like the shallow people in attendance. They were so eager to confine themselves to a role and make the correct impression that they'd forget to have any actual thoughts of their own. How would I ever figure out what exactly it was that I wished to do, stuck here in sleepy Bramhurst?

Gazing out the window, I wondered if I should try very hard to have a horrible time tonight to spite my mother, or if we were still close enough to home that I could just throw myself out the door and roll back down the hill. But since we had left, the light pattering of rain had become an angry barrage, while the lightning flashed and the thunder raised its voice in warning. Hopes for an impassable flood took root within me as our carriage swerved and slowed along the slick, muddy road. Suddenly, it jerked to a dead stop, and I believed my prayers answered until the driver shouted down to my father.

"Sir! There's a carriage stopped up ahead! Reckon they're stuck! It'll be just a moment!"

We lurched forward until we saw the outline of a carriage crookedly tilted halfway off the road. Our driver's voice carried: "Hello there! Can we be of assistance?"

Rose and I crowded to her tiny window and found three drenched men—a driver, a passenger, and a near giant—all attempting to push the vehicle back out of a muddy ditch. They paused upon hearing us, and the large man tipped his hat toward our window, the carriage light illuminating his tanned skin and pale lips.

Their driver wiped his brow with a handkerchief as he approached. "Thank you, sir!" he yelled, panting as he waved us along. "It's quite all right! Get your passengers to their destination! We shall manage—" The rest of his words were sucked up by another growl and crackle of thunder.

Whether it was the man's words or the storm that was convincing, our driver decided not to argue and sent the horses forward. As I turned back, watching the three men fade into the blackness, a flash of lightning unveiled them for one last glimpse, their shapes stark against the bright white rip across the sky. But it wasn't any figure that caught my eye. It was their carriage, which seemed to be *lifted* entirely off the ground by the giant man and heaved onto the road before they were swallowed by the darkness again.

"Did you see that?" I asked Rose.

Her raised brow answered the question, but then it furrowed

as she considered the matter. "Is the fair in town? Perhaps he's one of those strong men we always see advertised."

"But . . . still, to lift an entire carriage by himself?"

"Evelyn," Mother interrupted. "I don't wish to hear another story about hallucinations rendering you too ill to attend—"

"Rose saw it, as well!"

"Oh. Excellent. Then we need not risk the health of any of our footmen to fix that driver's foolish mistake," my mother said, in her infinite kindness.

Our conversation died in the din of the storm, but the unnatural image of those four wheels suspended in the air stayed with me as we rolled up the narrow dirt path to the congested entrance of Feydon Hall. Though there was surely a rational explanation, my nerves were now on edge, making Feydon's familiar details seem sinister. At the crest of the hill, the mansion loomed over the rest of the country, and thick clouds roiled menacingly over the magnificent estate. Cracked stone statues of Hades and Charon welcomed visitors in, while gnarled trees reached out to capture all who dared to veer off the path. Towering gargoyles stretched upward as if to attract an ominous flash of lightning. This was ridiculous. Was my mind so tired of Bramhurst that it was conjuring up these gothic images? This must be how girls go mad: It's the only alternative to boredom.

Shaking the absurd thoughts away, I followed Rose and my parents out of the carriage. Umbrella-wielding footmen led us to the front door and into the bright, breathtaking vestibule that set the tone for the rest of the mansion. Though our home was rather large and well kept, Sir Winston's home of Feydon was still awe-inspiring. Vivid paintings glowed in the gaslight against the dark wood paneling. Lush oriental rugs covered the floor, and the ceiling reached toward the sky, providing room for the second-floor balcony—a place where guests wanting for conversation topics had a steady supply of people below to scrutinize.

Still, in spite of the main hall's enormous size, the waves of fashionable men and women rendered it impossible to navigate. This looked to be by far the biggest ball our small town of Bramhurst had seen in years, which unfortunately meant I didn't have to worry about a sea of suitors, but an ocean. We had not gone three steps when my mother fixed her eyes on a boy frozen in perfect imitation of the bronze statue beside him.

She leaned in confidentially. "Evelyn, see there. The eldest from the Ralstons. I hear they have a lovely collection of stained-glass windows." Ah, yes, just my type: a stiff, prideful lord-to-be with impeccable, cold deportment to prove his perfect breeding.

"Set a date," I declared solemnly with a wave of my hand. "I shall marry him immediately."

Rose choked back her giggle, but Mother was far less amused. "Not this childish behavior again," she said through her teeth, which were still arranged in a polite smile for the guests. "You will give these men more than a second's thought or deeply regret this attitude in a few years' time."

"Yes, when I'm crying next to, God forbid, a plain window," I said with a sigh.

As we slowly made our way inside, my sister caught my arm and flashed me a commiserative smile. Only Rose seemed to understand how unbearable these evenings were for me. If I could just make Mother see that, or annoy her enough, perhaps she would pack me off in frustration. I reaffirmed my plan to show her how joyless a ball could be. For everyone.

She, however, seemed to have her own plan and reinforcements, leading us to Sir Winston at the foot of the grand stairs. With his round face, sizable nose, and wide smile, our host's jovial nature was easily apparent as he greeted his guests. But lurking beneath the surface was a slyness that most people missed; he was a Machiavelli who plotted marriages. Mine, mostly.

"My dear Wyndhams," he greeted, giving me a quick wink. "I'm so glad you could come! I am the picture of health, thanks to you, Miss Rosamund, and of course your sister, Miss Wyndham! You are so very welcome tonight. What a pleasure!"

"The pleasure is ours," I said carefully, wondering what he could be planning—for the man was always planning something.

"Sir, I am simply glad to see you so well recovered. The ball is beautiful." Rose, of course, was all sincerity.

"A wonderful evening, indeed. I am sure you have many new friends gathered here tonight," my mother said, stealthily shifting the subject. "Is there anyone of special acquaintance we should be sure to meet tonight?" They shared a mischievous look.

"Why indeed, Lady Wyndham, I must confess that tonight's ball is a particularly special one. For we are celebrating the arrival of my nephew, Mr. Sebastian Braddock. Sebastian! Come meet the prettiest girls I know, Miss Evelyn Wyndham and Miss Rosamund Wyndham!"

With another wink at me, Sir Winston stepped aside to reveal his nephew behind him. Good Lord. His appearance was nearly a caricature of the dark and brooding hero from every gothic novel. He stood very tall, even more so than my gawky frame, arrogance oozing from every inch of his broad-shouldered form. Alert, hooded eyes scrutinized me fiercely, as if trying to turn my blood cooler. His lips were drawn into a slight frown, presumably a permanent state, while the crease in his brow gave the absurd impression of perpetual deep thought. With a gloved hand he brushed away a strand of mussed, straight black hair to afford us a better view of his captivating face. I felt sure he knew exactly the effect this would have on most young women.

Most.

Standing as far from us as was possibly acceptable, he shifted awkwardly, eyes held on Rose, and murmured, "Good evening."

"Welcome to Bramhurst, Mr. Braddock," my mother said, taking charge. "I hope you are finding the country agreeable."

"It is . . . yes," he said, still looking keenly at Rose. My sister is quite pretty indeed, but this felt like something else. "I have heard much about you. I—I hope to see Miss Rosamund's . . . *miracles* myself." His eyes burned bright as he put on a strange sort of grimace that I could only assume was an attempt at a smile. Was he mocking her nursing expertise?

Eager for us to be further acquainted, Sir Winston stepped in to hurry the process along. "Sebastian, why don't you accompany Miss Wyndham and Miss Rosamund into the ballroom, and Miss Rosamund can tell you all about how she saved your dear old unc—What? Don't be shy, boy, give her your arm." Sir Winston gestured to Rose, who was closer to his nephew.

Mr. Braddock took a step back, his eyes flickering between all of us. "My apologies. . . . Perhaps they—you—uh—can find your own way in?"

He gave Rose a stilted bow and whirled away with nary a good-bye. We watched in stunned silence as he attempted to escape the main entrance hall, his initial route into the dining room too slow-moving and his alternative into the obstructed ballroom even worse. On his third try, he crossed back to the other side without meeting our eyes and finally disappeared into the game room.

"Ah, my nephew," Sir Winston said. "You will have to accept my apologies—"

Rose jumped in to save the floundering man. "Sir Winston, do not trouble yourself. He must keenly feel the pressure of meeting your many friends. I assure you, we are not offended."

Sir Winston relaxed at her kind words. "As usual, Miss Rosamund, you see straight to the heart of the matter. He is quite overwhelmed. I hope Miss Wyndham will also give him the benefit of the doubt!" Sir Winston beamed hopefully at me, and Mother's gaze cast a hot warning.

"Of course, I understand," I said. I believe it even came out sounding somewhat sincere.

With yet another wink, Sir Winston bade us a good evening and steered my father toward the smoking room. I let out a quiet snort that only Rose could hear.

"My, my, what an attractive, eligible young man," my mother proudly declared, ignoring my dropped jaw. "A bit odd and mysterious, yes? I know that's very popular these days. Mr. Sebastian Braddock—I shall have to ask about his parents."

"Mother, are you really trying to marry me off to the man who just snubbed your youngest and ran off in order to appeal to fashion?"

"It was not on purpose, Ev," Rose said. "He must have been anxious. And even *you* must admit he is extremely handsome. And tall."

"As handsome as he may or may not be, he couldn't simply walk you in like a gentleman?"

Mother glowered at me in an unwitting imitation of Mr. Braddock. "Perhaps he was running from my daughter, who could not make the slightest effort at politeness."

"There is a troubling Byronic trend you will see next year, Rose, where these men try to appear mysterious and brooding without

one true emotion among the lot of them. It will be nothing but exasperating," I explained.

"Surely it cannot be as exasperating as your complaints about them," my mother snapped, turning on her heels and all but dragging us into the crush.

The night already felt like an eternity. Yet deeper in we ventured. My mother's punishment meant deliberately passing the dining room, where the waft of fresh breads and pastries could tickle and taunt my nose before we closed in on a bright waltz tune. If there were a tenth circle of hell, it would most definitely be a country ballroom.

The crowd bulged to the edge of the white marble dance floor, and a flurry of twirling dresses revolved around the center. All eyes fell on Rose when she floated in: The orchestra struggled to concentrate on their unremarkable tune, and a man accidentally stepped on his partner's foot, while she withheld the yelp for propriety's sake. Sometimes I wondered if I simply imagined the effect my sister had on a room, but here it was undeniable. It isn't just her fair curls and bright blue eyes that draw attention; Rose has something indefinably wonderful about her—a coat of goodness she is unable to shed.

As a result, a mass of charmed suitors seemed to slink across the room to Rose. Mother, meanwhile, greeted several friends and fell deep into such giddy conversations about bachelors, one would think they were just out of finishing school. I could see her starting to arrange dances for us, but fortunately, a welcome sight intervened. He bowed before us, dropping his head full of silken brown hair and rising up with his face wreathed in an ever-present smile. Our dearest, oldest friend, Robert Elliot.

"Evelyn, Rose, good evening to you. You're looking quite lovely tonight." His brown eyes never left Rose as he spoke.

In fact, his eyes had not left Rose much in his eighteen years. Living on a neighboring estate, Robert had been our constant companion since childhood, suffering through many a doll's tea party and game of hide-and-seek. He grew into a kind, affable man, if slightly earnest. Not the man for me, but . . .

"Thank you, Robert," Rose replied. "A lovely evening indeed."

My sister never mentioned her feelings for Robert, but the attachment between them had always been obvious. Even when we were children, I often felt as if I were sneaking into their secret society without an invitation. I wondered whether tonight would be the night he finally made his intentions clear.

"It *really* is a lovely evening, isn't it?" Robert continued with far more passion than the topic called for.

I glanced at Robert, who looked at Rose, who looked back at Robert. Well, odd one out, then. Maybe he would propose if I disappeared.

"Oh look! Upholstery," I declared, feigning fascination with a side chair in the corner of the room. "I will be right back."

Creeping toward the chair, I looked around to be sure no one was paying me any mind. Then, ever so subtly, I slid behind a large green plant. Good. A place safe from dancing, where I could make sure Rose and Robert's romance flourished. The two were a good match, even if Robert was a little wanting in confidence. They were never at a loss for conversation, and when they got into the thick of things, Robert would actually relax, looking as if he were at home by a soothing fire instead of standing right in the center of a blazing one.

I gave a small, quiet cheer as he worked up the momentum to ask her for a dance, and her eyes lit as she nodded yes. Or at the least, I supposed she did. A large leaf was currently obscuring a quarter of the scene. She took his hand, while many disappointed faces watched her glide into the center of the room for the next song.

I sighed and patted the plant. Healthy, green, and stout as it might be, it was not the best company. If only Catherine weren't galloping across Moroccan plains or attending a risqué Parisian salon. My only other choice was to rejoin my mother and listen to fascinating facts about every eligible man passing by. (Apparently, Mr. Egbert collects gentleman's bootlaces! The wonder of it all.)

I peered glumly through the foliage at Rose and Robert, twirling on the dance floor. They seemed marvelously happy, and I had to question my own dissatisfaction. Was I simply too disagreeable, as Mother claimed? Would I grow just as bored of the Continent? And why was there a giant man staring through the window?

Him. The one who had lifted the carriage. I hastened toward the wall, maneuvering around conversations to afford myself a better angle, but when I reached the next window, he was nowhere to be seen. Nothing outside but night falling over Sir Winston's estate. I didn't know whether I wanted it to be him or my boredom manifesting itself as madness again. Hoping for any sort of answer, I spun back around for the first window and collided directly with a sleek black suit, and the gentleman in it.

"Dear me. I had no idea my absence would cause such distress."

Pulling back, I could see he also carried a surprisingly unspilled wineglass, despite the collision. He was just my height, but the confident way he held his square chin made him seem taller. Yes, it was certainly him. Mr. Nicholas Kent.

"What on earth are you doing here?" The question left my lips before I could decide if it was too blunt.

"I wanted to see the reaction my arrival would get, and I must say, it did not disappoint," he said with a smile.

I couldn't suppress the jolt of pleasure. Mr. Kent was one of the few people who managed to make these social functions tolerable. I hadn't expected him to make the trip all the way to Bramhurst. My plan to find no enjoyment in the evening was suddenly in danger of failing. "You've come all the way from London just for a joke, then?" I asked. "I guess I shouldn't be surprised."

"No, no, my reason is of much greater importance. The entire city is in chaos. Buildings collapsing, streets flooding, the population plague-stricken, the Thames ablaze. But it was when an orphan boy I rescued from the rubble asked me, with his dying breath, 'Why did this all have to happen, sir? Why did Miss Wyndham leave?' that I solemnly promised to bring you back and restore peace."

"You must have spent quite some time on your long train ride thinking that up."

"Not exactly. The greater part was spent forming and rehearsing a plan of convincing you to dance with me."

"Oh, I cannot wait for this. Let's have it."

He turned around, drained his drink, took an exaggerated breath, and then whirled back, eyes filled with false surprise to find me still here. "Ah, Miss Wyndham, hello, would you like to dance?"

"No, not really."

"Hmm. Then let me ask you this: If someone went through the trouble to compose you a letter and you were to receive it in front of them, would you callously toss it out without reading?"

I shook my head, playing along. "No, of course not, that would be shockingly rude."

He set his empty glass on a passing footman's tray. "Then is that not the same impolite behavior as refusing to dance to this beautiful music that was composed and is now being performed expressly for your waltzing pleasure?"

"There are plenty of dancers. I can't possibly be offending anyone."

"What about my coming all this way?"

"So you're offended?"

"Incredibly. If you refuse, I'll be forced to dance alone," he said, holding up his arms as if he were leading an invisible partner. "It will be dreadfully embarrassing, and it will be your fault."

I snorted. "Threats are only going to make me refuse you more."

His hands dropped to his side, and he let out a sigh. "Very well. What would you do if you could do anything at this ball?"

"I'd eat cake."

"Unless you eat upwards of two hundred cakes, that particular activity will not occupy your entire night."

My mind shuffled through all the possibilities—cards, suitors, copious amounts of wine—but nothing appealed. This was exactly why I avoided every ball I could.

"I don't know," I admitted.

"Then I present you with two choices. We stand here, observing our dull surroundings, racking our minds for ideas. Or," he said, putting his hand out, "we do our thinking while spinning in circles and forgetting where we are."

"As persuasive an argument as any," I said, surrendering my hand. He clasped it for an inordinate length of time before putting it on his arm, and I didn't mind where he led me. As we moved toward the dance floor, a new song hummed to life, and Mr. Kent, unable to restrain his smile, pulled me into a waltz.

With gentle pressure on my waist, he guided me in slow circles, weaving us through the dizzying stream of couples, our every step and turn on point with the beat. My head felt light, almost giddy with the rush of motion. His light brown eyes met mine, and they seemed to dance along with us.

"You were right, this is absolutely dismal," he said.

"Don't be so quick to judge," I replied. "Here comes the exciting part, where we continue to twirl in the exact same manner as before."

Mr. Kent scoffed. "Would you like to reverse our direction? Knock a few couples down?"

"But then there'll be nowhere to dance, with bodies all over the floor."

"My God, you are impossible to please."

As we bounced to the swells and dips, the room and its crowd revolved with us. Poor Rose whirled by in a flash of silks as another infatuated dance partner tried desperately to win her approval with his footwork. Robert stood idly on the side, eagerly awaiting his next turn with her. Mother, breaking away from her group of matchmakers, made her way along the outskirts of the room. And Mr. Braddock stood determinedly by himself, a slight space between him and a gaggle of giggling schoolgirls. He seemed to be directly in my mother's path. Or even worse, her destination.

"I've changed my mind," I told Mr. Kent. "We're dancing forever now."

"Ah, that'll be a difficult life, but very well, I will let no other claim you."

"Good, for I can see my mother getting ready to arrange a dance with Mr. Braddock."

"I see." Something lit behind his eyes as they landed on Mr. Braddock, and I couldn't tell if it was amusement or jealousy. "Would that be the fellow over there? He certainly seems to have gathered a following."

"Indeed, it is." And Mr. Kent was right. It wasn't just my

mother and a few young women. Every mother in the county was eyeing him, fans fluttering and bosoms quivering. Simpering misses subtly pinched their cheeks and smoothed down their hair. How absurd.

A tall, plain girl bravely stepped from the pack and marched toward him. She turned and stared daggers at her companions, who had renewed their giggles. Mr. Braddock scanned the crowd closely, as though looking for someone, but his stiff posture suggested that he knew what a stir his presence had created and wanted to leave immediately.

Mr. Kent and I watched with some delight as the brave girl came up behind him and very impolitely grabbed his arm. By reflex, he wrenched his arm away, but the girl held on as she fell into a paroxysm of coughing. And though Mr. Braddock tried to step away, she managed to climax her performance with a none-too-graceful faint directly onto his person with some well-practiced gasps for breath in his arms.

For his part, Mr. Braddock seemed unequal to the task of dealing with the creature and unceremoniously let her drop to the ground, where it seemed her false swoon became a true one. He hovered above her, shock and guilt lacing his features. The ballroom lay deathly still for a brief moment until he wordlessly whirled and dashed straight out of the room, guests hopping out of his path. I looked at Mr. Kent and saw my own puzzlement mirrored on his angular face. Then a small, gloved hand grabbed my own, and Rose pulled me toward the fallen girl.

Two

_____

THE GIRL SHOT up from the divan.

"Whe—what's happened?" she asked. "Why—"

"Slowly, slowly," Rose said, easing her to a comfortable position. "You had quite a fall."

Rose held her fingers on the girl's wrist, taking her pulse. A slight wrinkle appeared between her brows. "Your pulse is still quite fast, Miss—"

"Reid." The girl looked around the drawing room dizzily.

Rose held up her hand. "How many fingers do you count?"

"Three."

"Good. Are you in any pain?"

Miss Reid looked quite distraught still, though that was likely embarrassment. Many guests had trickled into the room to stare. "No, miss."

Rose nodded. "Then there's no reason to be alarmed. You just have a mild fever, and I suspect a day of rest is all you need. I will call on you tomorrow morning to be sure your condition has improved."

Behind us, the crowd murmured their approval. Some even began to clap, which our mother seemed to take as a personal affront to our family. Bursting through the spectators, she called with operatic tones, "Evelyn, Rose, come along. I am sure her family will help her to the carriage."

Rose and I exchanged looks but quietly obeyed. We followed Mother out of the drawing room and into a long, empty corridor, where she stopped and turned her full height upon us like a wrathful Hera.

"Rose, I am ashamed of you. While I expect this stubborn disregard for decorum from your sister, it is an extremely unpleasant shock to see you display yourself in such a way!

"I have allowed you to nurse our friends and neighbors so long as it was modestly, humbly performed as an act of ladylike charity. But to commandeer the room in front of all those eyes, actually ordering men about! I daresay you were excited, and your innate good sense took leave for a moment. It will not happen again. Do I make myself clear?"

"Yes, Mama."

"Thank you, Rose. Evelyn, I expect you to set a better example."

"I'll insist Rose lets her die next ti—"

She interrupted me with her deadliest glare and snapped, "We will return to the ball, and there will be no such spectacle again."

With that, she drew herself up, pasted on a sickening smile, and took our arms. After hauling us back to the bright lights of the ballroom, she immediately called over a nearsighted young lord, who eagerly asked Rose for the next dance. With Mother's attention on them, I escaped unnoticed to the dining room.

I was just filling my plate with far too many desserts when a voice spoke directly into my ear. "Ah! The hero has returned. And found her cake."

I jumped slightly, nearly dropping my precious food on

Mr. Kent's shoes. Beside him stood Robert, glancing around as though Rose might suddenly appear out of a tapestry.

"Yes, I am extremely heroic and wonderful," I declared. "It certainly wasn't my little sister who handled the whole thing beautifully and was then set down by my angry mother."

"Ah," Mr. Kent said lightly, "she was not thrilled that your sister's talents were on display?"

"No," I said, taking a bite of cake, "she was not."

"If it's at all reassuring," said Mr. Kent, "the ballroom is far more preoccupied with Mr. Braddock's sudden departure."

Robert frowned. "Yes. It was rather odd. Perhaps he went to find a doctor?"

"Or he was simply being dramatic," I countered. "Hoping that we would fall all over ourselves, wondering what could have possibly been the matter."

A particularly loud babble of conversation rose, and I turned to see Mr. Braddock entering the dining room as though summoned by our talk. Indeed, a swarm of eager guests converged to speak to him, and he hurried back out of the room in a matter of seconds.

"This entire ball has gone mad," I muttered.

"Why, Evelyn, he seems like the perfect man for you!" Robert teased gently.

"Ha! That mysterious act is a mockery of men who have suffered any real grief or pain."

The slightest gleam appeared in Mr. Kent's eye. "And yet your mother wanted you to dance with him—what *is* she thinking?"

"Oh, she thinks him highly eligible. Though she thinks nearly everyone is suitable as long as they propose soon. But because Mr. Braddock is now in Bramhurst, she's going to pester me about him this whole winter. It's already unbearable."

"I see." Mr. Kent met my gaze before I looked down at my pudding. "Is there anything I might do to help?" All the usual lightness had left his voice.

"No, thank you, Mr. Kent, I simply must wait and hope she'll learn patience," I replied.

He gulped down the last of his wine. "What would make her more patient?"

"If Rose were to finally promise herself to Robert," I blurted out.

I paused for a moment to contemplate. Dear God, did I really just speak those words aloud? No, no, I'd never. But Robert's slack jaw and wide-eyed expression confirmed the truth.

"Miss Wyndham, I'm—I'm sorry. I did not mean to—" Mr. Kent said, looking rather distraught.

"Excuse me," I muttered, thrusting my desserts into his hand and rushing away, deeper into the crowd.

Blast. Blast. Blast! What an idiotic mistake. I didn't even know why I said it. I'd had only one glass of wine! Possibly two. And a half. But it was foolish! Exceedingly! It *was* the truth, but it was not my business at all. Rose. I needed to find Rose and warn her before Robert tried to surprise her with a sudden proposal. This was not the way it should have happened.

Distressed, I wove through bodies, squeezed past fences of guests, and searched for my sister. She wasn't among those finishing the remains of dinner in the dining room. She wasn't dancing in the center of the ballroom, nor was she resting on the side. And she wasn't playing or laughing at the whist tables in the crowded game room. This was ridiculous. A ball with hordes of guests everywhere—half of them in love with her—and she somehow vanishes. Rose should have been in one of these rooms. She was the responsible one. She wouldn't have run off, unchaperoned, to some part of the house that was open to family only.

Twisting down another corridor, I calmed at the sight of her blue satin dress and blond head. But my heart quickly regained its rapid pace when I saw the two men who blocked the path to her, for it was not only the unwelcome Mr. Braddock but also the carriage lifter who had been slinking about outside the house. Fear knotted in my stomach as I gained on the trio.

"Rose!" I called. "What in heaven's—"

My words were drowned out by Mr. Braddock's: "Again, sir, as you were not invited, I must ask you to leave."

The giant studied Mr. Braddock, saying nothing. Behind them, Rose looked pale and uncomfortable, but unharmed.

"Now, sir." Mr. Braddock took a step forward, still not acknowledging my presence behind him. Rage lined his voice with a jagged edge. "I would hate to remove you myself."

It felt dangerous standing in the middle of the hall, directly between him and the giant's potential exit. Nervously, I shuffled to the side. A tense silence followed, and something indecipherable seemed to pass between the two until at last the giant conceded. His expression softened as he turned to Rose. "Thank you for your assistance, Miss Rosamund," he said with a light French accent. "It appears I must be leaving."

"But how might I help further?" she asked, glancing cautiously between the two men.

"I will send a message with my information," he said, giving her a quick bow. As he passed Mr. Braddock, he gave a final nod. "I'm sorry for the intrusion."

Mr. Braddock did not let up. "Leave the way you came in, and do not disturb our guests."

The giant passed me with a great whoosh of air and padded

down the hallway, the wood floor crackling as he disappeared around the corner. The corridor went silent. No drone of the orchestra, no pattering of raindrops, no explanation from Mr. Braddock. He simply glared past me, making sure the uninvited guest departed for good. What on earth happened? Whatever it was, I was getting my sister away from it.

"Rose, we must be going," I said, slipping by Mr. Braddock. "The ball is almost over, and Mother will be searching for us." I pulled my sister by two fingers back toward the ballroom, passing Mr. Braddock and the roiling energy emanating off him. I avoided all eye contact and any reflective wall hangings that might lead to it.

"Miss Rosamund, a word, please. My apologies for that man," he said, following close. "I don't want to bother you, but about your healing, your special power, really—"

My head snapped up. Her *special power*? "Mr. Braddock, that was much more than a single word," I said. "And it is much too late. Good night."

I pulled Rose along, but still the man stalked her, ignoring me entirely. "Please, this is important. Miss Rosamund, you have a rare gift—a miraculous power to heal—and I would be grateful for your assistance. I have a friend in London who is very sick—"

In a fury, I stopped and swung Rose behind me, putting myself between the two. "Rose, go find Mother. I will meet you in a moment."

She pressed my shoulder with concern but made no protest. She headed down the hallway, and Mr. Braddock began to follow until I blocked his path, glaring at him.

"Mr. Braddock. My sister is a talented nurse. I don't know whether you're trying to mock or deceive her with this miraculous *power* nonsense, but I suggest you take your brooding act and odd fixations elsewhere. You and that man have obviously upset her—now leave Rose in peace."

His eyes flashed fire, and I found myself thinking for the briefest moment that Mr. Braddock's behavior might not be an act. He strained a smile. "Your . . . interest is most appreciated, but this matter doesn't concern you."

He attempted to brush by me, but I sidestepped with him and drew myself up, annoyed to see that he was one of the few men my height had little effect on.

"Unfortunately, you don't get to decide that."

"Miss Wyndham, I *will* speak to her, with or without your leave."

"Of all the outrageous, presumptuous things to say—" But this time I was the one cut off as he gave a curt bow and turned, striding down the corridor toward the gardens and, I hoped, off a nearby cliff. Good riddance.

Exhausted from the whole horrible evening, I hurried back to find Rose before Robert could. Somehow, I managed to grab her, then hurried Mother and Father along to the carriage with no more than a hasty good-bye to a poor, perspiring Robert, who no doubt desired a tête-à-tête with his newly confirmed love.

During the ride home, I clutched Rose's hand, considering the feasibility of never letting go, to keep her from danger, particularly the odious Mr. Braddock. I tried to put him out of my mind. He didn't even deserve the thought. He *will* speak to her, he says! The nerve. I shouldn't have even responded to him. A man that eager for attention needs to be avoided, ignored. He was sorely mistaken if he thought I would let my sister near his pretense and folly. While I contemplated murder, Mother listed off the evening's many eligible men, "especially Mr. Braddock," she fluted, eyes digging into me.

A hand squeeze and an inquisitive look from Rose brought my mistake with Robert back to mind. What a mess this evening had turned out to be. I gave her a halfhearted smile, and she nodded. We both knew there was much to discuss. After bidding good night to our parents, I changed into my nightgown and sneaked back downstairs like a recalcitrant child.

Rose entered the musty library moments after me, but before I could ask what the large man and Mr. Braddock had been about, she spoke with a melancholy sigh. "Oh, Evelyn! The poor man, Felix Cheval, just wanted my help!"

"The giant?"

"He was looking for me! Apparently, talk of my nursing reached him all the way in London," she said, blushing and pacing about the room. I couldn't help but feel a rush of pride for my talented sister. "He has a sick sister in town. He has spoken to many doctors and is quite desperate."

"Enough to sneak into a ball, it seems. But how did Mr. Braddock get involved? They certainly seemed to know each other."

Rose nodded. "Indeed. Mr. Cheval found me as I paused from dancing, and asked to speak to me somewhere quieter. We were having a perfectly comfortable conversation until Mr. Braddock stormed in and ordered him out of the house, as you heard. They must have some kind of acquaintance."

Given that they seemed to be at odds with each other, I briefly found myself trying to choose a side. Mr. Cheval was simply an exceptionally large man with a sick sister, while Mr. Braddock, on the other hand, was rude, overbearing, and maddening. But they'd both been doing strange things throughout the evening. I shook away the thoughts. What mattered was Rose's peace of mind.

"You aren't responsible for anything," I assured her, settling into the nearby window seat. "There are plenty of other doctors out there for the case. It's not as if you're actively hurting his sister."

"But what if I am the only one who can help? And someone has to tell this girl, as she lies there dying, that the person who might have saved her could not make it because she has a family's reputation to uphold?"

"Rose, that's *highly* unlikely. And your reputation won't even be an issue soon—future matters shall be a bit easier."

She tilted her head and squinted her eyes.

"Robert would be rather understanding. . . ." I added.

Her lips pursed. She still had no idea what I was talking about.

"And I may have told him tonight that I assumed you would marry him, which is actually an ideal—"

"Evelyn! You didn't!" she exclaimed, stiffening.

"I'm afraid I did. I'm sorry, I wasn't thinking and it just came out that I hoped you and Robert would be married shortly."

"But he's like a brother to me—to us. Where—how did you even get the idea I have feelings for him?"

It was my turn to be confused. I didn't even know where to begin that list. "The endless hours you two spend together. The glances you give each other. Whenever we have a dinner party, you prefer his company over anyone else's," I insisted.

"You sound like Mother now," she said, slightly impatient. "None of that means I want to marry him. I don't wish to marry him—or any man, for that matter!"

I was the worst sister. I considered self-defenestration.

"I always assumed you were teasing when you spoke about Robert in that way," she continued.

I sank back against the window's drapes miserably. "And I always assumed there was an understanding."

She frowned and paced before finally settling down on one

spot on the rug. "Well, I will simply have to tell him you were mistaken."

"The man has been in love with you ever since I can remember," I pointed out lightly. "It's not like declining an invitation to a picnic. You have to be careful how you say it."

She glanced over at Father's desk and sighed. "Yes, I'll have to prepare something so I don't say the wrong thing—"

"I'm so sorry to have to put you in this position. I can help you—"

"No, don't be, it's quite all right. If he really is in love with me, we would have had the discussion at some point," she insisted. "I'm glad you brought up the matter. I simply don't want to hurt him."

Poor Robert. He'll be devastated. I tried not to think of the horrid poems that would spill from his fevered brain.

"But I cannot allow marriage to impede my work," Rose said, standing up with new resolve. "I must become a doctor. I must study in London so I can help people like Mr. Cheval.

"If I settle this with Robert tomorrow morning, I should also speak to Mother. I cannot allow her to interfere with my nursing as she did this evening. I didn't protest her restrictions when she made them—I was happy to be treating any patients. But lately, I've been reading Mr. Darwin's journals, and, well, he was only able to learn by traveling and venturing to a new place. That was how he formulated his brilliant ideas."

Rose spun Father's globe with a great push as if she wanted to leave at that very moment. Her words came out with a speed to match it as she explained all the difficulties that female doctors encountered in trying to get an education, take the certification test, and find a place to practice. "Oh, I wish I could do the same!" she said. "There are too many sick and poor all over the world and not nearly enough doctors to help. If only Mother would allow me."

"You have a better chance of persuading her than anyone else," I said. "Besides, what is one more mad daughter to her?"

"I should thank you for going mad first, for it makes me look rather sane," Rose replied with a laugh.

I unfolded my legs to let them dangle, but my feet kept hitting the floor. It took everything within me to refrain from complaining about my own situation. At least Rose had her passion. She knew her precise goals and the obstacles standing in her way. It was a difficult path, no doubt, but it was still a path, and that was enviable. I could not be a doctor like her, and I had no desire to run a household like my mother. What else was there to do? And how would I ever find out if Mother refused to let me see more of the world?

"Ev, you'll figure it out," Rose said, sitting down by my side. She saw through me with her piercing eyes, guessing exactly what bothered me. "There's still plenty of time. And Mr. Kent is quite understanding."

"What do you mean?"

Rose giggled. "That man is in love with you. And he would certainly be a wonderful companion in your world travels!" Something hot ran through me, starting at the crown of my head.

"I can't imagine Mr. Kent ever marrying. That's why I thought we got along so well."

"Well, if anyone can convince him, it's you."

Mother had always argued that there was more freedom during marriage than before. But I had never considered that an actual possibility until this moment.

Rose smiled mischievously. "It looks like we both have a lot of thinking to do, men to turn down . . . or not turn down."

"Indeed, it is exhausting being so in demand, is it not?" I asked archly.

"Speaking of which, I think it's bedtime. I can barely stand after all that dancing."

A yawn took over my mouth. "And all that hiding from dancing has exhausted me."

We clambered upstairs by the faint light of a nearly melted candle. Outside her bedroom, Rose came to an abrupt stop and enveloped me in a hug. "Thank you. Just talking about this makes me already feel better—freer even."

"I shall declare your love to men at every ball, then."

She snorted. "I look forward to it."

"Good night," I said, muffling the words into a kiss on her forehead. "Wake me up before you do anything tomorrow."

"Of course."

I started down the dim hall, and Rose's voice followed me, soothing like a summer breeze.

"Ev, whatever you decide, I'll help, too. Mother will be unable to refuse us both."

Those simple words reassured me more than anything else could have. An involuntary smile crossed my face, and I felt a bit lighter myself. "Thank you, Rose."

With a wave, she slipped into her room and closed the door behind her. For a moment, I stood in the dark, cozily silent hall—the candle flickering, my toes sinking into the soft rug—and I appreciated the present. No restlessness about the future bubbling up inside to keep me awake all night—just simple contentment.

The only lingering question in my mind was whether there had been some sort of mix-up with our births. Rose was far better at playing the older sister than I could ever hope to be. As I climbed into bed and drifted off, I promised myself that tomorrow I would be the best sister the world had ever seen.

Three

I WAS FLOATING on the Nile River under madly swirling clouds obscuring the pale pink sky, when a familiar, female voice sputtered through my dream.

"Mis . . . Wyn . . . am!"

I turned in the bath-warm water, struggling to see who it was. No sign of life on the riverbank, besides the prowling lions.

"Miss Wyndham!" it shouted, and a wave of realization shuddered through me. That voice. That stern reprimand. I'd heard it countless times from my former teacher and governess, Miss Grey.

"Ca—yo—hear m—?" her voice called out. My head absently nodded to my disembodied teacher's question. I stared around the dreamscape wildly, wondering why I was still asleep and not jolting awake with fear.

I endeavored to speak, but no matter how I tried, all that came out was a strangled moan. How—where, no—*what* was she?

"Yo—mus—list—" A pale face framed with wild hair formed in the clouds high above the river, her words sparking with urgency. Bewildered, I struggled to make sense of her mashed-together sentences, rearranging and testing out the sputtered half words. But even when the same sounds seemed to repeat in her desperate warnings, they remained impossible to fit together. Only one intelligible sentence stood out from the mess.

"Do not trust him—protect Rose."

"Who? Who can't I trust?" I tried to ask. But nothing came out. The river lapped against my shoulders as I shut my eyes and desperately tried to wake up, wake up, wake up!

But all I could do was lie rigid and paralyzed in the water, staring up at the rapidly changing clouds with her words resounding in my head.

"Do not trust him—protect Rose."

"Do not trust him—protect Rose."

I lay for ages in a horrible half-state, knowing I was dreaming but unable to wake from the horrid nightmare.

Until a scream, one not in my head, pierced the air.

Four

I FLEW UP and awakened, senses adjusting to the diffused sunlight, the smell of burned tallow, the sounds echoing across the house. The cries had not stopped.

When I scrambled out of bed and stepped into the hallway, a folded sheet of paper rustled under my foot. I snatched it up, but another loud yell sent me running into Rose's room, where Mother and two maids stood, hands clasped to their mouths in shock. Chills crawled down my back.

"What happened?" I asked.

No reply.

Rose was nowhere to be seen, and her room had the strange appearance of a hasty departure. Her bedsheets had spilled onto the floor, her dresser drawers were left open, and her wardrobe was half empty. A sizable number of her dresses were gone, but the selection made little sense. Her favorite green silk and other well-loved dresses were left behind, but some of the older, unfashionable ones were missing. Kneeling by her trunk, I flung open the lid. Her familiar medicine bag, meticulously packed away, stared up at me.

"Where is she?" No response again. My pulse jumped

forward. Something was horribly, horribly wrong. "What is all of this?"

"I don't know, Evelyn!" my mother finally erupted, pacing the room with her hand at her breast, as though trying to keep her heart in place. Her wide eyes scanned the floor. She bit her lip and cleared her throat. "No one has seen her this morning."

"And in the night?"

"Please. I must think."

My fists clenched, and the forgotten paper crinkled in my hand. A letter. The writing looked haphazard and rushed, but it was undoubtedly Rose's hand:

Evie—

I must apologize for my abrupt and secretive departure, but I felt it necessary for my own sake. A true good-bye would have been far too much to handle, and I fear I would never have gone through with it had we spoken.

I have decided to travel to London to provide care for Mr. Cheval's sister. I find that I cannot deny someone in need of my help, and if I do not take this request, I can never trust myself to do something of the slightest inconvenience to me in the future. I know I had planned to speak with Mother about the matter, but what you said is true—I am the last person who can persuade her. I know this request would not stand a chance.

I hope you understand my reasons and I will write to you immediately upon my arrival.

Rosie

"Mother," I said, handing her the letter with shaking fingers, "it's her hand—but this isn't her. This isn't Rose."

She drew in a sharp breath, her eyes scanning the document. "Heavens." The word escaped her lips unnoticed. Leaning against the wallpaper, she looked trapped by a congested tangle of flowers and vines growing around her. Gradually, though, the lines on her forehead smoothed, and her distress changed to her usual, if more strained, self-command. "Your sister has put us in a difficult situation."

"Mother, Rose would not write such a letter! This was written under duress—someone forced her to do it!"

"Stop it," she snapped, belying her composure. She drummed her fingers against her neck, where I could see the slightest tick of her heartbeat. "This is serious. Stay calm, and I will speak with your father to decide what must be done." She ordered the maids to clean up the mess and hurried out, folding the letter over and over.

I stared around the room blankly. I had told Rose that she was the only one who *could* persuade Mother—quite the opposite of what she'd written. And the names! Never had we used *Evie* or *Rosie* as nicknames or even as jokes. Rose would never have written a good-bye letter like that.

My hand flew to my mouth as I struggled not to heave.

"Do not trust him—protect Rose."

I failed her. Somehow I dreamed of the danger last night but remained asleep like a useless lump. It was entirely my fault.

Our maid Lucy cleared her throat by the door. "Miss Wyndham, your mother asked me to help dress you for church."

My guilt shifted very quickly to anger. Rose was kidnapped, and they wanted to go to church? Mechanically, I marched to my room and dressed, not knowing where Lucy put my nightgown or how she laced me into my corset with shaking fingers. My mind thought of nothing but Rose. Mother would not listen until I found some kind of evidence, and with two men showing entirely too much interest in my sister last night, I had my suspicions about which of them might be able to provide it. And he would be attending church with his uncle.

"For the time being, we will tell anyone who asks that Rosamund is visiting my sister in London," my mother informed me as the carriage took us into town for church.

Father nodded along in approval. "We will have to wait for her next letter. Then we'll send someone to retrieve her."

I refrained from saying anything and seethed silently, raging at both Mr. Cheval and Mr. Braddock. The carriage groaned to a stop outside the church, and as the small crowd of our neighbors meandered inside, I saw a solitary dark head lingering in the shadows. Of course he was in the shadows.

"Oh look, Mother, there's Mr. Braddock. I would so like to speak to him again!" I said as I climbed out.

Mother looked at me suspiciously. "I thought you didn't like him."

"Oh no, I simply didn't wish to give myself away!" Was a modest look down doing it up too brown? Yes, probably.

"Is it really the time for this, Evelyn?"

"It can't hurt to just speak to him, could it?"

My parents were too tired to argue any further and led the way to the church. I pretended to find the sky deeply fascinating until they were safely inside. When the last person shut the door, I marched directly toward Mr. Braddock, and the expression on his face turned stormy when he realized my target.

"Miss Wyndham, are you also angling for a seat in the back?" Dark green eyes judged mine for a brief moment before he bowed slightly.

Without preamble or forethought, the words spilled out. "What is your relationship to the giant?"

He stared at me as though I had grown a few extra heads, and in reviewing the phrasing, perhaps he had reason. "What are you speaking of?" he replied carefully. "What's happened?"

Straightening my back, I pierced him with a cold glare.

"Last evening at the ball—you obviously knew that giant French man, Mr. Cheval. What is the nature of your relationship with him?"

He glared back hard before answering. "I gather you are referring to the man I asked to leave, yes?"

"Of course I'm referring to him. It's rather difficult to confuse him with another."

He bristled and broadened his already considerable shoulders. "I have not been acquainted with him."

"If you were not acquainted, how did you know he was not invited?"

"I did not see my uncle greet him at the door," he said, his voice strung tight and low. "It was obvious he snuck inside."

No. The rage in his face had been deeper than that. I knew in my bones that he wasn't telling me everything.

"I apologize if you mistakenly received the wrong impression," he said curtly, moving away from the stone church wall. "But that was our first meeting."

Liar.

"Is he an acquaintance of your sister?" Mr. Braddock asked, attempting a guileless innocence and failing. "Is she here today?"

I ignored his question and latched onto his mention of my sister. "What is your interest in Rose? Why were you so intent on speaking to her with all that nonsense about her gift?"

Frowning, he spoke slowly to me as though I were a child. "I wished to thank her for helping save my uncle's life last week."

Ha! "You could have easily given her all the thanks and gratitude in one sentence. But you demanded a private word with her. You, sir, wanted to talk to her about her *'powers.'* What could you mean by that?"

His eyes narrowed in annoyance, and his lips twisted into a sardonic smile, a lazy, roguish attitude altering his features in a way intended to make a girl swoon. "Miss Wyndham, I think your problem is one that is common amongst bored country dwellers— you're scrutinizing meaningless details when there's nothing to be found. I simply wished to speak to your lovely, demure sister. Now, I'm sorry, but if there's no other problem, I believe a higher power is calling."

I gaped at the sweeping generalizations and mouthed inarticulately as he passed me with a smirk and a tip of his hat.

Finally, I found my tongue and my feet to follow him to the church steps. "My problem, Oh Lord Byron, is this secretive, mercurial behavior! First you make all sorts of strange, veiled suggestions, then you hide information and lie to me! I *know* you know Mr. Cheval, and you will tell me where he is!"

Confronting him directly on the issue was remarkably refreshing, like puncturing the skin of an orange. Still, he simply ignored me and stormed up the steps, taut as a bent bow. I flew after him like an arrow.

"Why can't you answer a straight question with the truth? Do you believe this brooding masquerade is somehow attractive? Just tell me what you know and stop wasting my time." His back tensed visibly under his jacket as he spoke without turning to me.

"Nothing would give me more pleasure. Except, of course, if you stopped wasting mine."

I felt all shreds of rationality flee my head. "Mr. Braddock!" I half yelled. "Stop at once!" He gave no sign of acknowledgment.

How dare he! Fuming, I flew up the steps behind him, hissing his name to no avail. As his hand closed on the church door, I reached and grabbed his wrist, catching the bare skin between his glove and shirt. At once, a rush of hot blood and some unfamiliar, sublime essence worked itself into my veins. Frissons of stimulation swirled up my arms—peaks and depths, vacuums and floods, compressions and explosions, endless contradictions fitting together like jigsaw-puzzle pieces. I was aware of every distinct, tiny part of my body. A gasp climbed out of my throat as I glowed brighter than the sun had ever shone. And then he wrested his wrist away, our connection severed. I was again normal and alive and existing here on earth, and he was gazing at me with horrified concern, his own breath coming in shallow pants.

"What on earth did you do?" The words left my still-trembling lips without permission.

His expression changed to wonder as he took me in, and his eyes darted to our hands, as though they had suddenly appeared at the ends of our wrists. Indecipherable emotions swam in the depths of those eyes, and his hand hovered up to my face, but with a snap, he pulled it back, afraid to cross some unspoken boundary.

"You . . . you're well?" The words fell softly, reverently from lips that curled into a soft smile. I stood transfixed for a moment before pulling away from him, away from the confusing sensations that warmed my skin.

"Wh-what?" I stuttered, stumbling away.

He followed eagerly, face utterly transformed by a strange zeal. "It must be something—my God!" He cut himself off with a deep, relieved laugh. "Miss Wyndham, you needn't hide it from me. It must have to do with your power."

Just then, the church door opened, and for the first time in my life, I thanked God for the unexpected appearance of my vexed mother.

"Darling," she said, "I am sure you and Mr. Braddock would like to attend church today, yes?"

"I—Mother, I am terribly ill, and I must go home at once," I said. Mr. Braddock drew a few steps back. Mother pinned me with a dark stare but gave a sympathetic sigh for Mr. Braddock's sake.

"How unfortunate. I will see you to the carriage. But please be sure to send it back for your father and myself."

She pulled me away, chastising me for my peasantlike arguing that she could hear from inside the church. Just because Rose was missing, she reminded me, did not give me cause to act like a hoyden. I bit my tongue and agreed, thankful to be left alone. Nestled in the moving carriage, I tried to keep my eyes on the church, my mother, anything, but Mr. Braddock's gaze held mine like a vise until he disappeared behind a rising hill.

I rapped on the roof. "James, we will stay in town. I must stop by the inn." The only way I could remain composed was to concentrate on one problem at a time. If Mr. Braddock wouldn't tell me anything about Mr. Cheval, I would just have to find him myself.

But the trip into town only supported the information in Rose's letter. At the inn, the owner explained that Mr. Cheval had left late the previous night with all his luggage. At the train station, an attendant recalled selling two early-morning London tickets to a large foreigner and his tired female companion.

As we headed back to my parents at church, I fretted, desperately trying to sort it all out. The obvious pieces of evidence supported the letter's veracity, but the little details said otherwise. Rose had planned to speak to Robert and Mother today and sort out all our problems. She did not have cause to lie to me about that and disappear. She would not have packed so strangely, nor written such a confounding good-bye letter. I knew how unlikely and ridiculous an abduction would be, especially in Bramhurst. I knew I sounded like a pliable reader of too many sensational mystery novels. I knew this outlandish conclusion went against everything I normally thought. But I absolutely believed she was taken against her will. I could feel it in my bones.

The problem, however, was no longer convincing myself that she was kidnapped. The problem was convincing my parents to do something about it.

Five

"**A**ND THAT IS why we must travel to London to retrieve Rose."

The parlor fell dead silent. Mother and Father gaped down at me over a wooden table cluttered with tea things. In my short chair, I felt like I was on trial.

I had explained everything to them: the clues in the letter, Rose's strange packing, my inquiries at the inn, the sighting at the train station, and my general conclusions from all the evidence. Too much was amiss for there to be a simple explanation. Surely it would be impossible for them to ignore the signs.

Yet Mother managed to exceed all my expectations. "Your sister has acted somewhat rashly, yes, but she has always shown uncommonly good sense, and we are sure she will do so now by remaining discreet. We have already decided to wait until Rosamund sends word from London."

A spectacularly awful plan. "Mother, I don't believe she is there by choice. We may never get a letter from her."

Both of them gave tight, condescending nods, as if I had con-cocted my own fantastic adventures in wonderland. My mother took a dreadful tone of authority. "It is entirely possible that in her hurry, your sister packed the wrong clothing and miswrote a few words in her note, is it not?"

"No! Of course not. And she wouldn't forget her medicine bag or leave such blatant hints! Don't be daft, Mother."

"I am not the one proposing this wild theory," she said, folding her arms. "What do you even mean for us to do in London?"

"Start a search for her."

She raised her eyebrows skeptically. "And if it turns out she really is helping this man, as she said in the letter, everyone will know she went to work as a doctor. Or worse yet, people will gossip and exaggerate and come to believe it an even bigger scandal. In any case, we cannot walk through the streets shouting her name, telling the police and publicizing this information. I have sent word to your aunt and uncle to give out that Rosamund is with them. If anyone asks to see her, she will be ill or in Bath. That is the way to handle this and preserve her reputation."

"Perhaps we should worry about preserving her safety. Or her life."

She leaned back in her chair. "I'm quite aware how bored you are of Bramhurst, but there's no need to be so melodramatic."

"This is not melodrama! You might trust me for once!"

"Evelyn, I know you. You've gone and gotten this idea stuck in your head, and now you're too stubborn to give it up. But you must consider the whole situation."

"And then do what? Just accept the most pleasing explanation with an utter disregard for any other possibilities?" I gripped the wooden arm of my chair, wishing I could crush it. They were ignoring everything!

My mother rubbed her forehead and glanced at my father, who was busy pouring himself another cup of tea. She changed tactics and spoke in a slow, soothing voice. "We have no other recourse. We're in debt."

What was she doing? Trying to distract me with poor jokes?

But the look of pity did not leave her face. "I hadn't wanted that sort of pressure dictating your marriage, so we decided not to tell you, and I apologize for that."

My mind was a blur. "What—how is that relevant?" I asked.

"There's no money for your dowries. All we have to offer is our reputation, and if word about Rosamund gets out, we'll have nothing."

I took in their grave faces. "How . . . did this even . . . happen?"

My father struggled to look me in the eye. He took a sip of tea and spoke into the cup. "I'm—I'm sorry, Evelyn."

"That's it? That's all you have to say?"

"Please," my mother cut in. "You've been through much today. Perhaps you need some rest."

"*You want me to take a nap?*" I yelled. Hang it all, she was infuriating! I looked to my father, whose eyes were now aimed downward at a Turkish rug. "Father, you actually agree with this?"

"About the nap or—?" He cleared his throat and caught my mother's eye before responding. "Yes, your mother is right. It would be wise to be prudent," he said.

"Ha! Like you were prudent in handling our money?" I asked, rising from my seat. I tried to be respectful, but it had come to this. "Thank you for all the help. I will see you both when I find Rose."

I stormed out of the parlor and bounded up the staircase. My mother's footsteps followed. "You are not going to London!" she called from the foot of the stairs.

"I believe I am."

"No. I won't have you running around there and jeopardizing everything for us."

"Then I won't run around. I'll walk."

She was silent. I never stopped. There was no need to look at her. I knew the expression of suppressed ire well. Just before I slammed my bedroom door shut, her voice rang out once more.

"If you leave this house, do not plan to return!"

Very well. If bearing the Wyndham name meant caring more for the name than the actual people who bore it, I'd rather not be associated with it.

Furious, I rummaged through my closet, unearthed a trunk, and started packing it. I had not planned to leave so abruptly. Now I had to determine everything about my trip in a matter of minutes.

The first issue was lodgings. I would have to try to beat my mother's letter to my aunt and uncle. They would surely take me in, even if I appeared on their doorstep without warning. Once they heard that I had left home without permission . . . well, that was a problem to be dealt with later. After finding Rose.

Within ten minutes, my trunk was packed with an assortment of clothing, some jewelry to sell, and Rose's medicine bag. All that was left to do was ride to the train station. But when I called for our butler, Pretton, to have my trunk sent down and the carriage readied, he met my request with a stony face. "I apologize, Miss Wyndham, but your mother has halted all carriage use."

"Is there a messenger available? I'll hire one from town, then."

His lips tightened. "No messages are to come in or leave without her knowledge."

So she was truly making matters difficult. Well, then. It was close to noon and a three-mile walk to town. I could make it by the afternoon, hire a carriage to take me to the station, and reach London by evening.

Already regretting the amount I'd packed, I slid my trunk down the stairs myself and heaved it out the front door. Slowly but surely, I trudged out of our estate, dragging the great wooden burden and crushing assorted plant life along my path, with no stops to wish good-bye to anyone.

As I passed through meadows and over hills, the house gradually receded into the distance. I took a moment for one last look back, wondering if this would truly be my final glimpse of the place. Had Mother watched me leave? Did she even expect me to go this far? A twinge of guilt for disobeying sparked in my stomach, but I knew it was nothing compared with what I would have felt staying trapped in that prison. Really, I was better off.

Onward I trekked, and my home shrank to a distant speck before disappearing behind the hill. After the first awful hour of the exodus, I stopped to catch my breath on a grassy field and consider how much farther I could realistically walk. It would only get more difficult, and my blind rage was turning into a frustrated self-doubt, which was not as great a source of energy.

While I rested, a low trotting sound slowly rumbled in from the west, and a rider emerged over a distant ridge. The gallops grew louder and closer, and a jolt of dread wriggled through me. It was either someone calling on my family, or the only other nearby estate, Feydon Hall. Oh, please, not Mr. Braddock. I couldn't deal with him now. Anyone but him.

And my wish was granted, but my anxiety was not much abated by the sight of Mr. Kent riding toward me. I had picked possibly the worst spot in England to stop for a rest. Nowhere to hide in this open field. I debated the effectiveness of squeezing inside my trunk, but before I knew it, he was dismounting his horse before me.

"Miss Wyndham, I was just coming to call on you because

I did not like the way our last conversation ended, or the fact that it ended at all. How do you do?"

"Very poorly," I spit out.

"I can see that. I almost mistook you for a packhorse. Why exactly are you doing poorly?"

"Because my sister is missing, in all likelihood kidnapped, and my parents refuse to believe me." Fine. Let's see what the man thinks of the truth.

Mr. Kent's face turned darkly serious. "When did you last see her?"

I am quite sure my eyebrows shot to my hairline. "Last night. You believe me?"

"I can't imagine why I wouldn't."

I sat down hard on my trunk. He smiled slightly before frowning again. "I gather there was nothing strange about the last time you saw her. . . ."

"We said good night and she went to bed. I—well, I had an odd nightmare. And then her room was in shambles this morning, plenty of clothes missing, and—I know this sounds odd—but there's a very strange man in town whom Mr. Braddock seems to know named Mr. Cheval who had snuck into the ball to get Rose's help in London, which is what this good-bye letter Rose wrote also says, but I know it's false—"

Fortunately, Mr. Kent cut me off before I babbled myself into the highest register man had yet to know. "I'm sorry . . . which man is this?"

I took a moment, trying to coherently arrange my thoughts.

"My sister was seen boarding a train to London with a strange man. And I know he forced her. So I am going to bring her back."

"I see. I imagine that trunk has become burdensome. It is still a mile or two away."

"My mother all but threw me out of the house and refused me a carriage. I have no other choice."

Mr. Kent furrowed his brow and tapped his riding crop meditatively against his leg. "And what do you plan to do when you arrive in London?"

"Explain my presence to my aunt and uncle before my mother's letter arrives. Though they will never stand up to her and let me stay if they know that my parents do not wish it."

He paced back and forth in contemplation, the grass swishing against his leather boots. "You believe your sister is in harm's way?"

"Yes."

"And she left a false letter?"

"Yes."

"And your family will not believe you or help you?"

"No, they refuse to bring more attention to it. You know, you are beginning to sound rather like a detective, Mr. Kent."

He turned sharply and exhaled. His eyes were wide as he carefully took my hand. "Not just any detective, my dear Miss Wyndham. I am the greatest detective the world has ever seen. And I will be escorting you to London to find your sister."

Six

THE TRAIN SQUEALED into Victoria Station with a deafening, bouncing finality, an excess of steam hissing out as the bells signaled our arrival. Coughing our way through the smog, we descended the train, found porters to retrieve our luggage, and shoved past the hordes to the exit.

Outside, the greasy London afternoon activity was even more overwhelming. A tall man bumped my shoulder as he rushed by, talking to himself like a madman without diverting his gaze from his gilded pocket watch. A young flower girl wove through the heavy traffic on the sidewalk, singing about the violets for sale in her basket. A fruit seller, looking like a shipwrecked sailor, growled at passing pedestrians. With three and a half million people in London, I could never just happen upon an acquaintance as I did in Bramhurst. That would help me avoid detection, to be sure, but what did it do for my chances of finding Rose?

Ignoring the crowds, Mr. Kent led the way down the sidewalk to fetch a cab. The driver loaded up our trunks, and Mr. Kent provided him the address of his parents' home, while squeezing next to me into the cramped two-seater. It wasn't the most appealing prospect for lodgings, as his stepmother had disliked me from the moment we met and his more amiable merchant father had set sail on one of his vessels, but it was a much simpler solution than my aunt and uncle's. All it took was one message to Mr. Kent's adoring little stepsister, Laura, telling her to pretend that my visit had been long planned, and everything was arranged without arousing suspicion.

Our cab set off down the crowded Victoria Street toward the heart of the city, trundling past drab buildings and gray street corners at an agonizingly slow speed rivaling that of a dying cow. To make the trip even more enjoyable, pungent city scents seeped through the hansom doors—strangely enough also reminding me of a dying cow. Nothing could be done but to put all bovine thoughts out of my mind, ignore the immodestly close proximity of my travel companion, and pray the house was not far.

Fortunately, Mr. Kent, as always, set about distracting me. "So, as the world's greatest detective, I prefer to give my solution last and put all the other proposed ideas to shame. Did you have a plan before I got myself tangled up in this?"

"I did—I mean, I do. You know, you don't have to continue this detective act for my sake. I appreciate your help all the same."

Mr. Kent cocked an eyebrow. "It's not an act. The only reason I've never called myself one before is I didn't want to put the other detectives to shame by association."

"Oh, I see. It all makes sense now," I said, dropping the matter. "I'll keep my inferior idea short, then. Mr. Cheval wants Rose's nursing expertise to help his sick sister. If her illness was tricky enough to make him search for Rose, I'm sure many other London doctors and medical societies were consulted for the case. One of them may know where to find Rose."

He made a noncommittal *hmm*.

"And failing that, I suppose we might inquire at some chemist and druggist shops. Rose will need to replace the medical supplies she left behind, and we've always had a little joke about how linseed oil seems to cure most of our patients. We can start there and compare the contents of her bag with recent purchases at these stores."

Mr. Kent nodded and clicked his tongue, thinking hard before he finally spoke. "You show promise, but allow me to demonstrate what my very real and true detective expertise can achieve."

"What do you suggest?"

"I had this wild idea that we might ask some doctors about recent tricky illnesses, or alternatively, we might check the sales records at chemist and druggist shops."

"Two brilliant ideas. Wherever would I be without you?" I said, trying my best to restrain my smile. Laughing should have been a relief, but it felt wrong, unearned. The warmth shared between us was both confusing and consoling.

After we sailed down another smooth thoroughfare and bumped over a few cobblestone streets, Mr. Kent rapped the roof, and the cab jolted to a stop by a corner.

"I will take a short jaunt around the block. Wouldn't want to give them the idea we traveled together." He paid the driver with a few coins, gave me a parting wink, and hopped out.

A little ways down the road, the cab found an open curb outside the Kents' small but pleasing redbrick townhouse. The horse halted and let out a huff, as if he could barely withstand the city smells himself. The driver handed me out and waited by the cab while I climbed the stairs to the entrance.

The front door opened to reveal the Kents' steward, Tuffins, who greeted me with a pleasant, formal air. "Miss Wyndham, welcome. Shall I send for your luggage?" he asked.

"Yes, thank you, Tuffins. How have you been? I hope I haven't come at a bad time."

"There is never a bad time for your visits," he replied.

As welcoming as I remember. I suspected his fondness for me stemmed from the fact that I was one of the few people who never made a request for "muffins" and snickered at the horrendous rhyme.

A footman dragged my trunk from the cab while Tuffins led me into the main entrance hall. The Kents' home was richly decorated with fine, full carpets, silk drapery, and the typical furnishings, but my attention was seized by the countless family portraits lining the wall as if they were the wallpaper. Images of magnanimous men looking into the distance and stately women folding their hands in their laps repeated endlessly, only with slight changes for fashion over the years. If I ever had any burning questions of whether the Kent family had reputable ancestors, this hallway would hit me over the head with answers. No wonder Mr. Kent had established bachelor's quarters elsewhere in London as soon as he could.

Tuffins ascended the main stairs. "Miss Kent has asked me to bring you upst—"

"Ev-e-lyn!" a voice chirped from the floor above.

I braced myself for the attack as Laura bounded down the stairs. Less fifteen-year-old girl and more pure energy that somehow took a human shape, she had the perpetual look of being about to fly apart at the seams: hair clinging for dear life, loose ribbons ready to untie, stockings half unfurled.

"I got tired of waiting!" she announced, embracing me tightly, her head tucked below my shoulders. She was almost my height, but the way she hugged me suggested she still hadn't quite adjusted to that. "Ooh, I hope you'll stay for a while. It's been so dreadfully boring without you or Nick here! I tried to get Tuffins to hire a French spy or a man with a mysterious sort of scar, but our new footman is neither!"

"Sorry to disappoint, my lady," Tuffins put in, leading us back up the stairs.

"You're quite lucky Miss Wyndham's arrival saved you!" she told him, then turned to gaze at me in her alarming, wide-eyed way. "Nick's message sounded ever so distressing and urgent! What's happ—wait! First, you must surprise everyone!"

"Surprise everyone? Laura—wait, did you even tell your mother I was comi—"

Before I could get in another word, Tuffins gently knocked and opened the drawing room door. "Miss Kent and Miss Wyndham," he announced as Laura pulled me inside to see two unwelcoming faces.

"How unexpected," an acerbic voice spoke first. It belonged to Lady Kent, the grave, small woman sitting on a Chesterfield by the fire. Though she could not have been more than five and forty, her bad back and knees gave her the weary look of a woman thirty years older, and she spoke with the same uncaring bluntness of one. "I did not know you were in town, Miss Wyndham."

"Mama, I meant to surprise you," Laura said, her pert nose scrunching up.

"You know I find surprises vulgar," Lady Kent said, waving her hand dismissively and shifting her gaze to me. "You are acquainted with Miss Madeline Verinder, I presume?"

"Good evening, Miss Verinder," I said, exchanging curtsies with the sweetest, gentlest, most accomplished, and most amiable girl in all of London. At least that is what I had continually repeated to myself the past season, so I wouldn't slap her by sheer reflex whenever she entered my conversations with Mr. Kent and turned them into competitions for his attention.

"A pleasure to see you, Miss Wyndham," Miss Verinder said, with the slightest dip in her sugary twitter of a voice. She must have been eagerly anticipating Mr. Kent's arrival, only to get me instead. "What brings you back to London?"

Fortunately, the train ride had given me ample time to create a sound story. I settled into the chair beside her. "My sister came to visit our dear aunt and uncle, so I thought it a fine opportunity to visit Laura as I had promised her."

"You're staying here, then?" Lady Kent snapped out.

"I—I had hoped to," I replied as humbly as I could, nervous that our flimsy plan would fall through before it was even implemented.

Lady Kent let out a strange, gruff harrumph, which, judging by Laura's giddiness, somehow translated into acquiescence.

But Miss Verinder's rosebud lips curved into a perfect smile and let the thorns loose. "Why, I thought you were in town to nurse one of your patients."

What a lovely and thoughtful girl.

My hands balled up into fists, and I stuffed them into my lap. Refusing to meet Lady Kent's disapproving eyes, I peered at Miss Verinder's and searched for signs of malice. "No, that is only for close acquaintances in Bramhurst," I insisted.

"Lady Wyndham still permits this?" Lady Kent sneered.

"Only as a charitable hobby of ours," I said.

Lady Kent rubbed her aching knees and shook her head. "A hobby is an activity done at one's leisure—an occupation is done at another's. Since nurses are called upon at all times of day, it is by nature an occupation, and a highly inappropriate one at that for two respectable girls."

I bit my tongue, resisting the thousand retorts in my head. I needed to stay in Lady Kent's good graces. With a herculean effort, I managed to even (Rose forgive me) agree with her. "That is true. We've tried to keep it a hobby, but it's rather difficult."

"Impossible, I'd say," she concluded.

An awkward silence settled over the room until Laura attempted to rescue me. "Oh, Mama, can we get Evelyn an invitation to tomorrow's dinner? Don't they need another for the table? It will be such fun! And there's the Lyceum Theatre on Thursday and our dinner party on Friday! She can meet Mr. Edwards. Evelyn, you will absolutely die when you meet him. But remember, please, that I saw him first and you have other—"

"Laura, enough," Lady Kent interrupted, pinching the bridge of her nose, pained by her daughter's enthusiasm.

Miss Verinder tucked a blond curl behind her ear. "Yes, my parents have a box for *Much Ado About Nothing*. Will you join us?"

I wished Laura had let me explain matters before rushing me in here. There was no time to be wasted on dinner parties and plays. "I don't wish to intrude on any plans," I said. "I don't mind missing the play."

"Why, you must come at least this time," Miss Verinder insisted. "I did not see you at the theater much during the season."

Lady Kent scoffed, and the fire seemed to snap in agreement. "In my experience, those who avoid the theater suffer from an excess of drama and scandal in their own lives."

Heavens, was Miss Verinder doing this on purpose? Or was there just no pleasing Lady Kent? I had not been here five minutes, and she was already trying to glare me out of the city.

"We're often most selective when it comes to our favorite things," I returned. "I would so love to come. *Much Ado* is a favorite of mine."

Lady Kent pursed her lips and assessed me as if she were searching a dress for imperfections in the stitching, while Miss Verinder's eyes lit up with delight or deviousness or both. I was bracing myself for the next potential disaster when a miraculous knock on the door interrupted, and in walked my rescuer.

"Nick!" Laura exclaimed, darting across the room to tackle him with a hug. Miss Verinder began smoothing her dress excessively.

"Hello, Kit!" Mr. Kent said with a laugh. He returned the hug and glanced about the room. "Good afternoon, everyone. Ah! Miss Wyndham, you seem to have beaten me here. What is your secret?"

"Taking the earlier train, sir."

"A radical choice," he said, nodding profoundly, "yet elegant in its simplicity."

"That sounds like a code to live by."

"Yes, though I find the best codes are the ones you die by."

"Seeing as I am the only one unaware of Miss Wyndham's visit," Lady Kent interrupted, "we've unfortunately had our tea already. Miss Wyndham, you are hungry, no doubt. Laura, take her to the kitchen and see what they can prepare. Nicholas, please sit."

She rang a bell, and Tuffins promptly appeared at the door to escort us. As Laura and I left the room, Miss Verinder beamed brightly, as if she'd won some pivotal battle. She turned to her spoils. "Welcome back, Mr. Kent. Did you miss London already? I understand Bramhurst can be a bit . . . slow."

"Yes, but that makes it the perfect place to settle down," I heard him say. "Speaking of which, I don't think I've eaten since leaving, myself . . ."

Moments later, he was catching up to us in the dining room.

"Thank you for getting us out," I whispered to him. "I feared that would never end."

"The old bat detests being left out of a conversation. Sometimes when she's summoned me, I've resorted to talking to myself so I might be dismissed."

"Well, if she didn't dislike me already, she absolutely detests me now."

"I'm glad to hear it," he replied. "I could not conceive of a better recommendation of your character."

In between bites of the blissful chicken and potatoes, we took the risk of explaining the crisis to Laura: the shocking events of Rose's disappearance, the precursor of the past day, and my plans for the search with Mr. Kent. She behaved as theatrically as I expected, gasping at each revelation, no matter how minor.

When I finished, she gripped my hand and nearly fell to her knees pledging her help to me. "Evelyn, I promise you, I will stand by you both through this. Tomorrow we will all search together, and then there is the Pickfords' dinner party in the evening! This is far too exciting! I've missed having a confidante to whisper to behind fans."

"Kit, Miss Wyndham is having a difficult time of it, with her sister missing," Mr. Kent said. "She is not here to have fun."

"And I cannot afford the time to attend," I added. "I have to refuse."

"Nonsense! You mustn't! Please, Evelyn? Say you will! I beg of you. And besides, you must at least make an appearance. If not, people will start wondering where you and your sister are, and then someone might question your stories. Oooh! This is ever so tricky and secretive!"

Mr. Kent gave me a sympathetic look. "She does have a point."

I couldn't help but sigh in defeat. Somewhere in her gaspings, Laura had hit upon the hard truth. I had to keep up the pretense as long as possible. Prove to Lady Kent, to society, that the Wyndham family was still intact and its girls still irreproachable.

Miss Verinder's nettling comments made it a struggle to be polite, but Mother's unwelcome voice resounded louder in my head. Our good name was all we had left. Not only did I have to protect Rose but her pristine reputation, as well.

She would need a life to return to when we found her.

Seven

"WHAT EXACTLY MIGHT you mean by no?" I asked.

"I mean, miss, that my customers value their privacy and wouldn't appreciate me sharing it willy-nilly with anyone who comes in off the street."

"Then you don't have to share the whole list with me. I'd just like to know if you've had any customers since yesterday purchase crushed linseed or linseed oil."

The druggist shook his head. "No."

"No? You have not?" I asked.

"No, I can't tell you," he replied.

"Please, sir, believe me when I tell you it's a matter of grave importance."

"I'm sorry, can't oblige you, miss." He crossed his arms to make the decision final.

I stared at the druggist. He stared back. This was his shop. He had nowhere to go. I couldn't waste the rest of the day trying to wear him down. I looked to the druggist's two apron-clad assistants. They immediately spun around and pretended to busy themselves with rearranging some shelves.

Hang it all, this wasn't supposed to be the difficult part! First the doctors from the Medical Society and the Harveian Society barely answered our questions. They all told us that there were too many hopeless cases in London, and they did not have the time to help narrow our search. And now these druggists were guarding valuable Crown secrets? Could no one in this damn city provide a simple piece of information?

With a sigh, I turned to the exit when the bell jangled, and in walked Mr. Kent with Laura behind him.

"Nothing from mine," he said. "Any exciting information here?"

"Only that he thinks their sales log is none of our business."

He frowned. "Oh. Well, that won't do at all, will it?" He took off his hat and floated down the narrow aisle of glass cases to the druggist at the back counter. "Hello, Mr. . . . . Mortimer, is it?"

"Yes, sir, but as I told the young lady—"

"Do you have a daughter, Mr. Mortimer?"

"Yes, I do, but I don't see—"

"Imagine if, God forbid, little Miss Mortimer went missing today. Would you scour the city, searching day and night, imploring any gracious citizen who might possess the slightest bit of information to help you find her?"

"Why, yes—"

"Then please take this opportunity to be that gracious citizen and answer this question for us: Have you had any customers since yesterday purchase linseed?"

"No, sir. No one," the druggist answered soberly, as if he, too, was disappointed by the answer.

Mr. Kent put his hat back on. "Ah, well, that was all we wished to know. Thank you for your assistance, Mr. Mortimer. I shall send all my sick and dying acquaintances here, should they ask for a recommendation. Good day."

"Good day!" Laura added kindly, unnecessarily.

And just like that, we had the answer and were back outside, the city bustling around us. As we crossed the road toward the next shop on the block, Mr. Kent whistled a tune, and I could hold my tongue no longer. "How in heaven's name did you do that?"

"Well, first you might notice the shop was called Mortimer's, rather than Mortimer and Son's, but the man wore a wedding ring and didn't look portly enough to own a successful shop *and* be childless. So you might look for signs of a daughter and find the display case in the back holding two dolls dressed to fit the distinctive tastes of two little girls. They were English wax dolls from the craze of 1876, but one wore a hat that was fashionable in 1879, which might make you wonder why one was more neglected than the other. The answer to that is sitting in a vase containing lilies and cypress, which any flower girl worth her salt will tell you means innocence and mourning the dead. So mentioning Mr. Mortimer's daughter would arouse his emotions for both the tragically deceased one and his precious living one."

"You . . . noticed . . . all that?"

"No, don't be absurd. It's not that complicated. I just appealed to his humanity."

In front of us, Laura spun around and pointed at a haberdashery street stall, as if possessed by some sort of hat demon. "Nick, can I try that one on? Evelyn, I'm terribly sorry, but Mama will be suspicious if I don't return home with anything! I only need one moment!" Before we could say anything, she hurried back to put that moment to good use.

"Just one, Kit!" Mr. Kent called after her, then turned to me with a shrug. "We all have our weaknesses."

The rest of the afternoon was spent repeating this dismal pattern. We started the search near Trafalgar Square and moved west, concentrating on the druggists and pharmacies in the wealthier neighborhoods under the assumption that Mr. Cheval's friend, who had the means to consult many doctors, would be living nearby. Most of the shops had not sold linseed in the past two days, and the several that had eventually led us to the wrong customers. If there were two constants to the day, it was that Laura could never own too many hats and that nothing brought us any closer to Mr. Cheval.

"I hate to say this right now," Laura cheerfully announced when we trudged out of another chemist shop. "But the Pickfords' dinner party is in two hours. We really must return home, otherwise Mama will have a fit."

A groan escaped my lips. The sun was setting, and the shadows of buildings and streetlights stretched long across the streets like prison bars. "We've made no progress," I muttered.

"No cause for alarm, Miss Wyndham," Mr. Kent said. "I will continue searching and questioning the druggists until the very minute they lock up their stores. And I'll pester them on their way home, too."

With a reassuring nod, he called for his own cab and promised to send a full report by the end of the evening.

Our carriage returned to the Kent home, where there was hardly a moment to reflect upon the day and consider our next plan. Lady Kent ambushed me at the foot of the stairs, wielding my dinner invitation to the Pickfords', and I was forced to graciously thank her for subjecting me to the last event on earth I wanted to attend. I took some lazy care to dress for it, but it did not occupy the hour and a half that Laura spent gratuitously analyzing her outfits.

"Should I wear this? I have been saving it for a special evening," she said, holding up a red monstrosity, far too low-cut to be worn anywhere decent and festooned with an assortment of colored lace, ruffles, netting, bows, and every other possible scrap the dressmaker could find on the floor.

"Laura, that dress is not suitable for today, I'm afraid. It's only a small dinner party," I said, hastily stuffing it into the abyss of her wardrobe in exchange for a simple, undecorated blue dress, which would, as Laura passionately claimed, "accentuate her sapphire orbs so Mr. Edwards could not look away." I sincerely hoped she meant her eyes.

When everyone was ready, we climbed into the carriage, and I prepared myself for the dreadful night, formulating answers and excuses for my sister's absence in my head. I wondered if we might try to escape after dessert, but unfortunately, Laura was not the type to quietly agree to anything, let alone leaving a party early. The second the vehicle began moving, she bobbed impatiently, and slippery brown strands dislodged from her coiffure. Unaware, she tugged at her mother's dress, completing the image of a child. "Mama, who all do you think will be there?"

Lady Kent was more than happy to provide a thorough list of all the guests and their many faults, while Laura traced Mr. Edwards' name in the fogged window (with a heart around it, of course) and waited for the name of this love of her life to reach her ear. Uninterested, I peeked out my sooty window, and a strange sight seized my attention: a large building with two statues posted like guards over the entrance. The Egyptian Hall.

During my season, I'd passed by the theater many times, annoyed that I might never visit Egypt herself. But this time, in front of the building, a simple square canvas overshadowed everything else. I nearly choked on my breath. An advertisement. A magic show was scheduled for "tonight and only tonight" at nine o'clock, and the name of the performer was none other than Mr. Felix Cheval.

Now, there was no conclusive proof the Mr. Cheval I had met was a magician, but once the prospect entered my mind, the pieces all fit together. Felix Cheval was not at all a common name. The show ran only for tonight, which coincided with his return from Bramhurst. Magicians were always far more popular and convincing to audiences if they were strange-looking men from exotic countries. All the things the man did in Bramhurst—lifting the carriage, sneaking into the ball, taking Rose without a sound—must have required clever tricks. And even my cautionary dream had taken place in Egypt. I couldn't pass up the chance. I had to attend the show. Even if it wasn't him, the possibility would be stuck in the back of my mind for all eternity, and I'd curse myself for going to a useless dinner party instead.

"Oh my. Oh no," I moaned weakly.

"Evelyn? What is it?" Laura peered so closely, she went cross-eyed.

"I am feeling terribly, terribly unwell." I tried to sound vaguely breathy and tightly screwed up my eyes, praying for tears.

"Oh dear! Mama, once we get to the Pickfords', we shall have to have her lie down!"

"Yes," Lady Kent said, avoiding the sight of me as if it might infect her. "They will have the necessities to make you comfortable."

Damn. Oh well, nothing for it.

"Oh, my dear Lady Kent, Laura, I cannot possibly make it so far. I fear I am about to be quite, quite . . . ill!"

"Turn the coach around!" Lady Kent rapped heartily, gasping and wrenching her skirts away. I convulsed my throat, getting into the role, Laura whimpered, and I nearly did feel sick as the carriage swung around in a tight U and bounced back to the house with great haste.

With my arm wrapped around her shoulder, a sweetly distressed Laura helped carry me inside and up two floors to my bedroom, while Lady Kent begrudgingly followed, masking her leg pain with her stiff posture. I insisted I should be quite fine on my own, that they absolutely must go without me, and Lady Kent took very little convincing, agreeing before I finished and hurrying out of the room. Laura needed a bit more, about five words' worth: "Mr. Edwards will be waiting."

When their carriage rattled away, I set to work, digging out an old brown walking dress and repinning my hair, doing my best imitation of a simple maid on her day off. I peeked out into the empty hallway. The grandfather clock showed 8:35. No time to send Mr. Kent a message, no one else to accompany me. A foolhardy plan, to be sure, but I had to try. Creeping out and down the main stairs, I managed to make it most of the way without seeing a soul. But as I slipped around a corner in the first-floor hall, my haste sent me almost barreling into a catlike Tuffins, who gracefully swung a hot tray full of tea things away from me in one smooth motion.

"Miss Wyndham," he said, his startled expression relaxing into relief. "I was just bringing you some tea."

"I—I am—" I sputtered, at a loss for any plausible excuse.

"Sleeping, I believe?" Tuffins offered, the barest spark of humor seeping into his oblong face. "Naturally, you won't want anyone to disturb you."

I could have hugged him, but I knew he'd much prefer a firm nod of the head, which I gladly supplied. "Yes, thank you. I shall sleep for an hour or two."

He gave me room to pass, and I continued down the hall, poking my head into a few rooms before finding one empty parlor with exactly what I needed: a window leading to the narrow alley by the side of the house.

Holding my breath, I rattled the window open, squeezed through the frame, and nearly twisted my ankle landing on the damp, uneven cobblestones outside. Goose pimples formed along my arms, and I sincerely wished I had grabbed my cloak beforehand. Too late now. No choice but to brave the bitter cold.

I smoothed out my wrinkled dress and set off through the dense fog toward the glow of the main street, a slight fear pricking in my stomach with every clacking step. Never had I wandered London alone at night, nor considered it even a remote possibility, which meant my mind hadn't yet found anything in particular to be terrified of and instead settled on everything in general. Every dark patch of the street rendered me vulnerable to criminals, and every yellow pool of gaslight exposed me to Society. Every passing pedestrian produced a flinch as I expected a thief or shocked acquaintance, while every stretch of silence meant no one to help me out of danger. Every moment, I alternated between keeping my head down inconspicuously and raising it to be aware and anxious of the entire street. Any lingering thrill of freedom that I might have had was completely swept away by the terrifying uncertainty.

A light breeze blew my skirts askew and sent stinging fragments of dirt and dust into my eyes. I swiped the debris away and tried to console myself with the resolution to send Mr. Kent a message at the theater, but at the present, the decision did nothing to calm my nerves. A few long blocks made it clear the theater was much farther than anticipated. Even as I crossed streets and sidewalks, recalling landmarks and memorable images from the carriage ride, part of me still worried this walk would somehow last forever.

It was only when I heard the dear, sweet noise of traffic from a nearby thoroughfare that I allowed myself a heavy breath of relief. Cabs, carriages, and omnibuses rattled by, and the facade of the Egyptian Hall beckoned me from across the street. The archaic style was completely incongruous with the surrounding buildings, but architecture hardly warranted a second thought, what with my heart racing and all. I stumbled through the pillared doorway, purchased a floor ticket for a couple of shillings, and slipped inside. The doors closed behind me like a tomb, and the lights above were extinguished.

It took my nearly sitting on several poor attendees before I found an empty spot in the darkness. Two men in the row in front of me, who smelled as if they'd bathed in spirits, turned around, gazed hazily at me, and offered a drink from their flask. I politely declined as I landed heavily in my seat. Smoke discharged in the center of the stage, and a figure seemingly materialized out of the air with a bang. When the smog dissipated, I almost cursed aloud. The magician was wearing a blasted mask!

The combination of his navy cloak, my distant seat, and the sheer spectacle of the show rendered it impossible to determine if he was the same Mr. Cheval. This one was certainly a big man, but his confidence set him apart. His physical movements at the ball appeared awkward and clumsy, but here onstage, he was in his element. Every motion was precise, every step graceful. He treated his act like a delicate experiment. He performed disappearing tricks with two beautiful assistants. He brought a woman from the audience onstage, demonstrated what he called "the science of mind reading," and guessed everything about her correctly. He blended vials of chemicals, dropped them in an empty box, and conjured up birds and rabbits from his compounds. He even performed surgery on an assistant by cutting off her head and miraculously restoring it within seconds. Perhaps it was entertaining, judging from the loud laughter and applause from the two drunkards in front of me. But after all this, I was no closer to confirming his identity. I did not have the patience or time to sit through the entire performance, then wait outside for another hour in the hopes of catching him after. That would run too dangerously close to the end of Lady Kent and Laura's night.

When Mr. Cheval announced in his light accent that we had reached the show's centerpiece—a death-defying escape from a locked glass box—I leaned over to the drunkards. "I have seen this trick before—he just uses a double! That's why he has the mask!"

Gratifyingly, one man gasped and the other let loose the same sort of wailing "No!" that Achilles might have unleashed at his discovery of Patroclus's body. I nodded significantly.

The more vocal one turned to the stage and loudly slurred, "Take off the mask, you fake! You have a double and we *know* it!"

The doubtful murmurs in the audience swelled into cheers of agreement as they all realized the scheme.

"Well, well!" the magician exclaimed. "What an intelligent crowd! I suppose it is only fair!" The audience cheered, and I thanked my drunken friends before scurrying down the aisle to get a closer look.

With flair, he flung away the mask to reveal a long, pale, bearded face with a protruding brow that looked nothing at all like the Mr. Cheval I met. I stared in disbelief for a moment, then found myself storming out of the theater, crumpling up my program as furiously as one could crumple up a sheet of paper. A fitting waste of time to end a perfectly useless day.

Once I was outside in the cold, my worries overtook my anger.

Perhaps Cheval really was a common name. Or did the giant at the ball lie to us about every little detail? If he were stealing my sister away to London, it would make sense for him to take on an alias. What better than a magician who put on an act and, before you realized it, disappeared?

I searched for a cab along the silent road, but the traffic had vanished within the past couple of worthless hours. A group of rowdy men hollered to me as they entered a nearby tavern, so I started in the other direction, hoping to avoid unwanted attention. The echo of a distant carriage called me down one unfamiliar street, then another. An attempt to retrace my steps only got me more lost and disoriented. Nothing kindled my memories. Not the darkened shop windows, not the half-torn advertisements covering every wall, not the slivers of gaslight casting shadows that twisted at my feet. After far too many turned corners, a familiar half-open window brought me down a lifeless alley littered with trash, vomit, and what looked like two vacant eyes staring up at me.

I did not remember that.

Shivering, I hurried away, splashing through foul puddles and dank recesses without hesitation. I rounded a corner chemist shop, found that the next street looked completely wrong, spun around to retrace my steps, and crashed right into the two reeking men from the magic show. My muttered apologies and attempts to slip by failed as their wide, swaggering frames blocked my path. They didn't look to be the friendliest of guides.

"'Ere she is! 'Ello, poppet. Whereya runnin' off to?" one voice scratched like sandpaper.

"'Ow much fer the both o' us?" the other said.

I endeavored to turn around, but one shuffled in front of me. "Oy, take a look at those lips! Come on, darlin', 'ow much?" he yelled.

My heart started to pound, furiously begging my legs to move. I made a dash, but the men were faster than drunkards rightfully should have been. One seized my arm and swung me back while the other clutched my neck with his grimy fingers. I struggled to utter words, sounds, anything as I heard the metal clang of a dropped blade and scraping as one of them picked it up.

"Lucky us. No one's 'ere," a voice in my ear cackled to the other man. "Who needs a room?"

"No, no! Please—"

The taste of dirt hit me as a thick, fetid hand smothered my cry for help. Another hand pulled my neckline apart with a horrifying tear, and my final, frantic lunge away was stopped short by two hairy arms pinning me to a strange, damp body. The edge of the knife pricked my burning throat as their whispered threats lingered in my ear. The suffocating stench of tobacco and ale filled my lungs, violating all my senses.

I kicked. I kicked so hard, and it did nothing but hurry them along. Hands seized my feet, and a voice cursed at me as they carried me off the sidewalk and down an alley—an alley far too dark to see what they would do next.

Eight

AND FAR TOO dark for them to see me.

My hand flew up, clawing at the closest face, fingers digging into hair, flesh, eyes with every shred of fury I could summon from within. Thick wetness dribbled down my palm, and a loud, gruff scream tore straight through my ears. The blade dropped away, and the holds on me loosened for a brief, startling second.

My feet kicked hard again, flailing and hitting and thrusting into what felt like a face, a stomach, a groin, and then they touched solid ground. I scrambled backward, bumping into a body and shoving it away and spinning around in the dark, looking for the yellow glow of gaslight. Hearing grunts and footsteps behind me, I dashed toward the street, my skirts tangling, my slippers half sliding off, my balance and breath leaving me. If I could just make it down the street, a constable would hear me. Someone. Anyone. And that was when a third silhouetted man arrived, standing between me and my freedom.

I flew at him like a feral cat, aiming for the eyes, trying to do what worked before, refusing to be taken again. The collision sent him stumbling back a step, but as I attacked with all my momentum to throw him off balance, that unmistakable sensation surged through my body, and I felt myself being whirled around and pushed into a pool of light. The world stopped spinning to settle on Mr. Braddock's eyes, glaring into mine as waves of energy passed between his hands to my arms, where he clutched me.

The scuffle of footsteps snapped his attention to the alley. He pivoted back and swung his fist at the man in front, catching him straight on his nose and sending him stumbling and slamming into the other. But they didn't fall. With a newfound rage, the two staggered forward.

"Lucky one that was," one of them said, wiping his bloody face.

The other pointed his knife at Mr. Braddock and smirked. "We'll be the lucky ones. I get his coat."

"Long as I get the bitch first."

And the one in front charged with his knife, thrusting at Mr. Braddock's head to avoid bloodying the coat. Mr. Braddock gracefully sidestepped the lunge and grabbed the unbalanced drunkard's wrist. Impossibly fast and forceful, he contorted the wailing man's arm and twisted him around. I heard the snap of bones. With a yell, the second attacker launched a hard, clumsy kick at Mr. Braddock's side but found his foot lodged in his friend's stomach. Mr. Braddock's human shield crumpled to the floor. As the second drunkard realized his mistake, his eyes widened, and his crooked jaw would have dropped, had a skyward fist not collided with it first and sent him sailing backward onto the hard pavement.

That should have ended it, but the first attacker clambered back into the fray, broken arm held in tightly, and tackled Mr. Braddock from behind before I could shout a word of warning. Surprised but still upright, Mr. Braddock hurriedly spun around, attempting to dislodge the desperate attacker, who was futilely trying to drag him to the ground. After a few punches from Mr. Braddock, the drunkard's tight hold with his good hand finally loosened, and he collapsed to the ground between us, while Mr. Braddock stood over him watching, his brow furrowed.

I could do nothing but gape at the sight. My knees buckled, and I sat down hard on the street, my skirts fanning out along the dirty pavement. My thoughts would not stop. They seemed to weigh down on me, every single awful thing that had almost happened. I did my best to push them away, to think on what really had happened. My heavy breath, held for entirely too long, escaped in a loud gasp and turned Mr. Braddock's attention to me.

"Are you hurt?" he asked quietly, slipping a pair of kid gloves over his blood-speckled hands.

I wasn't. I wasn't hurt.

Somehow, I managed to stand, and he scanned me for injuries until his eyes reached my torn neckline and his blinking grew excessive. He stared at the ground as I groaned, my hands flying up reflexively, doing little to cover the damage. Looking pointedly away from my bare skin, he slipped off his jacket and handed it to me without a word. The wool itched, and the sleeves awkwardly hung too long past my arms, but it sufficed. Something earthy and spicily familiar drifted from the fabric. Much better than the stink of smoke and alcohol, at least. I stopped myself before I took another long inhalation, realizing what I was doing.

"Miss Wyndham, *are you all right*?" His words came condescendingly slow and overly enunciated, as if he thought I no longer understood English.

I blinked. Anger, fear, astonishment, helplessness—a maelstrom of emotions still coursed through me. I grasped at one of the many questions flashing through my head. "How did you find me?"

"I was on my way to call on you at the Kents' when I saw you leave the Egyptian, clearly lost and frightened."

"I was chilled," I snapped. Strange, my hands continued to shake, no matter how I told them not to. "And so you followed me but decided to wait until my life was in danger, so you could jump in heroically, yes? No normal 'Hello, Miss Wyndham, perhaps I might escort you home?' A marvelous plan, Mr. Braddock. You're quite 'mad, bad, and dangerous to know,' congratulations."

Mr. Braddock prowled around me in half circles as if a trap lay hidden in the space between us. Then he stopped and gestured down the street. "Fine. Perhaps I might escort you home now. If you can stop the rudely unsubtle Lord Byron comments."

"As long as you don't walk with his limp."

"Do you do this to every man who helps you?"

"I—well—do *you* behave like this for every woman *you* help?" was my intelligent reply.

"No, you alone seem to inspire it," he said, leading the way. "I thought you might still be in shock, but this sounds like your usual incivility."

"Well, I thought I was abundantly clear in our last conversation that it would be our *last* conversation. But here you are."

He opened his mouth but stopped after an angry "You," clenching furiously at air, arms stuck at his sides. He looked like he was mentally counting to ten. I think I even heard a soft "Nine."

"I apologize for the other morning," he finally said, guiding us around a corner. "You caught me by surprise, and I went about everything the wrong way. It was not my intention to cause the distress I did."

The apology caught me off guard. It took me a few moments to break the habit of thinking up retorts. "And, and I . . . well, thank you, for coming to my aid. I was—I was overwhelmed . . . and not quite expecting you here. Why did you follow me?"

Broken shadows crept across his profile, bending around his Greek nose. "To tell you what I was trying to say when you ran off before. I should have been clearer, but . . . I thought you were already aware. Have you been able to accept it yet?"

"Accept what?"

"Your gift. The powerful healing ability."

"You are confused. That would be Rose. She studies for hours every day—"

"As knowledgeable as your sister may be about medicine, her success comes from the extraordinary power she was born with. When we first met, I had assumed it was her power alone and that she understood it. But until our meeting yesterday, I had not considered the possibility that *both* of you had the power and both of you were completely unaware of it."

He took a deep breath, pulling in my gaze with his own. "It is your touch that heals people, Miss Wyndham."

"Ha! Half of Bramhurst insists that Rose has some miraculous gift of God, no matter how much I try to explain that it's science, but I must admit, it's amusing you would fall for such an idea, too."

"What I'm telling you *is* science. There is a process called saltation that some scientists argue is a more precise theory of evolution. It finds that speciation occurs when select members of a particular species undergo sudden drastic changes in their development that suit them better for survival. This jump randomly occurs from one generation to another, and the new, advanced species are the ones to live on, while their predecessors gradually go extinct. That is how you and your sister acquired such rare gifts of healing. You are part of that jump. As am I. I have my own power. . . . I have lived with it for three years now—"

"Mr. Braddock," I interrupted, finally prodded into speaking. "I told you to stop this dark act. I'll admit, this is far more inventive than those moody men who knock over trays of appetizers to attract attention or loudly mumble bits of their poetry, but do you really think I haven't the faintest idea of how evolution works and that I'm willing to believe myself in some fantastic gothic novel?"

"No, of course not—"

"Good. Then thank you very much for your assistance, and please, let me go home in peace."

He stepped in front of me, crowding me back in an alley. "I cannot let you do that. I know this is unbelievable—it took me time to come to terms with it, as well—but do *not* simply ignore me."

His intensity and vehemence sent a chill down my spine, and my amusement vanished entirely. He really believed this. Was he completely unaware of what he was doing? If this was not an act, how crazy did that make him?

"You've told me your amusing story, now let's—"

"It's not a story."

"It is, unless you have any shred of evidence." I tried to move past him, but a tight grip on my hand twisted me back around. I drew in a sharp breath as a searing essence surged through my arm, prickling my veins from where his hand met mine, until a second later, his hand and the feeling were gone.

"Was that evidence enough?" he asked, voice hard as stone.

"You . . . did that?" I gasped, almost unable to speak.

"Did you think it was the flutterings of your heart?" He sneered, but I could see his lips tighten as he tried to control his own reaction. He resumed our course down the street.

I followed, maintaining my distance. "I think it's another magic trick. A hidden device."

"There's no trick. I told you, I have a power—"

"The power of vexation?"

Stepping up another crumbling curb, he rubbed his neck and his jaw tightened. (I was surprised it could tighten any further.) "Believe what you wish. But either way, I need your help. I have a very sick friend—"

"No," I replied with a sinking sensation. "Not another incurable condition."

"Why? Is that what the large man at the ball told your sister?"

"It was. And you want me to cure this friend, I'm sure, but I cannot do that," I said.

"Perhaps your sister, then?"

"She is unavailable."

"I can help you find her," he added with a steady sidelong glance.

Bloody hell. "Why would she possibly need finding? She is staying with my aunt and uncle." I attempted a carefree laugh. Judging by his startled look, it came out more as a madwoman's cackle.

"I see, yes, of course she's safe with them," he replied smugly. "Which is why her fiercely protective older sister came to me like a Fury yesterday, demanding to know what I had done after I showed an interest in Miss Rosamund at the ball. It also explains why the helpful attendant at the train station witnessed Miss Rosamund traveling to London with a distinctive man, and, oh yes, this older sister following with a 'Mr. Kent' by the day's end. You might guard yourself better if you wish to keep this a secret. If I could unravel this so easily, anyone else may be able to, as well."

He paused, savoring my defeat, before adding, "I gather it was not the right Mr. Cheval headlining the show?" A smile quirked on his lips.

I clutched my right hand at my skirts to keep it from flying at his cheek. "How do you know him?"

"I know him not as Felix Cheval but instead as Claude. And I know him because he is gifted with extraordinary strength. I am sorry for lying before. I needed to understand what was happening before I gave you even more cause to distrust me. Your absurd opinion that I fancy myself a gothic hero did not help."

"*My* absurd opinion?" My appalled voice echoed through the streets. "And *how* exactly do you know Claude? Does everyone with a special little power gather at a club for weekly meetings?"

"That would make matters much easier, but no. I don't know what Claude wants from your sister, but it must have something to do with these powers. There's no other reason he would have sought her out. Believe what you will, Miss Wyndham, but if you agree to try and help my friend, I will find Miss Rosamund."

"No. I cannot afford the time."

"The police are not an option, I'm sure. How else do you expect to find her?"

"I—I have many plans. And my friend, Mr. Kent—"

"Trust me. I know this city far better than most, and I know whom to ask about gentlemen with secret powers."

I did not know what to say. Against my best wishes, Mr. Braddock, in all his arrogance, had an answer for everything. But this insistence on those ridiculous powers . . . it bothered me that I could not guess his intentions for creating such a wild story.

He sighed at my silence. "Fine, ignore all I said about these powers. You were right. It was a jest, another false tale to make you fall madly in love with me." He walked slowly ahead of me.

"Don't mock me."

"I'm making this simpler for you. You *can* trust that I know Claude and he knows me—you figured that out easily enough at the ball. And you know how quickly I found you, so you cannot doubt that skill. And at the very least, I know this city better than you. Those facts do not change, regardless of whether I believe in these powers, or if I believe the lost city of Atlantis is easily accessible via a magical octopus just south of the Royal Docks."

"That sounds much more believable."

"We can be of help to each other."

"And when I am unable to help heal your friend with these nonexistent powers? What then?"

"You can try your medicines the way you usually do, and you'll either succeed or fail. No matter what, I'll help you. All I ask is that you give it one day."

One day. One vital day. Was it worth it?

"I'll even start the search tomorrow," he offered, eyes gleaming. "This way, you won't lose a day of searching—I'll just be taking your place."

The urge to refuse him was overwhelming, just aching to leave the tip of my tongue, but when I considered my plans for the search tomorrow and the hopeless questioning of more druggists and chemists, I found myself at an impasse. Rose. All that mattered was finding Rose. No matter how crazy, misguided, or deceptive Mr. Braddock was with this theory, if he truly had a sick friend, it was in his best interest to find my sister, so one of us would help find a cure.

After an eternity, I nodded and muttered, "Fine," as we rounded onto a familiar street. He had led me back to the Kents', and I had barely realized we moved.

"Good. Then I will have a carriage sent for you at noon tomorrow—"

"No, you will provide me the name and address of your friend, and I will come on my own," I insisted, watching his face closely for a reaction.

Not even the slightest twitch. "Very well," he said and paused, looking at me expectantly.

"What is it?"

"I will need my coat."

I hastily pulled it off, carefully rearranging my arms over the mess of my gown. He coughed, pulled out a pen and a card holder, scrawled an address on the back of a card, and handed it to me.

"I still think you're mad," I said.

"I'm sure you do." He stopped at the intersection of street and alley, on the edge of the greasy streetlamp light. "I trust you can find your way from here?"

"I'm not sure I can get inside. It's ever so difficult."

A spark of humor altered his features in a rather pleasing way. "I'm sure you can pry a door open with your quips," he said, gliding back into the dark street, blending into shadows. Typical.

I crept toward the window I left ajar ages ago and, standing on my toes, shoved it open. A figure flickered by an adjacent window, and my heart jumped along with the rest of my body. Desperately, I pulled myself up and over the sill, tangling my skirts, falling into the room with a thud, and nearly wrecking an expensive-looking Japanese vase. The noise brought rapid footsteps down the hallway to the door, and I frantically scrambled over to a nearby couch. With a final burst of effort, I climbed up and splayed out dramatically, only just remembering to cover my ripped bodice with a nearby blanket.

The doorknob squeaked, and Laura slinked inside, shutting the door behind her. "Evelyn! What in heaven's name have you been doing?" she whispered as loudly as her voice would allow.

"I barely even know myself," I groaned.

"What?"

"Never—never mind. I—I'm sorry. Did anyone else notice I was missing?"

"No, Mama is busy with company. Why aren't you in bed? I thought you were sick!" she exclaimed. I sensed a fit of theatrics ready to erupt.

"Shh, please, be quiet. I'm not sick. I went to find Rose—I believed the man who took her was a magician, and I went to his show."

"So . . . you lied about being ill?"

What could I say? "I had to. It was the only night for the performance."

"And you went alone?"

I nodded reluctantly.

"Oooh, Evelyn! That sounds so exciting!" she squealed, clutching her head as if to keep it from exploding. "I do so wish I could have accompanied you! You must include me in the future—investigating a dark magician who abducts sisters. It's utterly delicious! Almost as delicious as Mr. Edwards tonight. He was so handsome, and his conversation so witty and interesting . . ."

Well. Not the reaction I was expecting. "It was not the same man," I added, but Laura did not even listen as she continued to chatter and daydream her way out of the room. I followed her out into the hall, casually wrapping the blanket over the ruined dress like a shawl.

"Ah! Miss Wyndham, I heard you were unwell."

Like some eternal mosquito that never goes away, Miss Verinder sauntered up to us, perfectly coiffed. "I do hope you are feeling better?" Her voice was thick, syrupy.

"I was," I replied icily.

"The Verinders came to pick up music from my mother," Laura informed me.

"Something soothing, I hope," Miss Verinder put in. "There seemed to be enough excitement for everyone tonight."

"Indeed. Good night, Miss Verinder," I said curtly, nudging Laura up the stairs in front of me.

"Oh, and Miss Wyndham?" she called. "I know you're the expert on health, but I would recommend staying indoors. The cold must have been quite hard on you."

Rigid as a board, I glanced back, hoping no distress showed on my face. Pale eyebrows raised, and a faint, cruel smile played on Miss Verinder's lips. Refusing to let her bother me, I simply nodded before I pulled Laura up and around the banister toward the bedrooms.

Nine

My hand clutched the cold railing, my feet tested every stair, and my breath refused to come as I climbed up and up through the black void. Like a beacon, the strange, dim second-floor landing called to me. In the darkness, even the faintest light was better than nothing.

The moonlight brought me up to a dusty hallway and into an open laboratory furnished with tables, chairs, cupboards, and bookshelves. The walls displayed intricate illustrations of human anatomy and chalkboards filled with indecipherable notes. Grotesque shadows of containers, equipment, and book stacks twisted and stretched across the floor like ink spills.

Where was I?

The rattling and whistling of glass panes seemed to respond to my question. A large window looked out over London's foggy gray skyline, speckled with the orange glow of life and activity. I drew nearer, feeling the chilly draft seeping in as I peered out, but somehow the closer angle rendered it even harder to make sense of the view. The sights blurred, like indistinct smudges of paint. Colorful blobs took the vague shapes of buildings and streets below, but it was impossible to tell where I was in the city.

"Ev-lyn?"

I spun around to find a figure standing in the doorway, her red hair wild, her face wan. Miss Grey. "Is R-Rose still with you?" she asked, her voice quavering.

I shook my head.

"He took her?" she asked, eyes wide.

The way she spoke sent my heart racing. This time I managed to speak, slightly. "Who took her? Where is she?"

She gazed up at the ceiling. "Then—she must be here. Please, Evelyn, you have to find her before—"

And I saw past her, past the doorway, to the staircase leading up to the third floor, and nothing else mattered. I flew up the stairs, the darkness swallowing me back up and spitting me out into my bed, and I lay awake until the sun rose, hating these dreams that could solve nothing at all.

Ten

THE TICKING OF the giant grandfather clock grew as loud as life as I waited, resentfully, with Mr. Braddock in his friend's large and obviously well-loved London home. We stood in a drawing room lined with faded floral wallpaper and elegant chairs inviting us to delight in the rainy light, which, under normal circumstances, might have made for a cozy morning visit. But for the moment, it was quite the opposite. I crushed the folds of my gown in my fists and hovered in the middle of the room.

"Mr. and Mrs. Lodge will be downstairs shortly," Cushing, their quiet steward, said before shutting the door, imprisoning me inside.

I was even more confused than I was last night. This did not look to be a ploy. Laura had confirmed that the Lodges not only existed, but they were apparently a respectable family that had only recently withdrawn from social events because of their daughter's illness. But Mr. Kent had insisted Mr. Braddock was not to be trusted, when I urged him to continue the search without me for the day. And I hadn't even told him the whole story about the powers. Mr. Braddock surely had ulterior motives for creating such an elaborate explanation, but for the life of me, I could not determine what they were. Was the man cleverer than he looked or just crazier? The line separating the two seemed rather thin.

"So, who is this friend of yours?" I blurted out, hoping to distract myself.

Mr. Braddock glared at me as if I had just stepped on a kitten. "Miss Mae Lodge."

"Quite informative. Where did you meet?"

"A house."

"Do you willfully circumvent all questions?"

"As I recall from last night, my full, honest answers were not to your liking. At least cryptic responses require less breath."

"Then you admit to being purposefully cryptic and mysterious?"

"Sebastian!" a rich, friendly voice interrupted Mr. Braddock's elegiac sigh. An older man and woman stood at the door, both excited to see him—heaven knows why. With an elegant bow, Mr. Braddock greeted the couple, whom he introduced as Mr. and Mrs. Lodge.

Mrs. Lodge's puff of blond hair bounced gently as she turned her welcoming countenance toward me. "Thank you for coming, Miss Wyndham," she said, clasping her hands. "We are terribly in your debt for helping our Mae." I had done nothing yet.

Her husband, a thin, red-faced man with snowy hair, had the same honest smile as his wife. I was finally forced to discard the idea that Mr. Braddock might have me here for some other purpose. Their distress was written into every line that creased their kind faces. "Sebastian has told us the stories of your work. We find that dedication to be by far the most important quality, after some of the doctors we've seen."

"Has anyone given her a diagnosis?" I asked.

Mrs. Lodge gave a sober nod. "There have been a number of them. But more recently, the doctors have suggested Addison's."

I stared at them blankly. Addison's? Was that a real disease? I resisted the urge to burn Mr. Braddock with my eyes. He brought me here to cure a disease I had never even heard of. How could I let these kind people think there was anything I could possibly do to help?

"I am afraid that there may be little I can do," I started, giving voice to my thoughts, but their faces fell so quickly, I felt compelled to continue. "But I will do what I can to see to her comfort."

The Lodges nodded eagerly, and I felt like the worst of charlatans, peddling Evelyn Wyndham's Magically Useless Elixir.

"Shall we head upstairs?" Mr. Lodge smiled at me expectantly.

I forced out the words. "Yes, of course."

Miss Lodge's room was massive—at least twice the size of my own in Bramhurst. Her parents had spared no expense to make her comfortable. Buried beneath the silk sheets and quilts, she was barely visible. The shuttered windows blocked all but a few beams of sunlight. Beside her bed was a snug nook, settled with a plush chair and damask chaise, presumably to make bedside visitors more comfortable. A rather bleak consideration, really.

The Lodges roused their daughter, and she struggled to summon the energy to rise a few inches until Mr. Braddock stepped into her sight. She was up at once. Though she had little strength to express her excitement, it was apparent in her tanned yet obviously sickly face.

"Sebastian!"

"Mae, how are you?" Mr. Braddock asked with an affectionate smile so unexpected, I almost tripped. Who knew the man had teeth?

"I'm well," Miss Lodge replied serenely, though she hardly looked it.

He hesitated near the doorway as if he couldn't bear to see her illness up close. "I would like you to meet someone. This is Miss Evelyn Wyndham. She and her sister are talented nurses from Bramhurst."

My face burned as he raised their expectations even higher. I wished there was a cure to rid a room of Mr. Braddock.

"Good morning, Miss Wyndham," she greeted me as I stepped closer to the bed. Despite her sickness, Miss Lodge was an exceptionally pretty girl. Large, luminous gray eyes, a perfect upturned nose, and lovely golden hair that was probably even brighter when she was healthy—now it was plastered against her damp forehead. It was the shade of her skin that seemed strange. Oddly dark, yet unhealthy and at odds with her light eyes and hair.

Her parents informed me that Cushing was at my full disposal for all necessary medicines and supplies and they would only return to check on Miss Lodge's progress whenever I deemed it fit. They exited with hope lingering on their faces. I silently cursed Mr. Braddock for putting me in such a position. Deciding to curse him out loud, I asked him for a private word.

"Mr. Braddock, you are a very unthinking person to give these people false hope!" I whispered when we stepped into the hall. "I don't even know what this disease is!"

"I know you don't believe me about your abilities," he replied. "But I don't believe it as impossible as you say. And we have an agreement."

"Fine, I shall honor it by attempting to use my ever-so-magical powers to cure your friend of this affliction I know nothing about. But if you want your friend to actually recover, I suggest you start looking for my sister now. She is the only one who might begin to help."

"I told you already, I do intend to help you even if you are unable to cure Miss Lodge," he replied, frowning as though I had assumed otherwise. "I'll leave you to it now. If there is anything that can lessen her pain . . ."

"I will do what I can, but that is likely nothing!"

"Just please, try . . . holding her hand, measuring her pulse, anything. As mad as it may sound, I beg of you—I believe it works through direct contact."

I faltered, thrown by his apparent sincerity. Reluctantly, I nodded.

He continued: "I understand you feel quite thrown into a difficult situation—"

"A sterling observation."

He smiled determinedly and continued, taking a small step closer. "So truly, thank you. Thank you for even coming today. I will not forget it."

I had the clever response of opening my mouth and letting air run through it. The small space between us seemed to fill with a strange vibration. I finally just nodded again. He wished me a good afternoon and descended the stairs. My hands found the doorknob, and my feet brought me back into Miss Lodge's room, half dazed.

The first order of business was to liven up the dismal space. Rose detested the propensity to leave a sick person's room somber and miserable. She called it an early concession to death. I began by tying up the drapes, flinging open the shutters, and letting the light flood in while my patient observed me silently. Soon, the pale light of rainy London bathed the room in a soothing gray.

A paper and pencil in hand, I sat in the chair next to her bed. "Miss Lodge. How are you feeling today?"

"Better than most days . . . I was nauseated earlier this morning, but it passed. Thank you for seeing me, Miss Wyndham." She smiled serenely, quite willing to have my presence in her sickroom. I smiled back, completely unsure of what to do next.

"I am happy to do what I can. Now, can you tell me your symptoms?"

She listed them in such rapid succession that my hand struggled to keep pace. For the past month, she frequently suffered from nausea and vomiting, fatigue, lack of appetite, weight loss, and a change in skin color. The extreme weakness kept her confined to bed the past two weeks. The last doctor to see her said she would be lucky to survive the winter.

Truly, this strange disease dwarfed anything Rose and I had ever dealt with. Miss Lodge's calm disposition helped cover it up, but when she went quiet, tightly squeezed her eyes shut, and lay back down as a wave of dizziness overtook her, I wondered how much pain she was silently enduring. Calling for Cushing, I quietly asked him for willow bark and boiling water. He observed me curiously, surely doubting the country remedy, but he held his tongue and left to fill my request.

Returning to my patient, we sat in an uncomfortable silence for a moment, smiling politely at the bed linens. She was the one to break it by asking me about Bramhurst in her calm, inviting voice, and we slowly slid into exchanging the typical questions and answers of new acquaintances. The details and description of Bramhurst quite enthralled her, reawakening her childhood memories of the times spent in her grandmother's old countryside home with her brother, Henry. And drawing on our mutual acquaintance, she began to regale me with stories of Mr. Braddock and their many misadventures.

"And there was the day I almost jumped off the roof," Miss

Lodge said with a giggle and shrug, as if it were some small matter.

"I beg your pardon?" I asked. "You do not seem quite so desperate."

She gave a small laugh. "It happened just after I had finished reading a collection of Greek myths. Somehow, I had gotten it into my head that I could fashion a pair of wings and fly like Daedalus—I believe it was my brother, Henry, who convinced me. I could think of nothing else after the idea took root. For several nights, I constructed a set of wings by gluing together all the paper that could be found in the house. By dawn on the third night, I was ready and supremely confident.

"I climbed out the window on the third floor, crawled my way over to the edge of the roof, slipped on the wings, and never gave the danger a second thought. I wholeheartedly believed it would work. So I prepared to jump—"

"And Mr. Braddock heroically caught you at the last second," I said, with wicked pleasure, sure to my bones that I was correct.

Miss Lodge grinned at my impertinence. "Yes, exactly! I was just above his room, and he heard the racket. And I must mention that when he pulled me back, he tore the wings in the process. I was furious with him!"

"It seems Mr. Braddock has had years of practice, then."

Miss Lodge looked curiously at me. "Practice saving people?"

"Acting like a dark, brooding hero," I said, wondering if she could not see it herself.

A wrinkle appeared between her light brows. "I . . . suppose I can see it. But really, he's not like that at all, Miss Wyndham."

At that moment, Cushing returned with the willow bark and a boiling pot of water on a tray, and I left her bedside and set the willow bark to steep. The simple act only occupied a minute of time and needed a half hour to steep. Thoughtfully, Cushing had also brought us two cups of good strong black tea, and I decided they certainly could not worsen Miss Lodge's condition. I returned to her side and helped her prop herself up in the bed, her breath coming too quickly for the slight effort.

"How did the two of you first meet?" I asked as she took a shaky sip. "It sounds as though you have many years of acquaintance, but he has an incurable condition that keeps him from answering questions."

"He was best friends with Henry. They were schoolmates from a young age, and our families were also close."

"And your brother, is he away at school?"

Miss Lodge looked grave as she put down her spoon. "Henry passed away almost two years ago."

Not the pleasant teatime conversation I had expected. I choked on a sip and coughed it away. "I did not mean to—"

"No, no apologies. I am simply not used to telling others. It doesn't seem real, still."

"I'm sorry, it must have been . . ." I trailed off, for what does one really say?

"It was hard for all of us. And Sebastian had just lost his parents the prior year—"

"I beg your pardon? He—how . . . is that possible?" I asked, cold settling in my stomach.

"His parents were both stricken by the same illness. He lost his father first and then his mother a few months later."

"What sort of illness?"

"Consumption. The same as my brother."

I shook my head, as if that could change everything. "And now you have this . . . this Addison's disease. How horrible."

"You could also say I'm lucky," she replied with a smile. "I showed some of the symptoms of consumption myself after Henry, but I managed to recover. I'm still here despite the dismal odds."

I agreed but felt a little sick myself. Neither one of us spoke for some time. The faint sounds of traffic seeped inside. Miss Lodge's eyes glimmered in the glow of the sinking sun.

"Thank you for bringing him back, Miss Wyndham," she said.

"He brought me here to help you," I insisted, placing our empty cups back on the tray.

"Yes, but you see, when he was younger"—she paused to shift uncomfortably in the bed—"Sebastian was always the responsible one. The way Henry talked about him at school, he was the one other boys looked up to. But after all this happened, he was— he was distraught. He retreated further into himself. He never said it, but I know he feels guilty that Henry fell sick while they were traveling together. He'll hold himself responsible no matter what you say. He seemed quite lost after the funeral, and he rarely visited or wrote."

She looked up and gave me an earnest smile. "He must have faith in you if he decided to bring you here personally, and I'm glad of it. I want him to remember that this is a home for him. That he does not need to run away again."

"I doubt he will," I replied, unable to name the particular emotion running through me. "His desire to see you was apparent to me the moment he stepped in here."

"I hope so. He's still adjusting, but it's fortunate we've all been brought together."

Not entirely hearing her, I simply nodded. My cheeks burned as I turned away from Miss Lodge and poured her the willow-bark brew. Mr. Braddock truly had reasons for his grief, and I had mocked his pain. I winced inwardly, remembering my accusations about his fake tragic past. He had had every right to yell at me—indeed, he had been incredibly restrained for someone who had lost both parents and a best friend. With every breath, my perceptions seemed to rearrange until I was hopelessly confused and my opinion of him was reduced to a chaotic mess.

Serving Miss Lodge the tea, I endeavored not to betray my swirling emotions. She drank it down quickly, lay back, and began to drift away. Though I knew it was futile, I couldn't help but take her hands in mine, hoping that I really did have some ridiculous power. As Rose's assistant, I'd never held a life in my hands and felt that full, impossible responsibility. This girl did not deserve to die, yet here she was: weak, delicate as a bird, and wasting away.

I didn't know how many long minutes passed, my thoughts bounding back and forth between this girl I wished I could save and the man who was at every turn an enigma. When there was nothing left to do but pray, I noiselessly stood up and slipped out of the room. Before closing the door, I took one final glance at Miss Lodge, finding her color almost matching the ivory bed-clothes. Her fair complexion seemed to be returning. But as I looked closer, I realized it was just a combination of the faint sunset and wishful thinking.

I hated wishful thinking. It always made me feel useless.

Eleven

I WAS ABLE to return to the Kents' early enough for dinner. Lady Kent questioned me on my whereabouts the entire day, but Laura helped corroborate my hasty excuse about visiting my friend Catherine. To repay the favor, I spent far too long giving Laura an exhaustive account of my day with Miss Lodge. She almost fainted when she heard the drama of Mr. Braddock's tragic past.

Before I could take my well-deserved rest, though, Tuffins informed me that Mr. Kent had come to speak with me. I groggily shuffled into the drawing room and found him standing by the fireplace, eyes full of pity.

"How was the search today?" I asked, my voice high and worry pounding in my ears. "Did you find anything?"

"No, and I'm sorry. I almost did not come because I hate the idea of delivering bad news to you, but then I realized that my absence would in itself be the worst news you could possibly receive."

"Thank you for sparing me from such despair."

"But to be positive, the list of druggists grows shorter, and from a broader perspective, we *are* one day closer to finding Miss Rosamund."

"You don't always have to bring me good news."

"That comes as a relief, because try as I might, I cannot see the happy side to my other news."

I sat down hard in an uncomfortable chair. "What happened?"

"I was just coming out of a druggist's shop in Bloomsbury at about two thirty in the afternoon when I happened to see Mr. Braddock on the other side of the street. I followed him for—"

"Why would you waste your time—"

"Professional curiosity at first. I merely wanted to see where his 'valuable expertise' led him."

Curiosity? It sounded more like competitiveness. "And where, pray tell, did he lead you?"

"He went from public house to public house, drinking and carousing with his many drunk acquaintances, and when he was tired of that, he went to a gambling den, where he knocked some poor fellow unconscious. I'll admit the man had an abhorrent mustache, but Mr. Braddock went about it all wrong."

He kept his voice light, but I could see the concern in his eyes. I would have thought he was fabricating the entire story, were it not for the display of Mr. Braddock's fighting abilities last night after the magic show. "Is it not possible he was seeking information?"

"He capped off the night with a visit to a, uh, a brothel." His lips tightened as he mentioned the unmentionable.

"Excuse me?"

His eyes locked on a candle in front of him. "Ask any decent Londoner about the Argyll Rooms and you'll get a blush in response. They call it a dancing room, but that doesn't change what it is on the inside. What could he possibly be investigating there?"

The news should have rendered my legs lame and kept me

seated. Instead, it flared through my body, sending me up to my feet and almost out the window.

"There must be some mistake!" If it was true, I would kill, absolutely *murder*, Mr. Braddock.

"I assure you, there is not. Now, he doesn't deserve a second thought, Miss Wyndham," Mr. Kent said, seeing my anger. "Nothing will come of his assistance except distraction."

"So what do we do, then?" I cried back. My shaky plan had fallen apart, and the others were even flimsier. I felt suffocated, buried under it all.

Mr. Kent's steps moved closer. "If you wish to continue treating this friend of his, I will continue the search as I have until you're ready to join me."

I couldn't meet his eye, electing for the floor instead. "I don't know where else to search."

His head popped into view, looking up at me from a kneeling position. "Fortunately, as the world's greatest and all that, I have plenty of ideas, I promise you." He rose back up and, with the slightest touch, raised my chin along with him. "We should rest. It's been a long day, and you've done some kind and admirable work, regardless of the solicitor. Don't regret that. Miss Rosamund will be proud when she hears of it."

". . . Thank you."

He broke away and called for the footman, who brought his coat and cane for the brisk London night. "Call on me when you are ready," he said, gently taking my hand. It was reassuring to have someone tell me the truth after such a day. I squeezed it back, not quite wanting him to leave.

The remainder of the restless night was spent composing angry tirades to Mr. Braddock in my head, but when the servants woke early the next morning, I only had a simple message to send: I no longer required his assistance. Two hours later, Tuffins warily brought me an unexpected rebuttal. A Mr. Sebastian Wyndham, my *cousin*, was waiting for me in the parlor. The nerve.

Fortunately, Lady Kent had left to make her morning rounds, so I didn't need to explain the incredibly improper visit to her. I asked Tuffins to put him in the garden, bring tea, and make sure no one disturbed us. I couldn't keep him inside when I planned on shouting the roof down.

When I came down, Mr. Braddock was already seated at a small table, staring at the mysteries of tea things, and appearing extremely out of place among the bright, flowery surroundings. He looked up in relief as I entered, greeting my frostiness with an insuppressible smile and a giddiness that could barely be contained in his bow.

"Mr. Wyndham?" I asked caustically.

"There's always a distant cousin."

"And distant is how they should remain. Why are you here?"

"Your message. I apologize for calling on you like this, but I want to assure you, I will find your sister. Though I doubt even that would suffice to convey my gratitude for your help," he said, striding up to me. I had the oddest thought that he was about to embrace me in a hug. "Thank you, truly."

I backed away. Was he being satirical? "What do you mean?" I asked, entirely off guard.

"For Miss Lodge . . ." he said. Taking in my confused look, he asked, "Do you not know?"

I shook my head. "No, what's happened?"

"You restored her to full health, Miss Wyndham," he replied, stuffing his hands in his pockets as though he needed to contain them somehow. "I visited her last night, and she couldn't wait to see the sky and grass again." He practically leaped about the blooming paths, unable to keep to one place, his hands out of his pockets already and balled into fists. I imagined it's how Atlas would have looked after a comfortable nap. "I cannot thank you enough. Your powers are truly remarkable."

Was he serious? Or was he distracting me from his lack of a search yesterday by trying to convince me of these stupid "powers"? He must have made up her recovery—I just served her tea! "I would like to see her," I said firmly, testing him.

"This evening, perhaps," he replied. "She is extremely fond of you. And, of course, she wants to thank you, as well."

"That is impossible! I did nothing!" I choked.

His eyes seemed lighter, freer as he looked me over. "I don't think you truly understand the extent of your powers."

"Apparently not." I began to roll my eyes, but they caught on a decanter of wine that Tuffins had helpfully added to the tea things on the patio table. Too early? Too early.

"If she is feeling better, it is not due to anything I have done. And if you are hoping to deter me from asking after your progress, you are mistaken. Tell me, was my sister hiding away in any of the public houses you patronized last night? Was she in the gambling den? Or the brothel?" There was no keeping my voice as steady as I had hoped, and the final word emerged at a screechy, glass-breaking pitch. Also, loud.

Mr. Braddock's eyes gratifyingly bulged, though he swiftly composed himself, folded his arms protectively across his chest, and scowled at me as though I were the villain. "You had me followed. This Mr. Kent, I presume? You don't have the best taste in suitors, it would seem."

"So you admit it."

"I was meeting acquaintances. For information about your sister."

"And do you usually attack your acquaintances?"

He shook his head. "No, but I help when they are attacked by an angry patron caught cheating. Do you usually yell at the people helping you?"

"When they lie about being helpful, yes. What could you have possibly learned about my sister at a brothel?"

"It is a dancing room, not a brothel."

"I have it on good authority that it is a brothel."

"Mr. Kent is a good authority on brothels? How charming."

I glared at him, tired of the elusive act. Who cared about his stupid past? I stormed up to him, flowers be damned, and landed closer than he probably liked. He flinched back a step.

"Let's pretend I did as you asked and 'healed' your friend, Mr. Braddock. You are deeply in my debt. Now, would you kindly share your discoveries and tell me the truth *for once*?" I clenched my teeth and glared up at the obnoxiously tall man, ignoring the almost imperceptible current that seemed to live between us.

His face was back to a stony mask, all rigid lines and unwavering eyes. But it fell away as he sighed, unfolding a small piece of paper. "I wanted to handle it quietly," he explained, revealing its contents. An advertisement for the Argyll Rooms, announcing in red block letters its fifty-performer band, renowned conductor, and, at the bottom, the latest singing attraction:

EVERY NIGHT AT 8:00, OUR NEWEST STAR, THE WHITE "ROSE" OF BRAMHURST.

"And you believe that's Rose? My sister, the serious nurse, Rose?" I asked mockingly.

"I could go speak to her," he gently suggested.

"Did you see her last night?" I snapped, wanting no gentleness from him.

"No, but the staff had, and their descriptions sounded accurate."

"They were mistaken." My head ached and my stomach churned. I sat down blindly at the tea table.

Mr. Braddock looked down at me, pity swimming in his eyes. "Perhaps," he assented softly. "I had intended to speak to her tonight and, if it was Miss Rosamund, bid her to return. I did not think it proper to involve you in the specifics."

"That was not your decision to make! You agreed to help find her, and as absurd as it sounds, you seem to think you have. But this is the reason I came to London myself. There are certain things that only I can do," I said, more furious than rational.

"Which means?"

"I must go speak to whomever this woman is and sort it out," I said.

"No," he said simply. "That is entirely out of the question."

"You cannot presume to tell me such a thing!" I spluttered. "Besides, you said it wasn't a brothel. Why should I stay away?"

"It still has its share of . . . unsavory individuals. A woman like you does not belong there."

"If it truly is my sister, our family will have far greater worries, I can assure you," I said. "In any case, I will wear a mask, and no one will recognize me."

"It is not only your reputation I am concerned about." Mr. Braddock's civil demeanor was beginning to crack.

"I have no care for your concerns," I said. "This is the only way I will be convinced it's her. I came to London against my parents' wishes, and I am perfectly capable of doing this alone, as well."

He crumpled the paper in his hands, registering how futile it was to argue. He returned to pacing the length of the small garden, shaking his head, and fussing with the seams of his cuffs.

"Very well," he said. "Then I will be here this evening at seven."

"Unnecessary. I shall be fine myself."

"You will be eaten alive." His voice rasped with scorn. "If you are going to be so foolhardy as to go through with this plan, then I will accompany you."

"I don't need a chap—" I automatically snapped, but the memory of the drunken men in the alley was too fresh. I stood up, unable to resist the wine any longer. I poured it into a teacup and ignored the snort behind me.

"Ah, so you know what to do when a man takes you for a doxy?"

Mortified, I felt my face flush, but somehow kept myself from spitting out the wine. "When a man takes me for a . . . doxy? So you see it as an inevitability—why, thank you."

He prowled uneasily close to me, and I fumbled and dropped the cup. I only heard it shatter, unable to look away from the advancing oaf.

"Forgive me for sullying your innocent ears, but if you go to a dancing room unaccompanied, you will hear much worse. And you will inevitably be taken for that kind of woman even if you're wearing a nun's habit."

"Ah, and you know this with all *your* infinite brothel experience."

"Yes," he said firmly, not acknowledging the insult. "Now, seven o'clock—I will be here. It's no longer a question. Be ready and wear a plain, unadorned mask—the sort you might wear to a masquerade ball."

Insufferable. I had nothing left to say to the obstinate man.

"Fine," I muttered. "Now if you'll excuse me, I have better places to search this morning."

"Very well. But let me help—" he said, leaning forward to assist with the cup's sad remains.

I blocked his way. "I will be quite fine."

He nodded and drew back gracefully. "Do try to stay out of trouble today." I could hear the smirk in his voice. He buttoned up his coat and opened the door while I knelt to pick up the shards of porcelain with as much dignity as I could muster.

"You too. Try not to pick a fight with Tuffins as he lets you ou—!" But the final word became a yelp as a sharp ceramic edge drew a ragged cut over my palm, blood pooling up over the torn flesh.

Mr. Braddock was gone. I stared down at the glassy red coloring my hand, both nauseated and abstractly intrigued by the sight of my own blood. It welled into a small pool and dripped onto the wine-stained dirt below.

I carefully wrapped a handkerchief around my palm and headed upstairs to wash the cut clean. But when I took it off mere minutes later, only smooth, unbroken skin stared back up at me. I began to wonder exactly how much wine I had drunk. It could not have been enough for me to hallucinate, could it?

I hastened to my reticule, wildly grabbing a card—Mr. Kent's, actually—and sliced at my finger, causing a stinging paper cut. Though the graze still smarted, I watched closely as my skin knit itself back together in a matter of seconds.

The room spun. The blood on the handkerchief was all I could see, mocking me. I could no longer ignore the evidence.

I truly had the ability to heal.

Twelve

"I'M SORRY, MR. BRADDOCK," I forced out. "You were right. I believe you now."

My reflection managed to keep a mostly straight face.

Close enough. It had taken at least fifty tries in front of the looking glass before I had steeled myself to the point where I wouldn't gag during this. Though nothing could be done about the wince.

The only way I could even stomach an apology was by avoiding the fact that Mr. Braddock had been right and instead concentrating on my newfound powers. *Powers.* It still conjured up the same feelings it had hours ago—a sort of humbling awe at all the possibilities it opened up in the world. There was no word for it. It wasn't just *amazing. Spectacular* did not fit, nor simply *astonishing* or *fantastic.* Everything seemed to be an understatement.

I stared down at my arm, holding it up to the light. If I were a normal girl, my arm would still be covered with all the small nicks and scrapes I had given myself throughout the morning. Instead, they had all closed up within seconds, my skin left as smooth as it had ever been. Not even the faintest scar.

In a daze, I peeked out of my bedroom window and

concentrated on the street. There was no denying my body's ability to repair itself, but it still felt wrong to think I had the power to heal others. That had always been Rose! Perhaps Miss Lodge had simply had a good day. But an irrepressible smile found its way to my face when I contemplated every detail. My hand ran along the chilly pane, the sturdy sill, and the soft drapes as I asked myself the same question I had been asking myself through the entire blur of a day.

No, I *wasn't* dreaming.

A sudden knock at my door startled me and sent me across the room.

"Y-yes?" I asked through the open crack.

"Mr . . . Wyndham has arrived, Miss Wyndham," Tuffins said softly. "He waits in a carriage outside."

"Did Lady Kent hear?"

"She is currently occupied with Miss Kent in the parlor. I did not think it necessary to disturb them."

"Tuffins, you are a delight."

His head bowed, and his footsteps faded away. The time had come. I felt a certain giddiness and wondered what was more unexpected: these powers or the fact that I actually wanted to see Mr. Braddock.

With Laura distracting her mother and Tuffins keeping the rest of the staff busy, I slid on my mask, crept out into the quiet hallway, made a hasty dash down two flights of stairs, and flew out the door without anyone glimpsing my dress. In a flurry of red silk, I leaped into the hansom (and nearly onto Mr. Braddock), and we were off. I hoped to God no one was watching.

My breath returned as I observed my escort. He was wearing the same black coat and trousers from the evening of Sir Winston's ball. No strange clothes, altered features, or even a false mustache. He cared not one whit about his reputation.

"Fine disguise," I said.

He stared me up and down with wide eyes. He did not have to say anything—I knew I looked like a tart. But with Laura's hideous and inappropriate red dress barely secured on my shoulders (it was as bosom bearing as I had feared), her ornately carved, gilded mask fit snugly over my eyes, and the makeup painted on my face, I was also virtually unrecognizable.

"What on earth possessed you to wear that?" he finally asked, voice terribly low, averting his eyes to stare at his hands.

"You're all kindness," I replied.

He frowned. "You completely disregarded my advice."

"I'm sorry that I couldn't bring my extensive mask collection to London in my trunk. I had to make do. And you said nothing about my dress."

"That should have been self-evident. Instead of blending in, you will be the center of attention."

"Well, it can't be changed now. Do you want to pull out your copy of *She Walks in Beauty* and spend the next hour acting moody?"

"Why don't—" He stopped abruptly and took a breath. "Normally I'm good at being polite, but with you, I have to try *very* hard."

"Were you trying very hard the two times you've compared me to a prostitute today?"

He huffed and cleared his throat. "That was not my intention. I apologize."

"It's no matter, but perhaps it's better if we discuss something less hazardous for the time being. Say something about the weather, or ask me about my day."

He gazed out past the closed curtain. "The weather's fine, and I already know how your day went. You searched at more shops and discovered nothing."

Well, he was only somewhat correct. He didn't know Mr. Kent and I had visited more science societies to find nothing, as well. He didn't know that I hid tonight's plans from Mr. Kent, the idea of mentioning it flipping my stomach over and over. And he didn't know that I believed his wild stories now.

"I discovered something," I replied. "I have the power to heal. Myself, at least."

He gave me a withering stare. "Very funny."

Did I really have to convince him that he had convinced me? "Mr. Braddock, I—well, I am quite sure. Though there wasn't much grandeur for such a momentous occasion. No dramatic moment where I finally believed in myself and healed someone who was on the brink of death. I just cut my hand on that stupid teacup this morning, and it healed. So did the other cuts."

Mr. Braddock studied me, daring to hope that I was not teasing him. "What other cuts?"

"I gave myself paper cuts—which still stung and bled, mind you—but after a few seconds, the wound would close and the mark would disappear."

"That's . . . remarkable," Mr. Braddock said faintly, eyes wide with wonder.

"As the one who told me of this, you have no right to be shocked."

"It's just—still—hearing you describe it . . . it's impressive. I had inklings, but I did not know exactly how it worked."

"I was rather hoping you would be the one to tell me."

"I'm still learning about these powers. The little I know has only come from others."

"How many others are there?"

He shifted toward me, ensconcing me in the corner of the cab. I felt like it was just the two of us in all of London. "I couldn't say.

As far as I know, it's rather rare—otherwise the public would have noticed it. I've met several others, and that is only because I knew a man who was studying this phenomenon."

"Who is he?"

The carriage rumbled and creaked over a rocky road, and he steadied himself. "The originator of the saltation theory. And from the others, I learned that everyone who develops the power does so between the ages of fourteen and sixteen."

"We started nursing when Rose was fourteen and I was fifteen. . . ."

"And when they do start to appear, it is a weaker, more haphazard form of the ability. I would guess it took longer for your patients to be healed when you first started."

"We thought it was because Rose was still learning."

"That is the period when the ability is still developing. It does not appear consistently, and when it does, it is weaker—not quite as noticeable. From that moment on, one develops their power consciously or, in your case, unconsciously until it levels off."

I couldn't help but stare at my hands. Two years. Two long years of treating nearly every person in Bramhurst, and neither of us realized it. "What about you?" I asked.

"It took me some time to realize it, as well," he said vaguely and seemed to retreat into the corner of his seat.

"But what exactly is it? The power to locate missing sisters?" I asked with a smile.

He didn't find the joke amusing. Or perhaps he didn't find it at all. He blinked as if he were coming out of a dream. "No . . . it's a sort of physical protection. I can take a person's energy, put them to sleep."

"Ah, from your scintillating conversation?"

He shook his head uncomfortably. "Direct contact. My presence, to some degree."

"So that . . . sensation, it comes from you?"

"I had thought it was you," he replied, looking at the ceiling. "Maybe it is both of us."

"Who else is out there?" I asked. "What other sorts of powers have you seen?"

"Many of them are talents you might have even seen and not realized. It's sometimes hard to tell. There's Claude with his strength. Another who could not feel pain. One with an astonishingly quick mind for calculations. And two men, acquaintances, with gifted sight and hearing. They are the ones I spoke of before, who run the gambling den and make a living off the information they collect. They pointed me to the Argyll."

"Then you're convinced Rose is here," I said.

His hand raked through his dark hair. "We should be prepared."

"At this point, I might even be hoping it is her, just to be rid of this uncertainty. But if it is, I don't know what I will even do."

"If you'd like to wait outside while I speak with her—"

I interrupted. "I don't need you to play hero and protect me."

The corner of his mouth flicked up. "If I recall correctly, I have already saved your life once. Please let me know if the assistance is needed again."

My mouth let out an annoying squawk, so I shut it and settled for glowering at the man. Before I could say anything intelligent, the cab groaned to a stop at a crowded corner.

"Closest I can take you, sir!" the driver shouted.

Outside, droves of men and women alighted from their rides and converged on the establishment at the end of the street. We would have to walk half a block in public to get there. Splendid.

One deep breath later, Mr. Braddock was leading me down the sidewalk. It was a struggle to keep up in my dress, the tight bosom designed to treat breathing as an afterthought. Most of the women around me wore dresses in the fashions I'd seen during the season. The colors weren't as garish as I had expected, the cuts were more modest, and the trimmings tasteful, which only made me feel more naked as cool breezes nipped at my bare shoulders. Men leered at every woman who passed, and their eyes greedily lapped up any flash of skin. My skin crawled as the memory of the drunkards chilled through me again, and I stared stiffly ahead, blocking out everyone.

Finally, signs for THE ARGYLL ROOMS and THE WHITE ROSE welcomed us at the elaborately draped and gilded entrance. A few shillings gained us entry inside, down the marble stairs into a striking, airy hall furnished with lush red carpeting, polished gas chandeliers on high ceilings, and purple velvet sofas scattered about the room. More stares greeted me every step of the way. Mr. Braddock turned to me with a self-righteous look. "Still pleased you came?"

"Quite. I may just start coming here regularly," I said, hoping he missed the quiver in my voice.

He paused at the edge of the vivid crowd. A large band played on an elevated stage while couples waltzed scandalously close on the open dance space in front. The scents of perfumes and fresh flowers mingled in the air with the waft of liquor. Still, for all the supposed debauchery, the entire scene seemed oddly similar to Sir Winston's ball.

Rather than join the chaos, we found our way around and upstairs to a balcony area, where unaccompanied women scanned the dance floor with bored looks on their painted faces, sipped their champagne, and tapped their fans to the music. Behind them were a number of poorly painted scenes from Greek and Roman mythology, and I nearly gagged in disgust at one atrocious rendering of a disproportionate Hades (with a head as big as the rest of his body) and a one-legged Persephone. This was more offensive than anything else we had seen this night.

At an upstairs bar, Mr. Braddock abruptly stopped and ordered two glasses of champagne. When the pretty barmaid delivered the drinks, Mr. Braddock shouted something to her, inaudible to me over the din.

"Downstairs near the floor!" she said with a lascivious grin, leaning in intently.

Mr. Braddock shied away and nodded in thanks, maintaining a gentlemanly distance. He turned around and found a place at the chipped gold railing overlooking the dazzling display on the dance floor.

"Rose?" I asked.

"No."

"Who are you looking for, then?"

"A person."

He was infuriating. "Can we please go back to the full, honest answers?" I asked.

"They can wait till we have the time."

Knowing I would learn nothing further, I gulped the champagne, the delicious fizzle traveling down my throat, warming my chest, settling in my stomach, and hopefully steadying my nerves for the night.

Leaning on the railing, I glanced up at Mr. Braddock. He stood perfectly still while his eyes swiveled left and right, inspecting the crowd and inspecting them again. Between the tightness of his set, determined jaw and the hint of dark stubble under his chin, he looked like an intense gambler with too many cards to watch. The veins in his neck seemed to be under constant duress, and I had the childish impulse to poke at them.

Once he deemed our angle insufficient, Mr. Braddock took me on a slow lap around the room along the balcony path, checking for his mysterious contact from several vantage points. Eventually, the exciting odyssey led us back to where we started at the stairs connecting the two floors, and—

An extremely familiar voice floated upstairs, step by step:

". . . so I told him the reason Paris is cleaner is their minds take up all the filth!"

Hoping I had made a mistake, I peeked my head around the corner for a look. Smart suit, birch cane, sardonic smirk. It was most decidedly Mr. Kent.

I didn't know whether to feel ashamed for being here, angry about his being here, or guilty for lying to him. None of those feelings seemed particularly pleasant, so instinctively, I pushed Mr. Braddock into a nook just around the corner of the stairs to hide.

"You are aware that you have a mask?" Mr. Braddock asked in a strangled voice, as his back hit the wall.

"And you're aware you neglected to bring one?" I snapped back. "It's my—it's Mr. Kent. You may not remember him from the ball, but he will certainly recognize you immediately. Stop being tall. Put your head down."

At a loss, I burrowed further into the shallow space, mind whirring angrily as I tried to hide him. This was entirely his fault. We were trapped. Even if I was well disguised, once Mr. Kent saw Mr. Braddock, he'd see me, dressed like this, with Mr. Braddock instead of him, and he would not be happy. All my plans would fall down around our heads.

A warm, ragged breath disturbed the hairs on my forehead,

and my blood began pricking as I realized where exactly I had retreated: right into Mr. Braddock, our strange connection humming through the hairsbreadth of distance between our bodies, our faces. I froze, forcing myself to stop shoving against him further. Before I understood anything, a rough, large hand brushed my chin, my face tipped upwards, and his mouth caught mine, and suddenly my entire body was on fire. Whatever odd sensation had thrummed between us before was just the stroke of a violin bow to this clash of an orchestra. I felt the world pass between our lips, tasting champagne, hunger, and something indefinably darker, while his hand ignited sparks down my cheek to the nape of my neck. He wrapped an arm around my waist, pulling me closer, forcing that elusive essence to run deeper than my skin, deeper than my veins, until my very bones vibrated.

I stumbled back. My lips had never been so alive, and I was absurdly aware that my body both shivered from his touch and burned with embarrassment. My brain refused to work, and all my mouth could form was, "Mr. Braddock, w-w-why—"

"Why would you do that to avoid your suitor?" His voice was grave, breath broken, and . . . and he could not be serious. I looked up and found his nostrils flaring, brow bent disapprovingly, shadowing eyes flooded with reproach . . . for *me*. My stomach dropped to the floor, and it was all I could do not to let my entire body follow suit. "What—he is not my—and you are the one who kissed me—"

"Your masterful plan of leaning in and closing your eyes didn't present me with much of a choice."

"There was the choice of *not* kiss—"

"There she is," he interrupted, peering over my head at the lower level. "Wait here. Do not move."

"What? No. Stop!"

He brushed by, and the thumps of his steps faded down the stairs. Mr. Kent was nowhere to be seen, but I felt not a bit of relief. Damn them both! Mr. Kent here while he was supposed to be helping me—much like he accused Mr. Braddock of earlier! And Mr. Braddock pretending to be concerned about my reputation, kissing me in a brothel, and then suggesting that I forced him? Ridiculous. And where did he go? He had slipped around the outskirts and vanished behind the mob of dancers, drinkers, and dandies. Lovely. He had abandoned me. I rushed along the railing, circling around and searching from other angles to see the hidden spaces in the corners and behind columns.

A large, boisterous laugh erupted above all the other noise, and I traced it to a plump, extravagantly dressed woman who looked to be the center of attention. There was a matronly air about her. She looked like one of those older women in society who simply must have everyone around them married off at any cost. With a wave of her hand, she introduced a woman to a man, and the couple disappeared together through a side door. Ah, a brothel owner, conducting her business here. And next in line was Mr. Braddock.

She did not pair him up like the others, though. Instead, he somehow compelled the matron to send the other clients and girls away so they could have a private conversation. I tried futilely to get a more intimate look when a smooth voice to my left uttered a greeting, and I nearly threw myself over the railing right there.

"All this drinking and dancing and flirting," Mr. Kent said with a sigh, balancing a glass on the railing for me. "Dreadful business, isn't it?"

"Yes, I don't understand it," I mumbled, accepting the champagne as if it could magically transport me away. No, still here. What on earth was he getting at? Was he toying with me?

"That's just it. Perspective is a curious thing. One day, you see everything from one angle and you think you know what's important," he continued, looking out at the dancers. Then he turned to me, smiling wryly. "Then another day, from another angle, you see what's really important, and everything else just . . . melts away."

"I see," I said without meeting his eyes, hoping he'd be dissuaded.

He wasn't. His hand slid across the railing and caught mine. "I have never seen you here before. Are you one of Mrs. Shine's girls?" he asked.

Seen you here before? Downstairs, the tempo of the violins and cellos quickened. As my blood boiled, I could barely hear my own thoughts, and the response left my lips compulsively. "No."

"Excellent, then might I ask, who is your—"

"I'm sorry, I can't help you," I interrupted, hurrying away past the bar and the horrible paintings toward the stairs.

"Please, wait!" he called from behind, chasing after me. "What is your name?"

"Evelyn Wyndham," I said, giving him a false name.

Dammit. Champagne and Mr. Kent did not mix well.

"M-miss Wyndham!" he exclaimed. For a moment, it was rather strange to see the confident man look so confused, but he quickly regained himself with a smile. "I . . . I was just having a bit of fun. I knew it was you."

"Oh, was that before or after you propositioned me?"

"That is a question with no right answer, but keep in mind what I was saying about perspective earlier—"

"I've heard quite enough of your perspective," I said. Mortified, I broke off, ran down the stairs, and plunged into the most crowded part of the room to make my way to Mr. Braddock. Lost in the stuffy masses, I tore past amorous couples, cringing as I felt the wet stickiness of their drinks splashing onto my shoulders.

When I emerged at the other end of the room, I found Mr. Braddock speaking to the ruddy brothel owner. Hissing his name, I marched over, very aware that Mr. Kent was still at my shoulder.

"Ah, so you already brought a girl," she said, eyeing me like a slab of beef at the butcher's shop. I glared back in response, sick of all these hungry looks.

Mr. Braddock slid between the brothel owner and me, his eyes holding mine in reproach. "What is the matter?" he whispered harshly.

"Mr. Kent has joined me. Apparently he is familiar with this place."

Mr. Braddock glared over my shoulder, taking in Mr. Kent's slick appearance. He was clearly unimpressed. "Ah, your spy. And what is he doing here?"

"He's here because he thought it best to retrieve Miss Rosamund without exposing Miss Wyndham to such a place," Mr. Kent put in darkly.

"Well, this 'White Rose' is due to perform now, and we are meeting her after. You'll have to retrieve her from us." Mr. Braddock turned to the stage.

"He is certainly bossy," Mr. Kent grumbled in my ear, glaring at Mr. Braddock on my other side.

I shushed him and closed my eyes to calm myself. With a kissing Mr. Braddock and a propositioning Mr. Kent, I had had enough. Their bickering was the last thing I wanted to listen to when other, much more urgent questions constantly bubbled up inside me. Did I really want to find Rose here? Could I persuade her to come back? How badly would this affect her reputation? Would she believe me about the powers? Only a thrumming in my hand drew me back to reality, and I realized I had been clutching

Mr. Braddock's arm. Politely, I let him have it back. Mr. Kent had caught the exchange and was staring at Mr. Braddock with a renewed, vaguely hostile interest.

The lights dimmed, which fortunately helped hide me for the moment. We remained on the periphery, while the rest of the crowd shifted and squirmed for a better view of the evening's entertainment. With a flourish, the orchestra began a new tune, and out of the dark, a half-covered ivory leg peeped out to tease the audience. Licentious men shouted out vulgar comments and hollered like ravenous wolves.

Another half-bare leg followed, and the girl stepped in front of the band, igniting the cheers and chattering of all her devoted spectators. Her back turned to us, she glided across the space in a most definitely incomplete gold-and-white dress that matched the colors of the room. Her curled blond hair bounced with her movements as she swayed to each piano note, swung her hips at every wail of the violin strings, and waved her finger to the whistling of the flute.

The music crescendoed and cut out. Then came the girl's beautiful voice, ringing out over the silent hall. Her French words hung in the air, the moment lasting an eternity. The music joined back in as she finally whirled around to face us.

And there was no question about it. Those deep blue eyes, that porcelain face. No one could look quite so angelic. No one could fill you with such warmth in a glance. And no one could inspire so much hope from a single note of a song.

No one, of course, but Rose.

Thirteen

———

I FELT THE two men glance at me, presumably with sympathy, but I could not look at them. Nor at Rose. Nor the audience. Not even the stained floor. I couldn't look at anything in this damned place.

"This way, Mr. Braddock," the matron said with a greasy smile but stopped and frowned at Mr. Kent, who seemed to be hiding his face. "Not you, Mr. Kent."

He gasped theatrically. "Ah, my dear Mrs. Shine! Why on earth not? I am with these two."

"These two don't have debt." A snort came from Mr. Braddock's direction, and Mr. Kent looked rightfully embarrassed. I closed my dropped jaw before he could notice it, and the woman sniffed, turning to weave through the crowd.

Mr. Braddock ushered me ahead of him, while a man, presumably employed by Mrs. Shine, stepped in to keep Mr. Kent from following. Only his protests slipped by: "It's my father's debt, not mine!"

But we were already being led through the discreet side exit, down a dim red corridor, and through one of several black doors. The door opened on a small violet-scented room—golden and luxurious, matching the Argyll Rooms' theme. The far wall housed a lavish dresser overflowing with bottles of perfumes and makeup precariously strewn near the edge. In the nearest corner, a velvet curtain, covering what looked like a private changing area, swayed in the breeze from an open window. Next to it sat a large bed with red satin sheets.

"Just one small matter, Mr. Braddock," the matron said, holding out a bill. He compensated her with a signature. Satisfied, she slipped out, leaving us alone in the indecent room.

"Did you just pay for . . . ?" I half asked. I tried hard to not stare at the red sheets and imagine what normally happened between them.

"I apologize, there was no other way to speak to Miss Rosamund privately," Mr. Braddock explained, lounging against a bare wall.

"It's quite all right. You appear to be a regular customer already," I replied.

He flashed me a look of annoyance, then shook his head, refusing to respond as he roamed around the room. A collection of perfume bottles caught his attention. "Do you recognize any of these?"

I took a quick, cursory glance, but I already knew the answer. "None of this is hers."

The muffled music peaked and cut out, followed by cheers, whistling, and applause continuing for what seemed like hours. The clack of footsteps echoed down the hallway, the doorknob turned, and suddenly there she stood. Her wide eyes flinched in surprise and then relaxed when she put on a warm, welcoming smile. I stood paralyzed for a moment, studying her closely. Then, slowly, feeling returned to my limbs. It was her.

"Rose," I murmured.

A heavy flutter of relief set my feet in motion, and I lunged at her for a hug. Squeezing my sister's tiny frame, I expelled every single bit of tension, anxiety, and nervousness—naturally, it took a long time to get that all out. When I finally released her, Rose gasped a huge breath, and I could not help but laugh and apologize.

As my euphoria began to settle, Rose greeted Mr. Braddock with a pleasant smile. "And how are you?"

"Fine," he answered, his eyebrows curved in confusion.

She glided over to a stool in front of her looking glass and started to wipe off her makeup. "What brings you two here?"

Dumbfounded, I stared at her. "I should ask you the very same question."

She hesitated for the slightest moment before patting her eyes with a towel. "I like it here," she explained as if it settled everything.

"You ran away to London in the dead of night to sing at a brothel?"

"Please, it is a dancing room. I've always wanted to live in London, and I *do* enjoy singing. Let's not quarrel. This is only temporary, anyway."

I shot Mr. Braddock a quizzical glance. He returned the gesture. Something was not right. Out of the thousands of iterations in my head, I had not imagined my conversation with Rose taking this path. "Temporary until what?" I asked.

"Until I earn enough money for school."

"You didn't even ask Mother. She might have said yes."

"Oh, please. You don't actually believe that, do you, Evelyn?"

"I don't know. I'm just—I don't understand. Do you know how worried I was? Your note was so strange, and I—I thought you were kidnapped or—" I refused to tear up. Not for this. I had to convince her or, if need be, demand she come back.

She stood up and interrupted me with another hug. "I'm sorry for the mess. I did not mean for you to go through all of that. But there's no need to worry anymore. I'm perfectly well now, see, Evie?" She flashed me a smile to ease my tension.

My breath knocked out of me, I stared at Rose, not knowing how to react. Had I gone mad?

"What did you just call me?" I asked, regaining my power of speech.

Rose finished cleaning her face and threw her towel over the back of a chair. "What?" she asked back.

"You just called me Evie, did you not?"

She shrugged, pulling the window open wider with a screech. I turned to confirm the word (along with my sanity) with Mr. Braddock. "Did she not say Evie?"

Perplexed, he slowly nodded. "I believe she did."

"Are you well, Evelyn? I don't understand what you're going on about." Rose fidgeted with the edges of the velvet curtain, ready to cover herself up. Her gaze turned to Mr. Braddock. "Perhaps I could have a moment to change?"

He nodded and headed toward the door, but my hand popped out to block him. I marched closer to the curtain and found myself staring deep into Rose's pupils, hoping that would help extract all her secrets. There was something strange about all of this. Though it went against every bit of logic, I had felt it somewhere deep in my bones from the moment I walked in here.

"Who are you?" I asked her.

She cocked her head in disbelief. "What has gotten into you? It's me, Rose."

"Fine, *Rose*, then who am I? Just a simple question," I persisted.

"My darling sister. Now, I don't understand what's gotten into you, but please stop. You're worrying me." She shook her head and ducked behind the curtain to change her clothing.

"And who is he?" I asked, pointing to Mr. Braddock.

Rose peeked out. "I think it's best that you two leave now."

Mr. Braddock stepped up by my side and held his ground. "Answer the question," he demanded.

"Your husband, of course."

A thick silence dangled in the air. Unsure how to act, Mr. Braddock and I exchanged baffled looks when suddenly, the curtain flew back in a blur and not-Rose leaped out of the window and out of the room. Quick as a wolf, Mr. Braddock rushed to follow and hurdled through the gap. Blast it! My skirts would not fit through there. I regained control of my legs and went for the door, hurried down the dim hallway, and burst out the back exit into another dreary alleyway.

The cold air hit me hard, prickling patterns of awareness onto my bare skin. I drew a sharp breath, held up my skirts, and awkwardly pursued them in my unwieldy outfit as rats squeaked and skittered at my feet. Mr. Braddock flew down the passage, and it seemed a hopeless struggle to catch him. His shrinking figure led me across the empty stone street into another connecting alleyway, through a cracked wooden fence, and to a sharp right turn at the end of the passage. As I emerged onto the main road, Mr. Braddock escaped my vision, vanishing around a distant, gaslit corner. His long shadow chaotically bounced across the streets and buildings, serving as my only guide.

Hastily crossing the road to follow, I barely dodged a whinnying horse and its carriage and splashed through a puddle of what I hoped was water. The icy jolt shot a rush of energy up my burning legs, and I pushed forward, panting and stumbling up and down high sidewalk curbs and around piles of sharp gravel by a half-constructed building.

After the next block, I stopped at the intersection, lost and gasping, the chase out of sight. A cough echoed down the vacant street, leading me to the entrance of another concealed back alley, where a collapsed woman wheezed and coughed as she climbed to her knees. Next to her, a blushing, bearded man bent down to inquire about her health.

As I approached, Mr. Braddock stepped out and raised his eyebrows at me before centering his attention back on the woman. She still wore Rose's dress, hidden under a dark cloak from her dressing room, but her skin was now a caramel color, her hair charcoal black, and her blue eyes narrowed.

"How did—you catch her?" I asked Mr. Braddock through my staggered breath.

"She believed kissing a man on the street would hide her from her pursuers," he replied with an accusatory glare.

"Little did she know her pursuer was such an expert," I shot back.

"Miss, are you all right? W-what have these two done?" the bearded man asked meekly, as if he really didn't want to get involved.

"They are advising you to continue on your way, sir," Mr. Braddock growled.

The man flinched, but he still shook his head and stood his ground, unconvinced.

"We are from the . . . London health department," I added. "This woman has a highly contagious fever. I suggest you see a doctor immediately and rest."

The woman tried to say something, but she coughed again,

punctuating my suggestion. It was enough for the man. Wide-eyed and wordless, he hurried away.

"We will return to the Argyll Rooms to talk," Mr. Braddock told the woman as he led the way. "Are you hurt?"

She was well on her way to recovery—no injuries, just tired out from the chase. Not that it mattered: Either way, I lacked the patience to let this go on any longer.

"No, we're not waiting!" I exclaimed, grabbing her arm and stopping in front of her. "What is—why did you do all of . . . this?" I gestured to the remains of her disguise.

"I was hired," she replied in a nasally French accent.

"By whom?"

She scoffed. "I am a professional, and I enjoy getting paid large sums of money for my secrecy."

I looked to Mr. Braddock, unsure what to do as she sauntered past me. Perhaps he could be more threatening.

"The only thing I enjoy more is getting paid a larger sum for my betrayal," she added coyly over her shoulder.

Without a second thought, Mr. Braddock reached into his pocket and handed her a small bag of coins. I was beginning to owe this man quite a bit of money that my family didn't have. Her eyes glittered as she turned, snatched the money, and smiled sweetly at us—her new clients. "How can I be of assistance?" she purred.

"Who are you?"

"Camille. I do not give out my last name for any amount of money."

"Do you know where my sister is?" I demanded.

"Yes," she said with a wink. "She is quite lovely, you know. Easily the most beautiful girl I've ever been."

That sent a chill down my back. "Where did you see her?"

"No need to be so threatening. I will explain. You'll get your money's worth." She looked at her dim reflection in a storefront window and adjusted her hair as we walked. "I don't work for the men you are seeking or whatever their organization is. I work for myself."

"Organization?"

"There were three men, but they appeared quite well funded, so I presumed there was a source for the equipment."

"Three men—" I started.

Camille interrupted. "Try to be patient." I was ready to hit her.

"I have always had a talent of sorts for disguising myself. Some people are naturally fast or strong. I am naturally skilled at studying and imitating others. My makeup, costume, and acting abilities are flawless."

"You have a power?"

Camille looked at us skeptically. "I do not know what you mean."

"She does," Mr. Braddock jumped in. "I've heard stories about her."

"I have a natural skill, yes, but it was nothing without training. I've done this for the last twenty years and developed a reputation for my services as London's specialist."

"There are people who hire you to impersonate another?" I prodded.

"That is only half my work. I can also disguise clients however they wish," she replied, delicately tapping her forehead. Had those wrinkles been there before? "Three days ago, a man arrived at my home. He asked for a week of my services."

"Was his name Claude? Or Mr. Cheval?"

"He was a very large, swarthy, singular-looking man. He spoke with a quiet voice *en français*."

Good—we had the right one this time. Mr. Braddock's attention was fixed on Camille as we turned a dark corner under a broken gas lamp, and she continued: "He briefly explained the job, the payment, and asked whether I had the appropriate resources and abilities, to which I said yes."

"Who was the employer?" Mr. Braddock eagerly questioned.

Camille shot him a glare. "He did not give his name. Now, please stop interrupting the job you paid me to do."

He narrowed his eyes and stopped in front of her as a threat. "We are in a hurry," he said. "She may be in danger."

She brushed by him, unperturbed, and continued down the street. "She is safe. It is in their best interests to keep her well, it seems."

Mr. Braddock turned and followed, confusion lining his brow.

"How do you know that?" I asked.

"The large man brought me to a house to meet the two others in a laboratory room. The first man was pale, thin, and did not speak much. The other—a short man who appeared to be in charge—he told me to play the part of your sister for a week and build up a public reputation for her. When I agreed, they led me up one floor to your sister's room and gave me some time to speak with her so I could study her face, voice, and mannerisms."

"Was she—was she well?" I asked.

"Well enough to trick me. When I spoke with her, I pretended to be a servant trying to help her escape. I asked about her nearest relations and who to contact first for help."

I felt a surge of anger. It was both a horrible lie and a clever trick. "So you would be prepared with enough details to fool anyone who came looking for Rose," I said.

Camille nodded. "But it seems she did not entirely trust me. She told me she calls you Evie sometimes, and that you are married. I gather that isn't true."

I shook my head, unable to withhold a proud smile. Imprisoned in that room, Rose still outwitted them.

Mr. Braddock rejoined with a renewed charge of urgency. "What were you to do after the week was over?" he asked Camille.

"After I made a reputation for your sister, they would supply me with a body to be disguised as her and discovered, so any search by the police or the family would be ended." For such a horrible topic, she was rather nonchalant about the matter.

"You—you must be joking," I said.

"Not at all. I gathered he did not want to be bothered by a wealthy family's search," Camille replied, sashaying down the street.

"If I can provide you sufficient compensation, will you abandon your next few days of work?" Mr. Braddock asked.

Camille nodded greedily. "That can be arranged."

He handed her another set of notes. "Very good," he replied.

The elaborate kidnapping plan left me further unnerved. Whoever had taken Rose planned for and anticipated everything. Why was she so important to a man with a laboratory? What were they planning to do with her? If there were scientists who knew about powers, did that mean Rose could be someone's research experiment? My anxiety gave way to anger, and stamping on a discarded newspaper provided little relief.

"We're going now," I said firmly to Mr. Braddock.

"Were they settled in this house?" he asked Camille.

"I believe so. I was to receive half my payment there next week."

With those hopeful words, we found ourselves back in front of the Argyll Rooms. Hundreds of cabs waited along the street for the night to end so they could take passengers home or to a hotel. Drunken couples occasionally sauntered out, oblivious to their surroundings. One gentleman somehow procured his lady's shoe and vomited in it.

Mr. Braddock found a pencil and a card in his pocket. He handed them to Camille. "The address, please."

She wrote down the information. When she finished, she handed me her own card and, as a good-bye, made me one last offer: "If you have the money, I can disguise you much more convincingly!"

I resisted the temptation to tell her it wasn't bloody likely as she disappeared back into the building.

We made our way back to the street, where Mr. Braddock found an open cab and helped me inside. "This will take you back to your lodgings, and I will call on you when I retrieve your sister."

"What?" I yelped, jumping back out. "No, I am going with you. I need to see her for myself."

"It's too dangerous."

"Then we will alert the police first."

He scoffed at the suggestion. "The police will not believe anything about these powers, and I do not trust them to handle it while we wait elsewhere."

"Then let me at least fetch Mr. Kent from inside. If it's dangerous, he will help make it less so."

Mr. Braddock seemed to be searching for an argument, but he found none. "Very well, fetch him."

As I spun around to head back to the Argyll Rooms, I felt Mr. Braddock climbing into the cab behind me and realized his trick. I refused to let him leave me behind.

"I don't trust you to wait," I said, climbing inside.

He admitted defeat and tapped the roof, the hansom rushing forward with the clatter and clinking of wood, stone, and horseshoes. We traveled westward in silence, past Hyde Park, through Knightsbridge, and into Chelsea, where I lost all sense of direction as the cab careened through narrow streets and pulled to a sharp stop in front of an ugly, small building.

"So this is your plan?" I asked as Mr. Braddock paid the driver. "The two of us will walk in and forcefully retrieve Rose from three men?"

He opened the cab door and climbed out. "Not quite," he replied, shutting it in my face. "I will do it myself."

Fourteen

"MR. BRADDOCK, WHAT do you—"

The driver took off down the street with me still inside.

"Wait! Let me go! I'm still here! Stop the cab, sir!" I yelled.

"Sorry, ma'am, fella paid me well," he shouted back.

As the cab picked up speed, the whole of Mr. Braddock disappeared, shadowy as his stupid past. Damn it all.

I grasped for excuses. "He's mad! You must turn around! He's a thief who stole from me!"

"Then—then I say we best get as far as we can!"

A frustrated scream grew within me, climbing through my chest, crawling up my throat. I banged on the roof with all my might. The whole cab rattled, but the driver said nothing. He was only going faster and getting farther away.

Dammit. I pushed open the hansom door and watched the dark, painful-looking road rush by below me. A gulp as the cab slowed to make a turn and I leaped out, hitting the ground hard, rolling, tumbling across the pavement, pain bouncing around my body and then filling it as I slowed to a stop.

I pushed myself up to my feet, reminding myself that the

damage wasn't permanent, and limped my way back around the turn and down the road, scanning building numbers and hoping I'd be able to find the house.

Nearing the end of the road, I slowed in front of a building that seemed familiar, and a heavy bang conveniently rang out to confirm it. Movement and shadows in the glowing second-floor window. Images of bloody Roses and broken Mr. Braddocks flashed in my mind. No time for nervousness. The front door was unlocked, the shattered window next to it presumably Mr. Braddock's subtle work. A strange feeling of familiarity chilled me as I padded up the bare-board stairs to the second-floor landing and rounded the banister. Mr. Braddock had paused at the threshold of a room at the end of the hall.

He looked back over his shoulder, briefly shooting me a grim, frustrated glare as he removed his gloves. But something more important immediately spun his attention back. Before I could reach his side at the doorway, he clutched the jamb and blocked me out.

"I'm here to see what you are—" I said, my harsh whisper cut short by the sight of the towering Claude, whose head nearly grazed the ceiling.

In his gentle voice, Claude spoke with a stilted politeness: "Miss Wyndham."

"Go back downstairs," Mr. Braddock breathed, betraying a touch of panic.

I started to protest, but a voice interrupted. "Mr. Braddock *and* Miss Wyndham! Two pleasant surprises. You need not have broken in. I would have gladly invited you, had I known you were in town."

At the far corner, a short, lean man in a white coat stood up at his desk and crossed the room to greet us. As he passed glass jars, tubes, microscopes, and all sorts of equipment that stood in perfect ranks throughout the laboratory, I remembered that I *had* been here before. In my dream two nights ago.

The searing, clean smell of chemicals sharpened the air, growing stronger as the man approached. Large, almost silver eyes stood out in a waxen face. A normal man, unremarkable in every way, but for those eyes—watery, intelligent, and too pale. He stopped beside Claude and bowed to us.

"It has been too long," he said. Was he speaking to me? Or Mr. Braddock?

"Where is my sister?" I demanded, refusing to be frightened by this man.

A glint of unexpected intensity and vexation jumped into those eyes. "I'm sorry?" he asked. And seeing that glint of danger, suddenly I was the one who was sorry.

Still, I refused to let my voice fall. "Rose. Small, fair, beloved sister. You took her, now give her back."

He peered up at Claude in mock confusion. "I apologize. . . . I believe there has been a mistake," he replied.

"Where is Miss Rosamund?" Mr. Braddock demanded—a darker, more potent anger emanating from him.

"She healed my sister yesterday," the giant claimed, a horrible liar. "I have not seen her since."

"Camille saw her locked in here," I spat out, feeling like a pesky child as I bobbed behind Mr. Braddock's shoulder, trying to glare at them.

Claude had no response, except a sidelong glance at the smaller man for their next lie.

"Where is she?" Mr. Braddock persisted. He took two steps closer to the scientist. It would have been intimidating, if Claude were not there.

The scientist attempted a soothing voice. "No need for any unpleasantness. I don't want you breaking all of my doors."

In the silence, the house creaked rhythmically above us. Footsteps. Claude's gaze flickered upward for the briefest moment. I glanced back out of the laboratory, noticing another staircase to the third floor. Was my dream right about that, too?

Before I could take a step back, the scientist flashed me a courteous smile. "I don't believe we have been properly introduced, and Mr. Braddock seems to have quite forgotten his manners. I'm Dr. Calvin Beck—"

Mr. Braddock interrupted with a growl and charged straight at Dr. Beck, who simply looked bored. Claude stepped between the two and caught Mr. Braddock's tackle. The momentum sent the giant stumbling back, but he managed to stay on his feet, while Mr. Braddock took the chance to wrap himself around Claude. From behind, Mr. Braddock reached under Claude's armpits and clasped his hands tightly together behind Claude's head, like a wrestler, locking him in an uncomfortable hold.

Unable to break the tenacious grip, Claude spun around and forced Mr. Braddock backward, slamming him hard into the walls, crashing into bookcases, and finally, in a desperate move, throwing himself out the street window. A shrill, useless scream escaped from my throat as the glass shattered and the cold London air rushed in. The pair disappeared out the window. There was the briefest silence, a thud, and a rattling.

"No!" I rushed forward and could just glimpse Mr. Braddock below, rising to his feet to face his wheezing but uninjured enemy.

"Get yourself out!" Mr. Braddock yelled up at me.

Thank heavens. Still well enough to order me about. But Rose was here, and I would not leave without her.

Legs quivering and hands shaking with nerves, I stumbled past Dr. Beck, who called after me.

"Miss Wyndham! Don't run away just yet. I wish to speak with you."

Ignoring him, I made my way out of the room and up to the top of the stairs, where two doors faced me. One opened on a sparse bedroom with three empty beds, so I turned to the other, finding an unlatched padlock on the floor and the door half open. I heard shuffling and movement from within and shoved my way desperately inside to finally find her directly in front of me.

Rose.

It was her. Not some copy, not some actress. I knew it with every beat of my frantic heart. Then terror filled her eyes.

"Evelyn," she gasped. "He's in here—"

A hand appeared out of the shadows and clamped over her mouth. And she vanished.

"Rose!"

Without a second thought, I took a desperate lunge into the darkness, reaching for her, her captor, anything. My hand caught fabric—an arm. I squeezed tight and pulled with all my strength, but suddenly I was the one pulled right into the pitch black.

The cold ground hit me. Hard. Somehow I was outside again, lying on wet cobblestone. A blast of fishy air filled my lungs, and I gagged back waves of nausea as I pushed myself off the ground in the filthy alley to find a pale, wiry man clutching Rose tightly, his arm around her mouth.

He took a slow step back, then another. He couldn't carry her and run away. I could catch him. With a gasp, I scrambled to my feet and charged. He dove out of the way, to his left, straight into the wall, into an opening that wasn't there a moment ago and wasn't there when I reached it a second later. I grasped and scratched and pounded and screamed at the brick wall, at the shadows, at nothing. The alley was completely empty and silent.

Gasping back sobs of frustration and pain, I hurried toward a streetlight in a daze. Where was I? And where in God's name was Rose? The passage brought me to the main street, where glass shards, dirt, and blood littered the ground and Dr. Beck's house loomed over me.

As I made my way back to the building's entrance, Dr. Beck emerged and chuckled. "There you are. I was worried we wouldn't get the chance to speak."

"Where is she?" I screamed.

"Your sister? Why, she's gone. My associate—no doubt you noticed, he's very gifted—why, he has probably snapped her clean out of London by now. Let's not worry about that. What's more important is that you listen to me—"

Suddenly, a loud screech echoed down the street. I turned to see Mr. Braddock and wasn't sure my eyesight was working so well. His fight with Claude had continued to where the cobblestones met the long wooden bridge over the river, and Mr. Braddock was crouched low to the ground, slowly circling his enemy and waiting for a chance to strike. But Claude rendered that nearly impossible, wielding a gas lamppost as a normal man might wield a mace. Upon Mr. Braddock's every advance, the giant swung his massive weapon with unexpected quickness, always sending Mr. Braddock back in retreat.

I rushed over, not knowing what to do, desperately trying to form a plan. The streets were empty—no one to call. Fear for the obnoxious man clouded my head. Could Mr. Braddock's power really help him defeat a man strong enough to rip a lamppost from the ground? All it would take is one small mistake, and Claude could kill him with a single blow.

He needed help.

My sights sharpened on a broken stone in a nearby pile of debris. I darted for it, lifted the weight, and hurled it with miraculous accuracy straight at Claude. It soared through the air, thickly thumped his head, and dropped to the ground. Claude simply looked over his shoulder at me and scratched his head, then turned back to Mr. Braddock.

We needed to run.

"I keep trying to explain the matter, and you keep acting very rudely," Dr. Beck's voice crept in from behind me.

My dizziness immediately turned into a sharp-edged alertness, and I spun around with a desperate attack that he stopped without hesitation, lightly pushing me away. "What is wrong with you?" I screamed. "What are you doing with her?"

"Your sister is now part of my research that will change the world. There's something in her, on a cellular level, that accelerates and heightens the human body's regenerative properties."

The grunts, the scuffling, the thunderous crashes behind me continually distracted me from the madman's quiet voice. I feared each attack would be the last, but each one also meant Mr. Braddock was still on his feet.

"It's a result of a jump in evolution . . . a process called saltation—"

"I know what it is!" I growled, flinching as another attack seemed to shake the street. But Mr. Braddock apparently took that as his cue. Like a bull, he charged straight at Claude, entering the dangerous range of his weapon, daring him to attack again and end the fight.

"Oh, he told you? Splendid. Then you understand the amazing possibilities of isolating this ability of hers. Think of the advances. Any disease curable, any injury reparable."

Swinging low, Claude and his lamppost tore through the bridge's wooden planks, just missing Mr. Braddock, who jumped over the first slash and slid under the hasty second with the help of the slick cobblestone street.

"If you're so altruistic," I snarled, "why did you kidnap her? She would have gladly helped you."

Mr. Braddock landed right at Claude's feet, vulnerable, and the giant seized the chance, stomping his boot straight down.

"I cannot be restricted in my experiments," Dr. Beck sighed.

With a quick roll, Mr. Braddock barely escaped the attack, while Claude found his foot lodged deep in the stone rubble.

"I cannot deal with hesitation, guilt, or caution if I am investigating something so important."

Mr. Braddock leaped to his feet and tried to seize the giant from behind, but Claude, desperate to escape, took a leap forward himself—his foot tearing apart the road—and dodged the grab.

"I must have the freedom to do whatever my research requires."

Claude landed at the edge of the bridge and quickly spun around, once again keeping Mr. Braddock at bay with the lamppost. Breathing heavily, they both circled each other at a distance, ending up back where they started, locked in another stalemate. How much longer could Mr. Braddock keep this up?

"The greater good is all that matters."

My stomach flipped. This scientist was rationalizing the pain and suffering he would inflict on Rose for his success.

"You're mad," I got out. "You're all stark raving mad. She's just a girl."

"There are thousands of people out there every day, forced to watch their sisters and daughters die of diseases. And they're saying the same thing."

I turned to glare at Dr. Beck. "When I tell the police of this—"

"They will do nothing," he interrupted, looking exasperated. "I have plenty of persuasive friends who are highly invested in my research. Not that it matters, as neither of you are leaving here alive anyway."

The words sliced right through me—his matter-of-fact tone, as if our death were an inevitability I was too foolish to realize.

I tightened my fists and took a deep breath, holding back my tears of frustration. "Th-then what are you waiting for?"

He didn't deign to respond. Instead, he just watched as Mr. Braddock dodged and Claude advanced, winding the lamp-post back for another swing, digging his foot into the broken ground below him, and aiming a powerful and unexpected kick right in Mr. Braddock's direction.

It happened in the blink of an eye. The cobblestone debris hit Mr. Braddock's face and sent him tumbling down, his forehead smacking the wooden bridge as he landed. With the slightest hint of satisfaction, Claude balanced the lamppost on his shoulder and made his way across the bridge to Mr. Braddock. *Get up, get up, get up*, I pleaded.

He didn't.

Claude raised the lamppost high above his head for one last blow, his grip crunching into the metal post.

"Wait!" The cry ripped itself from my chest. "Take me!"

Silence. Dr. Beck looked at me, incredulous. "I'm sorry?"

"I can heal, too! Please, just call your other man back and take me in Rose's place."

Dr. Beck narrowed his eyes skeptically as though I were the

insane one. Without a word, he turned and headed for Claude and Mr. Braddock.

Somehow, I found the legs to follow. "And you must let Mr. Braddock go."

Dr. Beck motioned to Claude, who obeyed and lowered the gas lamp as we drew closer. "If you can heal," he said.

"I can," I insisted. "I promise."

Dr. Beck knelt beside Mr. Braddock. In one swift motion, he pulled a knife out of his jacket pocket and slashed a long, cruel cut into Mr. Braddock's back as I screamed. "Then prove it."

My stomach sank, along with the rest of my body, and before I knew it, I was on the ground pressing my hands over Mr. Braddock's gushing wound, willing it to close, to fix this whole mess, to bring Rose back.

With Claude and Dr. Beck standing over me, I swallowed my fear, removed my blood-drenched hand, and found the open cut staring back at me. *No.*

Dr. Beck shook his head. "As I thought. Just because you're siblings does not mean you and Miss Rosamund both have the same ability. I've found no such correlation in my research."

"It's t-true, I promise you, it's true." My voice was as broken as my newfound power, and tears fell fast down my cheeks.

"I hope this same sense of selflessness runs in your family. Then Miss Rosamund and I shall get along very well," he said, turning to go. "Finish it!"

Claude's heavy tread approached, the lamppost scraping and rattling along the wooden planks. Clutching Mr. Braddock to myself, I slid us backward, inch by inch, as if the extra step would somehow keep us from Claude.

Suddenly, Dr. Beck spun around, calling out urgently, "Claude, watch—"

A gunshot cracked through the silence, striking the railing near Claude. A carriage screeched behind me as the bridge started to vibrate. Claude froze, watching its approach, then turned to find Dr. Beck already backing away.

"Let's go!"

Another gunshot rang through the air, and Claude retreated, not waiting to see if our savior's aim would improve upon his approach. He disappeared down the street and into the distant darkness as the carriage rumbled close. Only when the horses whinnied to a stop and Mr. Kent leaped down next to us did my breath return in a gasp of relief.

"Miss Wyndham! Are you all right? What's happened?" he asked, reaching out to calm me down. I wanted so badly to close my eyes, collapse in his arms, and sleep for days.

Instead I ignored his hand on mine, concentrating on the injured man in my lap. I forced back a wave of nausea as I stared down at the deathly pale face. The only color interrupting Mr. Braddock's gray pallor was the sticky red blood still issuing from his forehead.

"I don't know—Rose is gone—she's gone—and he was protecting me from Claude," I babbled. "We—we have to help him."

I pressed my cheek against his, feeling his faint response tingle in my blood: weak, but it was there. A ragged breath scratched along his throat.

"Mr. Braddock, if you don't wake up, I shall kill you myself."

"It will be all right," Mr. Kent reassured me as we tugged Mr. Braddock up, pulling his arms around our shoulders. "God, he is much heavier than he looks, isn't he? Must be that large head."

We laid Mr. Braddock down in Mr. Kent's carriage, then squeezed ourselves in. "The closest hospital!" Mr. Kent called out to his driver.

"No!" I shouted, shaking my head fervently. The hospital would contact the police, and the police would contact Dr. Beck. We needed a quiet, safe place to treat him. With no other choice, I provided the driver with the Lodges' address. Mr. Braddock had to live. Then we could worry about the rest.

"How did you find me?" The words slipped out of me. I needed a distraction as I pulled Mr. Braddock onto my lap, cradling him as if my arms were the only things keeping him in one piece.

Mr. Kent's jaw set, but he answered civilly enough. "I saw a strange woman in the dress your sister was wearing earlier. Curious business, that. But she told me where you were—after enough money changed hands, of course."

"Yes, of course, I will explain . . ." But I couldn't. My words drifted away, leaving me unable to think on anything besides Mr. Braddock. Blood still seeped out of the cut on his back, soaking my hands, my dress, my thoughts. He had said I was a miraculous healer. He said I restored Miss Lodge to full health. I'd seen my hands heal. It was true. And I wanted it to be true. As we rolled down the bumpy streets, I closed my eyes, willing my body to access my power, whatever part it was that would make him better.

Please. I believed. Damn it all, I believed.

Fifteen

T HE ENTIRELY HEALTHY Miss Lodge greeted us at her front door and let out a soft gasp, taking in the entirely bloody Mr. Braddock. With the quiet, incurious assistance of Cushing, we hauled Mr. Braddock's body up the stairs and into a dark-paneled guest room. My arms trembled with exertion, and my eyes itched with tears I would not allow to fall. As we set him on the bed, I held Miss Lodge's disbelieving gaze, unnaturally shiny over the candle.

It was true. She really *had* recovered. And now I burdened her with this.

"I'm terribly sorry for troubling you," I whispered. "We just needed to treat him quickly."

At that, she snapped into action, swiftly rearranging the bedsheets around Mr. Braddock with an agitated energy. "No, no, please. Thank you for bringing him," she said with a rushed imitation of a smile. Her eyes finally landed on my dress and widened. "You're—you're covered in blood, Miss Wyndham. Are you hurt? We will call for a doctor."

"It's all—it's his blood," I croaked. "Please, let me help him . . . I must, he saved me."

Miss Lodge looked hesitant but gave in before I did, asking Cushing to fetch me the supplies I needed. In a flash, he returned with a cart of bandages, gauze, towels, laudanum, a sewing kit, and a bowl of warm water. Even if I couldn't magically heal him, I could still do this.

Whereas Miss Lodge's illness had baffled me, Mr. Braddock's treatment came naturally, recalling the countless farming accidents that Rose and I tended to in Bramhurst. First came the knife wound, which required peeling off the blood-drenched jacket and shirt with Cushing's help and trying to ignore the fact that Mr. Kent and Miss Lodge were waiting and watching in the corner. The cut ran six inches across his back, but fortunately it ran fairly shallow—Dr. Beck had not hit anything too serious. Silence fell upon the room, and I fell into a trance with my ministrations, carefully cleaning up the cut with the towels, stitching it closed with the sewing kit, wrapping it with the bandages, and then repeating the process for the cut on his forehead. The whole time, the faint sensation from Mr. Braddock tied us together like a delicate thread, and I did everything in my power to keep it from snapping.

Only when I stood up to fetch the laudanum to help Mr. Braddock with the pain did the exhaustion of the night hit me in full force. The dizzying room lurched like a boat, and my feet struggled to find stable ground.

In an instant, Mr. Kent was by my side, supporting me on his shoulder. "Miss Wyndham, you need rest, and I doubt this floor is the best place for that."

I let go of him and grabbed the bottle from the cart. "He still needs some laudanum. And some ice for his bruises."

Miss Lodge gently took it from me. "You've done all the difficult work. We can manage some simple nursing. Please, you've given me my health back, and I am truly thankful that I can do this for him." She looked past me. "Would you be able to escort her home, Mr. Kent?"

He nodded, and I gave Mr. Braddock one more glance, no energy left to argue or obstinately plant myself down by his side. This was Miss Lodge's home. She was already busy asking Cushing for more supplies and preparing for the rest of the night. Mr. Kent turned my exhausted body away and led me downstairs.

The dismal trip back to the Kents' felt like it took hours as Mr. Kent and I rolled through black, vacant streets, our silence thicker than the London fog. I hardly knew what to say to him, and he didn't press me with questions. My lips managed a thank-you and a promise to explain everything the next morning. He nodded and helped me to the house, where Tuffins politely greeted me as if I weren't a horrible mess and had a maid draw me a bath.

In the warm water, I gazed at my limbs as if they belonged to someone else. If my powers weren't working, there should have been at least a bruise or a scrape from my fall out of the carriage. But my skin was unbroken, unblemished. I tried to think, to analyze the evening's events, but my brain refused to process anything. I was numb, detached, empty. The last thing I remembered, as my head finally hit the pillow, was making a final prayer for Mr. Braddock's recovery. For my strange abilities to somehow do their work.

It was a good sign that the Lodges hadn't donned their mourning weeds the next morning when they welcomed me into their drawing room, but they weren't exactly the portrait of happiness, either. They both had expressions of equal parts trepidation and optimism, a fear of hoping too much.

"Miss Wyndham, it is good to see you safe and sound," Mr. Lodge said. "Is the rest of your party well?"

As I took a seat on a settee, I settled on a vague enough answer. "Yes . . . a bit shaken up, perhaps, but no harm came to them."

"Something must be done about these drunk ruffians," Mr. Lodge declared. "It's a shame that you cannot even attend the opera without worrying about an unprovoked attack. You must be able to identi—"

Mrs. Lodge rested her hand on her husband's. "Dear, I am certain Miss Wyndham does not want to revisit the event so soon. For now, we must count ourselves fortunate it was not worse."

"Thanks to Mr. Braddock's bravery," I added. Did this mean he was awake? He must have provided the Lodges this story. "How is he right now?"

The Lodges exchanged a brief glance. "He left early this morning."

What? He was close to death just hours ago. "How could he—did Miss Lodge not stop him?" I asked.

"She was watching over him but started to feel rather unwell herself. That is why Sebastian left. He did not wish to slow her own recovery."

"Terrible, terrible business," Mr. Lodge concluded, his weary, kind face drained of all color.

A silence settled over the room. I should have anticipated this. Both of them cared too much for the other's health, to the detriment of their own. Had Miss Lodge's illness returned? Had I even cured it in the first place, as Mr. Braddock claimed? My fully healed body gave me some hope, but I dreaded the thought of failing Miss Lodge. I had to be sure.

"Is Miss Lodge still resting upstairs? May I see her?" I asked.

From the way both their faces lit up, I could tell I'd made the right decision, even though the same doubt and dread (which seemed to accompany every visit here) seeped into my stomach as I followed Cushing upstairs to the bedroom.

"Miss Lodge?" he asked with a light knock.

No response.

"Miss—"

"No need to wake her," I whispered to Cushing. "I just want to see her condition."

He nodded and left me alone in the dim bedroom. This would be better anyway. With her asleep, I wouldn't have to flounder about trying to explain my lack of medicines.

Quietly, I approached Miss Lodge, planted myself in a bedside wicker chair, and attempted a diagnosis. Her breathing was heavy and labored, her forehead burned from a fever, and her nightstand held a handkerchief spotted with blood. This wasn't the Addison's disease that I last saw. Something else ailed her, and it looked very much like the consumption she had survived before. My goodness, was she the unluckiest girl in all of London?

I waited stupidly, hoping for a sudden, newfound understanding of my powers. No such luck. There was no reasonable explanation. Sometimes my healing worked. Sometimes it didn't. There was nothing to do but hope this would fall into the first category.

I clasped Miss Lodge's hand, closed my eyes, and waited. One minute. Two. I opened my eyes. No change. I shifted my left hand to her arm, my right hand to her burning forehead, and clenched my jaw, as if the strain might squeeze out my dormant power. Unsurprisingly, my orange-juice-inspired attempt did nothing. The persistent fever would not abate.

Neither would the thoughts and questions and doubts swirling about my head. How long did I have to sit here, futilely trying to cure her, before I was dragged away and declared mad? The last time, I had held Miss Lodge's hand for at least a half hour and sat with her for half a day. There was no telling how long was needed to heal her, or if it could even be done. I felt like some sort of useless steam engine, lifting my hand up every minute, sucking in a hopeful breath, then returning my hand back to her body with a sigh. Until finally, the cycle broke, and a yelp escaped my mouth instead.

Her face looked less flushed, and the sweat I'd wiped from her brow had not returned. And her breathing, it . . . looked more relaxed. Had her fever really decreased? I went absolutely still, afraid to break the spell. For several more minutes I just sat there, a curious and astonished lump, holding Miss Lodge's hand as she regained a healthy glow, steady breathing, and a stable temperature—completely cured right before my eyes.

I had seen my own hand heal. And I had heard of Miss Lodge's prior recovery secondhand. Nothing compared with this, though— I had helped save someone, restored their health in full. Me, alone. Was this giddy surge what Rose felt every time she cured someone back in Bramhurst? It was as if pure light flowed through me. Energy, renewal, *life*. I paced around the room several times in a daze.

How many people could we cure? Could Rose and I heal London? England? What would people say if we suddenly turned medicine on its head, performing miracles at every turn? I wanted desperately to run to a hospital and heal every person I could. But that fantasy was not complete without Rose. It would have to wait until she was by my side once again. Then I could think about the future.

Back downstairs, I assured the Lodges that their daughter would be perfectly healthy after a little more rest. On my way out, I asked for the address of Mr. Braddock's lodgings so I might inquire about his recovery. And in the cab, I provided my driver that address, instead of returning to the Kents'.

I had to speak with Mr. Braddock, and I cared not one whit if I was unaccompanied. All the rules of society had flown out the window with the rational rules of the world.

Sixteen

B ROKEN GLASS WAS never a good sign.

Afraid to knock, I reached through the broken window, groping around the other side of the door for the lock. A click brought me inside the dark, empty Braddock household. The door closed behind me with a faint rasp.

It looked as if no one had been here for months. Every piece of furniture in the entrance hall had a white sheet draped over its surface, with an extra layer of dust over that. The barest slivers of light were creeping in through the closed drapes. I waited for a moment, listening and hearing nothing but the sound of my heartbeat. I didn't know if that was a good sign or not.

I tread a few steps forward, wincing and pausing at the creak of the first stair under my weight. Nothing else stirred. I continued upward and reached the second-floor landing, finding three rooms before me. I chose the first bedroom to my left, the only open door, hoping I'd simply find a resting Mr. Braddock in there and I could finally get back to breathing.

An oak four-poster bed proudly stood in the center, with soft wallpaper and opulent furniture announcing the Braddocks' wealth. The weak gas lamps along the wall barely lit the room, but I could tell it had been used since the servants packed up the house. The bedsheets were a rumpled mess, there were bloodied bandages on the ground, and—

A strong arm wrapped tightly around my neck, pulling me against its owner's body. A warm, bare chest pressed hard against my back, and the sharp scent of mint-like medicinal salve and leather filled my nose.

In a panic, my elbow jerked back into the body, but I regretted it the moment it made contact, recognizing that familiar glow wherever my body met Mr. Braddock's. Whether it was my elbow or the same realization, he loosened his grip and staggered back, taking labored breaths as I tried to regain the use of my lungs, as well.

"I'm . . . sorry . . . Miss Wyndham," he said. "I thought you . . . an intruder. Are you hurt?"

I tried to respond but was immediately distracted by the picture of Mr. Braddock, braced against the wall for support. A large patch covered his forehead, one cheek showed some minor abrasions, and the other had the blue tint of bruising to match his black eye. His half-naked torso had fared better, but the looking glass behind him revealed a red, bandaged streak across his back, sending a shiver down my spine. I tore my gaze away and forced it back up toward his less confusing face.

"I . . . saw the glass broken downstairs," I finally said. "I didn't know what to think."

"I should have cleaned it. I had no other means of getting in when I first arrived."

"Where is your house staff?"

He pushed off the wall and closed in on me, trying to steer me out of the doorway. "You should not be here," he said. "It's not . . . proper."

"And you should not be out of bed." I sidestepped him and took a seat in the room's only chair. "It's not healthy."

He frowned, refusing to come closer.

"Mr. Braddock, from what I can tell, there's no household staff to make a fuss. Not that it should matter, seeing as I'm simply playing the part of nurse. So come. I've already healed Miss Lodge today, and I don't intend to leave until I do the same for you."

He took an eager step forward and almost fell. "With your power?"

I nodded. "Her symptoms disappeared within ten minutes, and she looked perfectly healthy when I left."

Mr. Braddock's expression changed from one of surprise to surprising warmth. "Thank you, Miss Wyndham," he said. "I believe I owe you two sisters in return now. Though I . . . I'm sorry I have been unable to deliver the first."

"The sooner we sort out your injuries, the sooner you can," I said, gesturing to the bed.

He gingerly took his seat, ramrod straight on the edge of the bed, as if he didn't quite trust it with his weight. That would not do.

"Lie down," I told him. "You really don't know how to rest, do you?"

His face was drawn and his lips thinned. Accepting help was obviously not something this man often did. But finally, he begrudgingly lay down.

I dragged the chair closer, wood squeaking against wood. As he squirmed slightly and adjusted, I severely misjudged where to set my gaze and found myself staring again at his uncovered skin. A very annoying blush warmed my cheeks. I had seen a torso here and there while helping Rose, but this was different. There was no emergency, and no Rose, to distract me. I could safely say that this was the oddest situation I had ever been in: trying to use a magical power to heal a strange, half-naked man in his bedroom.

"Your hand, please," I said, pretending to have some logic to what I was doing. As I grasped his hand, my blood warmed, but I held on tightly. His hand trembled in mine. Maybe it would work better directly touching a wound. The cut on his forehead or on his back? Forehead. Definitely the forehead first.

My left hand swept back his silk-soft hair and settled on the pale forehead, fingers brushing gently over the small contusions. The air grew heavy and thick around us while we waited, as if all the world's miraculous potential were building up right here in the room. Neither of us took a breath, afraid to suck it away.

"Is it healing? Does it still hurt?" I asked after a long minute.

He poked his forehead patch and grimaced. "I'm not certain. There is that same . . . sensation from your touch."

I took his hand, placing it between both of mine. "I never felt it when I healed Miss Lodge, though. Only you. I can't help but wonder if it's connected to why I couldn't heal you last night."

"I suspect it has something to do with my specific ability. I must confess, I haven't been honest with you about it."

"How so?"

With the slightest wince, he repositioned the pillow propped behind him. "When—when I was sixteen . . . my father and—" He inhaled sharply, and a cold mask seemed to descend over his face. His words came out clipped, sharp, and detached.

"Three years ago, within a few months of each other, my father and mother both suffered from what the doctors said was consumption and passed away. At first, I thought it a horrible coincidence, but the doctors worried it was contagious or an incurable sickness passing through my family. They advised me to leave the country for some time to protect my health and to get out of that unbearable house.

"So my friend Henry Lodge, Miss Lodge's brother, accompanied me on a trip around the Continent, happy to follow wherever my fancy or grief dictated. But before we could even settle in our first lodgings in France, Henry fell sick—from the same illness. We called for different doctors, but nothing ever seemed to work, and he grew worse and worse—much faster, too. The night he passed . . . I—I was with him. He asked me to promise him a number of things. He—he died before I could finish.

"It was during those moments I saw his eyes, and I—he made me see the truth about myself. It was me. There was a spark, a realization: We both knew *I* was responsible for his illness." Mr. Braddock let out an exasperated, humorless laugh.

"I developed an ability to . . . hurt others. My touch is like infecting someone with an illness . . . or . . . draining the life out of them. And this power, I cannot control it. When it first emerged, I was too foolish and blind to realize it, until I killed my parents and my closest friend."

"How could you *possibly* know it was you?" I spit out.

Mr. Braddock reached for a glass of water. He gulped down some (and spilled the rest) before speaking again. "I didn't at first. Because of the development period, sometimes I was hurting them; sometimes I was harmless. There was no clear pattern. Until I returned to the city for Henry's funeral and spent time with Miss Lodge. Within the first day, she, too, fell sick with the same symptoms. That was proof enough for me.

"So I left and hid in the city, cutting off all contact with society. I wish I could say it was because I knew that would fix everything, but I . . . I couldn't bear to be there and feel responsible."

"And she recovered because of your absence?" I asked.

"Within a few days of my leaving."

"What are the symptoms?"

"It starts with coughing and a fever, which quickly intensifies, leaving the person light-headed, weak, and coughing up blood. Then they fall unconscious until death takes them."

I dropped his hand by instinct. If he even noticed, it didn't seem to bother him. "And your touch is what causes it?"

"And my presence, to a lesser extent. When I am within ten feet of anyone, the symptoms emerge after two hours, and if I do not leave by the twelve-hour mark, they will die."

My every question felt like the twist of a knife. "And what happens if you make direct contact?"

"A few seconds at most for the coughing and fever. Twenty seconds to lose consciousness. Thirty for death."

There was nothing I could possibly do but look down at his hands in disbelief. I took them back in mine, feeling a little ashamed for stopping my healing when those symptoms clearly did not affect me.

His teeth were clenched together, his jaw protruding from behind his cheeks. His words came out strained. "Gloves and clothing help dampen the effects by a few seconds, but no matter what, I must take precautions and keep these times in my head to be sure I never do permanent damage. If I am with someone for more than an hour and notice their health deteriorating, I leave immediately. As far as I know, they are able to make a slow but full recovery when I am gone."

"Does Miss Lodge know any of this?"

Alarm crossed Mr. Braddock's face. "No—I don't know how I would ever tell her. How can I look her in the eye and say that I was responsible for all her pain and her brother's death?"

"It's not." I grasped at ephemeral strands of logic, unable to hold what I meant to say. "It's—"

"You need not say it's not my fault, Miss Wyndham. I've heard that said in excess."

"Well, no, it *is* your fault. No need to shilly-shally around that."

He paled and raised his eyebrows. "Have you had no practice in bedside manner?"

"It was an accident, though, and one you could not have thought to prevent—you must accept that. I can relate . . . albeit on a smaller scale. I myself could have—no, *should have*—protected Rose. If I had simply noticed these abilities earlier, we might have taken the proper precautions. But if there is a bright side to any of this, it's that guilt can be rather persuasive motivation to fix everything else around you that requires fixing. One becomes a better person for it."

I peered down at the rumpled damask bedding, unsure what else to say, and followed the chaotic details as they blossomed into a pattern of perfect symmetry. The bedsheets shuffled and Mr. Braddock sat up straighter, sliding his hand from mine, though it seemed to linger somewhat.

"It appears some things can't be fixed," he said, checking his forehead injury.

"No improvement?"

He shook his head. The corners of his mouth struggled to conceal his disappointment. "When I asked you to cure Miss Lodge, I had been hoping our powers were diametrically opposed, and it seems my wish has inconveniently been granted. You cannot give life to someone who sucks it away, as I cannot hurt someone who gives life. And if that is the case, then it might explain a few other strange things."

"Such as?"

"In the last two or three years, did anyone in your household ever fall sick? Family, servants, guests?"

I scrambled through my memories, failing to picture myself by someone's bedside in our house. "No. The last I remember was my mother. She fell ill during a trip to Paris, and when she returned home, Rose helped nurse her. That's when we first took an interest."

He nodded fervently. "Indeed, perhaps our powers are similar in more than one way. My presence also made many of our servants sick, while your household's good health suggests that your presence might help those around you."

"What would that mean?"

"Not only do our powers fail to work when we make contact, but perhaps also when we are near each other. The two instances when I attempted to use my powers in your presence, they did not seem to work."

"The fights?" I asked, cold at the memory.

"I had more difficulty with the drunkards than I should have. And Claude should not have reached the window."

My stomach felt sick. "So my being there nearly got you killed, and I can't even heal you . . ."

"I'd say Claude nearly got me killed more than you did." He tried to smile but just made a miserable mess of the process.

My overwhelmed mind raced through what all this meant. "If my presence cancels your power," I said, pulling out a card from my reticule. "Then does the opposite hold true?"

The thin edge sliced my skin open, but when I wiped the blood away, the paper cut remained. It didn't close within seconds, as it had when I was alone. I rose out of my chair and took slow steps backward, pausing and watching as the cut stubbornly stayed open, until I nearly reached the wall. In the blink of an eye, the cut vanished like it should have.

I glanced up at Mr. Braddock. "It healed immediately, after that step."

He looked at the distance between us. "Ten feet?" he suggested.

I sighed, returning to my chair. "This would be far easier if we had a guidebook. How can there be thousands of handbooks on the proper ways to bow or how to arrange forks for every possible occasion, but not a single one about how far you must be to keep from accidentally killing someone?"

For the first time and for the briefest, tingling moment, I made him laugh. "Perhaps you might write it."

A voice replied from behind me. "It might prove to be more revelatory if you were to write it, Mr. Braddock."

I spun up and out of my chair to find the intruder.

"Mr. Kent, what are you doing here—were you just eavesdropping?"

"Of course not. I was waiting for the perfect moment to enter the conversation with a witty rejoinder, but I had to settle for that. I didn't mean to interrupt. Please, continue as you were." He ambled in, appearing perfectly at ease. But there was a set tension to his jaw.

"How on earth did you find this place?"

"When you were not at my parents' home, I checked with the Lodges. They mentioned Mr. Braddock's address."

I did not know what to say. I found myself embarrassed, for some reason, as though I had been doing something I shouldn't. Mr. Braddock also seemed to be at a loss for conversation. Was Mr. Kent angry? Disappointed? Appalled? It was impossible to tell with the light air he gave his words.

"Very well. Then I'll take this opportunity to formally introduce myself," he said, marching up to the bed. "Mr. Braddock, it's a pleasure to meet you. I'm Nicholas Kent, the man who saved your life last night."

"It seems I am greatly in your debt," Mr. Braddock replied, not looking particularly thrilled about that.

"Excellent. Then I'd like to call in your first payment now with some questions. Have you known all along who took Miss Rosamund?" Mr. Braddock was visibly disturbed but still answered the question, as Mr. Kent paced haughtily around his bed, back and forth.

"No, I wasn't sure."

"But you had your suspicions?"

"I did."

I couldn't hold back. "You already *knew* who Dr. Beck was?"

"I once . . . worked for him," Mr. Braddock answered.

My breath disappeared, and my stomach slammed into my heels. Mr. Kent broke the silence, his voice grim. "When?"

"A year ago."

"Are you still in league with him?"

"No. As you can tell, we aren't on the best of terms."

"Then why would you *ever* help a man like that?" I asked.

"I thought he could cure me. I'd killed my parents, my best friend, and nearly killed m—Miss Lodge. I spent months searching London for anyone experiencing the same problem, and it was then I read of Dr. Beck in a newspaper article. He made wild claims and speculations about evolution, the development of abilities, and the future of mankind. It turned him into an object of ridicule within the scientific community—everyone thought his ideas unbelievable—but if there was a sliver of a chance he could help me, I had to take it. So I offered to pay him anything for a cure, or at least a proper explanation."

The floor groaned as I stepped closer to the bed. "What did he say?"

"He was enthusiastic, but he did not want my money—he had plenty of funding. He wanted my assistance. While I worked with him, he shared all his theories and findings with me. He told me what I told you before, about our abilities being the result of saltation."

"And what assistance did you provide him in return?" Mr. Kent asked.

"Information about my ability. I answered his questions, gave him blood samples, and allowed him to test and observe the effects."

"What did you test it on? Animals?" I asked.

"Animals aren't affected."

My thoughts had moved ahead and frozen at one question with the sudden realization. How far had they pushed the tests?

Mr. Kent asked the question I could not. "Then you tested it on human subjects, who I assume were less than willing?"

Mr. Braddock fixed his eyes on me, all mirth drained out. "I tested the milder effects on Claude, but . . . I—there was an impossible situation. Dr. Beck asked me to test on others, and when I refused, he . . . he locked me in a small room with a man who was just looking to earn a sovereign. I tried to sit at the farthest corner, I tried to convince Dr. Beck to let us out, I tried to control my power, but nothing worked, even as the man wasted away in front of me. I begged him. I begged him, and still he forced me to stay, slowly killing this poor soul."

"And after, he simply let you go free?" Mr. Kent continued, unaffected by Mr. Braddock's apparent pain.

"He wanted me to help with his other subjects, to see the value of his experiments," he said, blanching. "But I wanted no part."

"And you drew the line at killing an innocent man, but not the men who forced you to do it?"

There was no need to respond, but to his credit, he did anyway. "Yes. I didn't want to take *any* lives, even his."

"So you let them continue doing it . . ." I said, my voice coming out thin and high as a reed.

Mr. Braddock said nothing, and I had nothing more to say to him.

My sister's terrified face from last night swam in my head, and I was backing out the door away from both of them before I knew it, unable to say whether or not they might have called after me.

Perhaps it had been better when Mr. Braddock was hiding behind the lies and mysteries.

Seventeen

I FLEW DOWN the sidewalk, heart hammering in my ears, tears welling without permission. I couldn't see the road, nor the people in my way. Instead, my vision was filled with a faceless body falling, drained and withering at Mr. Braddock's hand while an elated Dr. Beck held up a pocket watch. Over and over I watched him kill Dr. Beck's victim till eventually I slowed, exhausted and nauseated.

He didn't *want* to kill that innocent man. Dr. Beck had forced him. At least that's what Mr. Braddock claimed. But after that, Dr. Beck simply released him? And Mr. Braddock left peacefully? How did I know these weren't more of his half truths? He'd lied about his ability and his connection to Claude, only admitting the truth later, when he could justify it with some noble explanation. Honesty wasn't quite honesty when it came reluctantly and piecemeal. It called everything into doubt, made it impossible to fully trust him, and I hated that one insurmountable fact. Our hopeless situation was almost starting to make sense during that brief moment when it seemed I'd finally found the real Mr. Braddock. But now it felt like he was further out of reach than ever.

A hand grasped my arm.

"Miss . . . Wyndham . . . wait . . ." Mr. Kent gasped, trying to catch his breath as he caught me. "I brought a carriage . . . and my driver will be . . . quite offended . . . if we choose to run instead."

From one confusing man to another. "So what do you suggest we do?"

He tapped his cane on the ground and stood straighter. "We forget this . . . unpleasantness and continue the search. I've already checked this Dr. Beck's location from last night, but it's been abandoned. Perhaps Camille or one of the science societies will know more about him or where he's gone."

So, he meant to completely skirt the topic of Mr. Braddock and proceed as if he never existed. That sounded better than fixating, to be sure. He offered his arm, and I perhaps leaned a little too heavily upon it, for he added, "That is, if you're up for it. How are you feeling?"

"Exhausted," I said. "And sick. But I want to come."

"Then we'll stop at home first," he said. "Because I'm sure you haven't allowed yourself a moment to eat in the past day. And whether or not this healing of yours helps out in that regard, it certainly isn't a substitute for a good cake."

Between his soothing voice, easy questions, and optimistic plans, Mr. Kent's foremost concern for the entire carriage ride seemed to be my comfort. I appreciated the warm gesture as the cold, indifferent London streets streamed by my window, but the moment he handed me out of the carriage, his touch brought to mind his disconcerting behavior last night. It seemed such a small matter after all we'd been through, but whether he saw through my disguise and put on an act to have fun with it, or that was simply a hasty excuse to cover his mistake, it planted a worrisome seed in my mind. Perhaps lying came easier to him than I thought.

As I climbed the stairs to the Kents', wondering if there was anyone in London entirely trustworthy, Tuffins answered the door—and my question. And as he let us into the entrance hall, he gave me a bit of news I would not have believed coming from anyone else.

"A Miss Alice Grey is here to see you."

The name took me a moment to comprehend, and even then I needed confirmation. "Miss *Grey*?"

Tuffins nodded politely at the stupid question. "She arrived looking rather distressed and insisted upon waiting for your return."

"Who is Miss Grey?" Mr. Kent asked.

"My former governess."

"Well, Tuffins can send her away—"

"No—" I interrupted. After one year of silence, with no visits or letters, she somehow tracks and finds me here. Not to mention her appearances in those recent vivid dreams of mine. It was too strange. There had to be some meaning to it. "Mr. Kent, I don't think I can accompany you on the search today."

Perplexed, he gaped at me. "Are you sure?"

"Yes, I must speak to her. It's important."

He frowned and nodded slowly, seeing my resolve. Or perhaps seeing signs that I truly needed rest. "I—very well. I'll send word if I learn anything."

Once I regained my ability to walk, Tuffins showed me into the drawing room, where I once again lost it.

"Evelyn," the visitor breathed. It was her in the flesh, not another apparition in a dream. Her footsteps ruffled the carpet. Tears streamed from her face, splashing down onto her blue dress. She rushed over and embraced me, looking worse than she had in my dreams: sallow, bruised skin framing her bloodshot eyes; nose and cheeks a bright pink; loose strands of her red hair messily stuck to her brow. She was only twenty-eight, but whatever she had been through seemed to have stolen away that last bit of youth. Frantically, she clutched my shoulders and pleaded, "Where is Rose?"

I could not answer. My hesitation seemed to nearly destroy her. "Evelyn!"

"She's . . ." I wanted to tell her, but I lost the words.

My governess closed her eyes with a sigh. She sank gracefully into the nearest settee and clutched her hat in painful meditation. "He still has her?" she asked, looking back up at me steadily.

Surprised, I peered deep into her grave eyes as I collapsed next to her. I nodded, and she pushed herself back up to her feet, pacing to and fro, weaving around the tables and chairs until I broke the silence. "Miss Grey?"

She stopped and looked at me, her eyes wet. "P-please, please forgive me—I am so sorry!"

I gaped up at her, unable to imagine what she could have possibly done.

"I—I tried to send warnings about Rose! I truly did!" The words poured out of her mouth so fast she started to cough on them. "But there was no way! They intercepted every letter, and no one would help me."

"I saw you," she continued, back to wildly pacing, hands in the air. "In your dreams. We spoke. You could discern me, Evelyn! Do you remember? Oh dear, I'm not describing this well at all. This must all sound absolutely mad!"

"I have been well acquainted with the mad lately, believe me," I said. "I remember the dreams, although I only heard fragments. Are you saying you had the same dreams?"

Miss Grey sighed in apparent relief and gingerly sat back down. "It's more than that. I'll explain everything. All I ask is that you listen first, and *then* call me a lunatic and send me on my way."

"I would never do such a thing."

"I didn't believe my parents would, either. That was the last time I told anyone about this, and it—well, it did not go as I wished."

She cleared her throat and clenched her hands in her lap as her eyes met mine. Her breathing slowed. She began much as Mr. Braddock had. (Not that I was thinking of him.) Her tone had the same sad resignation: "Since I was fifteen years old, I've had an affliction. Whenever I fall asleep, I have very particular dreams about people I've never met. I used to believe they were parts of my imagination or characters from stories, because I would witness them perform extraordinary feats. Things no human can conceivably do."

"I dismissed them for years until one evening, I had an encounter while I was awake. When you girls were about thirteen and fourteen, I traveled home to visit my parents for Christmas holiday, and while I was waiting at Victoria Station, a number of familiar faces caught my attention. They were all in a group, and I found it strange that I couldn't recall how I knew any of them. Then I saw a dwarf of a man and had an even stranger realization: They were from my dreams. I had memories of them performing in a traveling exhibition. . . . They called themselves human curiosities."

"What did you do?" I asked.

"I followed them, but I wish I hadn't. I was curious to see if my dreams were true, and when my cab followed theirs to a small theater, my curiosity only grew. I watched them perform acts that seemed to take advantage of the powers I'd dreamed they had. A man who could create fire was a fire eater on stage. A woman with a powerful voice broke objects with just her song. And the longer I stayed, the more I hoped something would contradict my dreams, prove they weren't all true. But nothing ever did, so I just kept watching.

"I watched from the street as they left the theater, I watched one of them get caught pickpocketing a man, I watched the man lunge at the pickpocket with a punch, I watched the man disappear through a door in the air before his punch hit, and I watched him reappear in the middle of the street, right in front of a moving carriage."

Dear God. This sounded like the same man from last night. "Did he . . . kill him?" I asked, wincing.

She nodded steadily, her eyes distant and stuck in the past. "That was the most horrifying truth to realize. Not the fact that these powers existed, but the fact that there were people who did such awful things with them. When I returned to your home, I tried to pretend the nightmares weren't real, but the harder I tried, the more vivid they became—it nearly drove me mad."

I remembered mornings when she came downstairs pallid, exhausted, and reticent. She would assign Rose and me work that required plenty of writing and little talking, then spend hours looking out the window, endeavoring to keep awake. It finally made sense.

"Eventually, it became too much. Your mother was concerned for my health, and we decided it best that I leave."

"Where did you go? We wrote you many times."

I could see her withdraw into her memories as she rose again, walking stiffly to a streetside window.

"When I was sent back home, my parents demanded an explanation, so I poured out everything. They sympathized and told me all would be well." There was a cold anger lacing her words that made me freeze, almost frightened to hear more.

"But they had decided I was mad," she continued, shaking her head in disappointment. "My two sisters also work as governesses, and my father could not risk my condition becoming known. I don't blame them, but I can never forgive them. They bundled me off to Belgium and shut me in a place worse than a prison—an asylum."

"No! They couldn't have!"

She clutched the windowsill to slow her trembling. "I cannot tell you the particular horror it is in such a place. Surrounded by strangers, treated like a dangerous, deranged criminal, I was made to drink vials of concoctions that kept me sick and sleeping most of the day. Of course, as I slept, I was forced to dream more. Sometimes it was pleasant. Mostly it was not. I did not know what I hated more, my waking moments or the dreams. I wanted to escape from both. But then, I dreamt of . . . I dreamt of you and Rose, Evelyn."

"Of course," I said, nodding.

She whirled to face me, the light from the window turning her into a silhouette.

"I've recently become aware of my healing ability," I said. "Rose's, as well."

The smallest bit of tension seemed to leave her body. "I was afraid I would somehow have to prove your abilities," she said with a slight laugh.

"No, there have been many chances for that over these last days."

Again, her eyes filled with guilt. "I am so sorry, Evelyn."

"It is not your fault!"

"When I saw the two of you healing patients, it was the first time I had seen someone using their gift for good. I felt the slightest bit of hope and clung to it. I made an effort to better understand my power. I kept a diary of my dreams to remember more details. I discovered that when I dream of someone who is sleeping, I enter their dreams instead. I even found I could sometimes control whom I dreamt of. But then I dreamt of *him*.

"The scientist. The one I dreaded most. Cold, empty, heartless. In my dreams he sought others with powers, convinced them to aid his experiments, and performed atrocious tests on them without remorse, all in the name of research. And in my dream, he was discussing Rose with his two partners: a giant and the murderer I'd seen in London."

"Calvin Beck," I said, strangled breath wrenching itself from me. "He . . . has a power? What is it?"

Miss Grey shook her head. "I never witnessed it. I dread the possibilities. Perhaps it is the lack of a conscience."

My head felt cloudy, stormy. Not only did Claude have an abnormal amount of strength and the other man the ability to travel anywhere, but Dr. Beck had a mysterious advantage, as well.

"I tried to warn you," Miss Grey continued, "but the caretakers refused to send my letters, and it was impossible to escape. Out of desperation I tried what I assumed was impossible. I entered your dream, Evelyn, and endeavored to speak to you. But I lacked the proper control."

"No. You have been wonderful. I simply didn't realize." It was my turn to stand and pace, trying to push away thoughts of *what if.* "How did you come to me now?"

"I met Emily Kane. She was a young girl recently transferred to the ward. You see, the asylum itself held a number of gifted patients who were also deemed mad by their families. Emily and I were not friends—not exactly. She was almost as insane as they wished her to be. She was too scared to leave, no matter what I said, but she used her fascinating ability to help me, God bless her."

"What did she do?"

"She could move objects without touching them. When one of the nurses fell asleep, Emily managed to acquire the keys to the gate and pass them to me. Unfortunately, they caught her. When they questioned the poor girl, she had a wild fit that nearly destroyed the entire building—fires, crumbled walls and ceilings, flooding. With the distraction, I was able to make my escape." A long silence settled as Miss Grey collected herself. She wandered to the pianoforte in the corner, gently running her fingers along the ivory keys without pressing them. "Although it seems I've arrived too late to be of any help. I failed you and Rose," she muttered.

I walked over to her and forcefully hugged her, as if to squeeze away that lingering guilt. Somehow I became the optimistic one. "Don't say that. Heavens, you did everything possible, and you have been through too much."

That did little to rest her spirits. Neither did telling her about my many mistakes over the past few days. The missed opportunities weighed heavy on both of us as we tried to find a solution.

Then the obvious answer hit me. "Miss Grey, could you not dream of Rose and find her?"

"I have tried," she said, her shoulders slumping even more. "If I think of the specific person before I fall asleep, it sometimes works. But my perspective is limited. Rose would likely be confined to a room, and that is all I would see. Even when I dreamt of Dr. Beck, I rarely saw him leave his laboratory. I never learned where it was."

"What about Claude or . . . that man who can create doors, what do we call him? The door man? My God, we don't even know their names."

"Gabriel Hale, I believe," Miss Grey said. "But he often travels straight to his destination with his own doors."

I felt a strange fear of breaking a fragile memory with too direct a question. "Can you remember anything else about them? Do they have homes or families?"

She shook her head, displacing stray wisps of hair. "I wish I had paid more mind. I cannot recall. My dreams are fragmented like anyone else's, and it's hard to remember details. All I have is my diary from the recent months, but I don't know if it will be of any use."

She handed me a small, ragged notebook from her reticule, and I skimmed through the delicate thing, finding the pages for Dr. Beck, Claude, and Mr. Hale. They were filled with brief, horrible memories and unfamiliar names. A couple of names were labeled as patients, but the unlabeled ones piqued my curiosity. Were they colleagues of Dr. Beck? Patrons? Camille had mentioned his funding last night. Surely Dr. Beck would need to meet with someone if he were moving to a new laboratory. Could this be our way of finding him?

"Miss Grey, do you know who these men are?" I asked, pointing at the names. A pang of guilt struck me when I looked up. She had taken several steps back, as if she did not wish to relive those memories with me.

But she stepped forward, glanced them over, and shook her head. "No, I only heard them mentioned in Dr. Beck's conversations. I'm sorry."

I closed the diary. "No more apologies, Miss Grey. This is a very promising start," I said. "I'm sure Mr. Kent and Mr.—will recognize a name, and we will find her soon."

She smiled and looked like she was starting to believe me. "What happened to that cynical pupil of mine?"

"Oh, don't worry, she's usually here."

"Well, you've grown since I last saw you—" Miss Grey broke off with a yawn. "Oh, dear. I'm terribly sorry!"

"No, no, you've had a long day," I said. "We will continue tomorrow."

With evening fast approaching and the many stresses, memories of horrors, and guilt pressing on her, Miss Grey needed her rest. She gave me her lodging information, and a footman escorted her to a cab. As I waved good-bye, I couldn't help but wish, despite all she had gone through, that she might continue searching in her dreams.

I had three wonderful seconds to myself before Laura leaped out from around a corner. "Evelyn!"

My heart stopped. An embarrassing scare, considering everything. "Heavens, don't frighten me like that."

"I'm sorry," she said. "You promised this morning we would talk! Who was the woman who came to visit? I thought of eavesdropping, but the last time I tried was positively dreadful. I got trapped in a cupboard for hours!"

"My former governess. She heard I was visiting London, and she wished to see me. Not worth getting trapped over," I said, unable to imagine Laura sitting still for minutes, much less hours.

She bounced across the entrance hall and to the next subject. "And what happened last night at the . . ." She trailed off, coyly lifting her shoulders and pouting awkwardly, which I could only take as the universal sign for *brothel*.

"It wasn't Rose who was there," I said and gave her the abridged version of the tale as we climbed the stairs to my room.

"You'll find her soon! I'm sure of it," she said with an optimism she must have learned from her stepbrother. "But there must be something more! You spent an entire night there! Was anyone's virtue . . . compromised?"

I shook my head, feeling a faint envy for Laura's boredom. Between the horrors befalling Rose, Mr. Braddock, and Miss Grey, there seemed to be merit to the comfortable tedium of my life a week ago. "The Argyll Rooms were much like a ball or dance," I said gently, slipping behind the dressing screen to begin removing my attire. "Nothing terribly special."

"Oh! Oh! What about Mr. Braddock? Was he still dark and mysterious and far less charming than my brother?" I gave her a harsh look over the screen as she squinted her blue eyes and sucked in her cheeks to remind me what dark and mysterious men look like. Like fish or Miss Verinder, apparently.

"Mr. Braddock is a reprehensible man, and we will not talk of him again."

She must have sensed something in my tone, because she immediately pounced on the idea and my bed. "Oh, Evelyn! Don't tell me you are in love with him! Oh, you are! Look at how red you are, Evelyn! My poor brother. You love him!"

"Goodness, I'm in love with no one, least of all him. He has done horrible things, and he's dishonest and dangerous, and, well, he has many awful qualities. Not that I ever think about him any-way—no, no, Mr. Braddock is nothing to me. Nothing at all! In fact—" I could hear myself rambling, and a certain quote about protesting too much flitted through my head.

Judging by her subject change, Laura still seemed to think I was putting on an act. "Well, since you won't admit to anything, I have exciting news about our theater outing for tonight!"

"The Lyceum . . ." I sighed. I didn't quite miss society yet.

"I know, they are performing some ancient play, but more important, Mr. Edwards will be in attendance! Sadly, he was not able to join our party because the family already had a commit-ment, but we will surely see him during intermission!"

"How lovely," I lied. "Did you say our *party*?"

"Yes! We have a box, remember? It will be us, the Verinders, and of course my brother!" Oh hell. Could I fall sick again?

She sighed and fell back down, staring at the canopy over my bed in utter contentment. "Oh, Evelyn! I don't think Nick would have come if it weren't for you! What it must be like to have two men in love with you!"

Eighteen

THE LYCEUM THEATRE might have been a magnificent sight, had the night's plans not been so unappealing. Six gigantic Grecian columns planted by the curb created a portico that loomed over the sidewalk, like a monstrous mouth threatening to devour the entire street. Arched doorways led into a vestibule that opened on a large, warmly lit lobby decorated in dark shades of purple, green, and elegant glints of gold. Thick hangings and portieres were serenely draped about the room, interrupted only by the wide staircase at the center, leading up to the box tier.

Waiting by this staircase was Mr. Kent, who managed to both grimace at his stepmother and smile brightly at Laura. I received a knowing nod and a quick smile as he met us with bows. I gave him a curious look in return, wondering whether he had news and whether he'd have the opportunity to tell me. We should have arranged a secret code beforehand.

Lady Kent, with the air of a street cleaner getting a foul task done quickly, greeted her stepson. "Nicholas . . . a . . . most welcome surprise to have you here."

"Yes, well, life would be so boring without a surprise here and there. You certainly have given me a few," he said, the joke rather too dry. Lady Kent forced out a guttural, clacking laugh that I hoped never to hear again.

Mr. Kent managed to keep his eyes from rolling too high in his head by rolling them toward Laura. "And my dear Kit, are there enough dinner parties and outings keeping you and Miss Wyndham busy?"

"There are less and less!" Laura whined, her voice shaking querulously. "After tomorrow's dinner, there'll be nothing to look forward to for the whole winter!"

"Don't worry just yet. I've spoken to some friends all over London this afternoon," he said, flashing me an enigmatic smile. "Not everything is set, but I hope to have good news tomorrow."

Well. It seems we did have a secret code.

Laura beamed. "Oh, I cannot wait! Please be sure to invite—"

"Ah, here they are!" Lady Kent interrupted. Her eyes lit up, and she smiled broadly, exposing too many teeth. "Nicholas, do you see Miss Verinder has arrived?"

With their grand entrance, it was rather impossible to miss them. The impeccably dressed Mrs. Verinder and her tall, shrewd-eyed husband floated through the archway, sending smiles to their numerous acquaintances, while the golden-dressed Miss Verinder followed close behind and was currently killing me twenty different ways with her eyes.

"I did see, but tragically, I've been blinded by that sun she's wearing," Mr. Kent replied, but then they were upon us, and introductions were made all around. Mr. Kent made a valiant attempt at politeness while Miss Verinder somehow managed to find herself at his side, clutching his arm, shooting me a gloating smile.

The ladies nattered on about nothing, and I kept quiet, knowing Miss Verinder would twist around anything I said. My thoughts began to slip to my search for Rose, or rather how it had come to a complete standstill. My sister was trapped somewhere in this city (I refused to consider that she might be anywhere else by now), and here I was, acting just like my mother, trying to keep our family's good name by wasting hours at a play.

Not that I even knew where to start looking. Dr. Beck's planning, preparation, and power made this far more complicated than any of us had anticipated. Mr. Kent was confident that we'd find them soon, but he always sounded so confident that it was getting harder to believe him, especially when Miss Grey's power to see them wasn't even enough. Every plan I imagined with the three of us came down to the same unfortunate conclusion: We needed Mr. Braddock. And it wasn't despite his past mistakes, but precisely because of them.

I closed my eyes for a moment, trying to force away the imagined scenes of his past. But when I opened them, Mr. Braddock was still there. Only now he was in evening dress incongruously paired with the bandage on his forehead, and curiously, he was attempting to hide behind a large fern. I withheld a gasp as I realized it really was him and not a conjuring from my imagination. Before I could investigate further, Miss Verinder's voice buzzed in my ear.

"Yes, when will the elusive Miss Rosamund be able to join us? She always seems to be with the sick."

"Sadly, she's actually taken sick herself. She's been resting," I said.

Of course, Lady Kent couldn't miss an opening like that. "That's what happens when you work as a nurse!"

I might have been unable to hold back a rude retort there, but fortunately I was still too busy darting glances at the plant. Mr. Braddock looked exceedingly silly and was entirely visible, which meant when Mr. Kent followed my line of sight, he had no trouble determining who had captured my attention. He shifted his weight, his expression turning rapidly dour.

A bell chimed brightly, alerting us that the show was to begin. "Shall we take our seats?" Mrs. Verinder suggested.

If Mr. Kent wished to speak to me, he was given no chance. The group followed Mrs. Verinder, except Laura, who tugged me aside like her rag doll. "Mama," she said. "Evelyn and I must go to the dressing room!"

Lady Kent, hanging onto the Verinders' story of a recalcitrant servant, waved her aside without a glance. Before I could protest or even decide if I wanted to protest, Laura steered me down a narrow hallway and into the lavish, lavender-scented room, where bored theatergoers could escape to gossip or tidy up their appearance.

Laura set me down onto a red velvet settee and bore her eyes into mine, spots of pink surfacing high on her cheekbones. "Evelyn, this is a matter of life and death." She managed to sit completely still and composed as she said this. No bouncing around the room or high-pitched squealing. Even her hair appeared serious.

"Are you ill?" I asked.

"Yes! My heart is aching," she said, sighing overdramatically and snatching up a bolster to hug.

"What on earth is the matter?" I asked, sick of the theatrics. And the play hadn't even begun yet.

"Did you not see Mr. Edwards when you came in?"

I couldn't say that was my first priority. "No . . . I don't even know what he looks like. Is he not here?"

"He is! He was the magnificent-looking man in the lobby! I must have a tête-à-tête with him during intermission. You must help. I can't do it alone. Please!" She attempted a small dive across the sofa toward me, almost kicking a vase of flowers behind her.

"Yip! Help with your . . . tête-à-tête? About what?"

"Whatever he wants!" she said, grasping my hands tightly. "The subject does not matter in the least."

"Why do you need me? What have you talked about before?"

Distressed, she sat back up, looked down into her lap, and swung her legs back and forth under her seat. "We've been introduced. And he had marvelous things to say about the weather!"

I should have expected this. He'd probably spoken no more than ten words to her, and she'd fallen in love after the third.

"I need you to be my foil!" she wailed. "I need someone to disagree with him, so I can agree with him and support him like a good wife should! Please, Evelyn! I cannot become a ruined spinster!"

I didn't think fifteen-year-olds had to worry about spinsterhood. I had the urge to shake her by the shoulders and snap her out of it, but the despair in her eyes and the belief that my disapproval would only render Mr. Edwards more enticing, in a forbidden sort of way, left me with no alternative.

"Fine. We'll do it," I said with a sigh.

She just about exploded at those words, jumping up in a dance of silk and joy (a shame, the hair had looked quite nice) and thanking me a million times over. A woman in the corner, whom I had not noticed before, caught my eye, and her lips pinched into a look of pity.

Eventually, Laura remembered that there was a play to be watched and dragged me back out into our double box overlooking the dull, bluish theater. With people crowding every seat, there was no way to make out a certain dark-haired man, and there was no time to learn what he was doing here. Two empty seats waited for us: Laura took the space next to her mother, leaving me between her and her brother, whose other arm was caught in Miss Verinder's clutches. If only it were Mr. Braddock she were interested in. I spent a few happy moments imagining the results of her grabbing *his* arm.

"My, my, it's a surprise to see Mr. Braddock here," Mr. Kent said, a hint of acrimony lacing his voice.

"Yes, it is."

He leaned in confidentially. "Perhaps he's come to apologize. Or maybe that also needs to be done in his bedroom."

I strained to keep a whisper. "You know very well why I was in his bedroom! He was injured, and I needed to check on him."

"No one is going to make an exception for that where your reputation is concerned."

"I had other concerns at the time."

He put his hand on his chest. "I'm feeling quite injured myself. Perhaps we might—"

"Mr. Kent! This is not an appropriate place for that kind of talk!"

"Very well," he said. "If you wish to speak about it somewhere much more inappropriate, just say the word."

At that moment, Miss Verinder rapped his arm and pouted for his attention. Fortunately for all our ears' sake, the lights dimmed, and the crowd's rumble of anticipation covered anything she wished to say.

Normally, this was one of my favorite Shakespeare plays, but with so many thoughts, emotions, and anxieties boiling within me, I wasn't at all in the mood to waste my time here. While the rest of the audience was drawn into the world onstage, I couldn't help but find the sets, costumes, and acting completely fake. There was not a single true note in Beatrice and Benedick's witty conversations. The "love" between Claudio and Hero was based on nothing. And all the men were too foolish to see Don John's comically obvious lies.

After the disastrous aborted-marriage scene, the curtain closed and the lights were relit. I didn't have a chance to speak one word to anyone before Laura—treating the intermission as if it were the play—seized my hand and pulled me straight to the lobby to find Mr. Edwards.

Sneakily, she wove us through the shifting crowd and arced us behind him rather than charging him head-on. She seemed to have a lot of practice in the clandestine maneuver, and against my will, I was half impressed and half amused. When we were close, Laura turned her back to her target, leaned, and gracefully bumped into the tall, thin-mustached man, feigning astonishment.

"Oh! Mr. Edwards. Ever so sorry. What a pleasant surprise to see you here!" she simpered. "May I introduce my good friend, Miss Wyndham?"

"Ah, yes, a pleasure, indeed," he replied, bowing and looking as if he'd just discovered the hard way that there was a fly in his soup. "How do you do, Miss Wyndham?"

"Excellent," Laura replied, somehow mistaking my name for her own. "And you?"

"Quite . . . well," he said, regaining himself after a momentary befuddlement. "The play is very good, is it not? A true example of drama at its best."

"If this play is the best drama that can be mustered up, Mr. Edwards, I'm afraid it's fighting a losing battle," I said.

"Evelyn, don't be so critical," Laura scolded theatrically. "I think this show exceedingly good so far."

"I wholeheartedly agree and applaud your taste, Miss Kent. I especially like the blend of this production's dreamlike opulence with the truthful, human performances," he said superciliously.

"Yes! Just the words I was about to say! A striking compromise between the real and . . . a lavish dream!"

Mr. Edwards raised his thick eyebrows and seemed to find Laura more attractive as she repeated his opinion back to him. "Mr. Irving always does a wonderful job, doesn't he?"

"I don't find him particularly unique," I cheerfully lied.

He waved his folded program as if it contained his proof, and he almost hit a passing couple. "I doubt you'll find anyone in London who is better."

"I especially liked his *Hamlet*," Laura proclaimed. "And last year's *King Lear*."

"Oh yes, I saw *King Lear* four times!"

"How unfortunate for you," I said, finding my role as a cynical baiter rather easy and enjoyable.

"I find it an unfortunate shame that you feel that way. You are missing out," he returned, straining to remain polite.

"Yes, honestly. You should be more agreeable." Laura's voice had a sickening shade of honey in it when she turned back to Mr. Edwards.

"Did you know that they originally planned to stage *The Merchant of Verona* last year?" Mr. Edwards asked, looking at Laura with a speculative glint in his eye.

"Truly?" Laura asked, looking utterly shocked—and not at his error. Heavens. Who would have thought this would actually work? She didn't even need my help. The two blathered on, both agreeing that Mr. Edwards was deeply fascinating, while I just stood and watched, silently amused, until someone brushed by my back and a familiar tremor ran up my spine.

"Pardon me."

Mr. Braddock. I spun around to see him slinking away from me, while awkwardly keeping a safe distance from others. His slow gait was enough to fool almost everyone else, but I could see the attempts to hide his pain in every step. Why had he come in this condition?

"Excuse me, Laura, Mr. Edwards," I said and stepped away before there was an objection.

I marched across the room toward him, keeping my eyes on his feet, struggling not to make a scene with the hundreds of people surrounding us. I seized his jacket and pulled him into an alcove. We were a snug fit, and I couldn't help but be acutely aware of him and the few inches of breath that separated us. The bitter scent of medicinal herbs seemed to sharpen all my senses.

"What is it? What are you doing here?" I hissed.

He leveled his gaze, chin up, and when he spoke it was determined, as if he had been waiting all day to tell me. "This morning, you said guilt can be effective motivation . . . and, well, I'm feeling too motivated to sit by idly. I've made terrible decisions that I regret to no end, and you have every right to distrust me, but I can only apologize and try to do some good by finding Miss Rosamund before any harm or pain comes to her." His eyes refused to drop mine.

"And what? You decided Rose was probably an actress in *Much Ado About Nothing*? Or are you simply here for your own fun?"

"Is this outing with Mr. Kent part of your search?" His eyes flashed with something that looked suspiciously like jealousy as he drained a glass of liquor in his hand.

"Don't be absurd. We can't all just mysteriously vanish from society for a year. I have a reputation to uphold."

"And I am upholding our bargain. I am following a man connected to Dr. Beck."

I stiffened. "What? Do you have more information? Why did you not inform me?"

"I am informing you now. It is a delicate situation, so I must handle it myself."

"What is it?" I whispered, pitching my voice low. "You cannot keep something like this from—"

"When Dr. Beck was trying to convince me to join him, he wanted me to meet this man. I never did, but Camille's mention of Dr. Beck's funding last night made me consider their relationship. I believe he may be the benefactor or part of a society funding Dr. Beck's research."

It seemed we had the same thought. "Who is he? What is his name? What society?" The words tumbled from my mouth as I looked around for this man I knew nothing about.

"I'll spare you the details," he said with an infuriatingly condescending glint to his eyes. "We can't startle him. If he is funding Dr. Beck's work, he will undoubtedly be secretive about it."

"And you think he is in attendance?"

"He is."

"Good. Let's go."

"Absolutely not. This is far too dangerous." I thought he was about to take my hand, but he pulled his own back and stuffed it in his pocket, looking uncomfortable.

"It's dangerous to everyone around you if I don't come," I persisted. "You'll be sitting in a row of sick, unconscious people, or is that part of your testing—" He paled so much that I immediately regretted the words.

"I purchased seats in different parts of the theater and will move every hour. But by all means, continue. The guiltier I feel, the less likely I'll be to give you life-endangering information."

"Ah, so that's what you're doing? Protecting me by neglecting to mention this mysterious man's name? Like you kept the fact that Dr. Beck has a power from me? Ha!"

At those words, he fixed me with such an intense stare, it seemed as if the rest of his world lost all significance. "What did you say?"

It was strange to see him so perturbed. "You did not know?"

He shook his head urgently. As quickly as I could pour out the information, I explained Miss Grey's sudden arrival, her abilities, and her visions of Dr. Beck.

"And she has no idea of what the power may be?" he asked at the end of it.

"She's never witnessed it."

"Then that is more of a reason to be cautious. Dr. Beck could be capable of anything."

I gritted my teeth slightly, refusing to be swayed. "And I'm capable of recovering from anything."

"Your healing is not instantaneous. We have no idea if it is fully effective for every situation, and I do not want to test its limits. I want you to stay out of this. There are worse fates than death, especially in the hands of that man. You must trust me to get her back."

This time he did take my hand—imploringly. Behind the drapery no one could see us, though my mind was far from propriety anyway. I idly wondered how many more times Mr. Braddock and I would find ourselves in odd corners and too close. The spinning current was dulled through our gloves, but I knew he felt it, as well. My legs trembled as I looked up at him, and I could see he was equally affected—skin flushed, lips slightly parted. The heady feeling was almost enough to make me agree to stay away. But not quite.

"This is precisely the problem," I said, pulling my hand away. "I keep foolishly wanting to trust you, and then you always provide another convincing piece of evidence for why I shouldn't."

He peered down at me, and the air practically hummed with our competing powers and annoyance. "Very well. I'd much rather lose your trust than lose"—he frowned at the turn of phrase—"anything else."

The bell chimed. The sea of people began drifting back into the theatre. Refusing to give in, I drew back, crossed my arms, and prayed as I grasped for the most likely name from Miss Grey's diary. "Perhaps I'll just visit Lord Ridgewood at his home and ask him myself."

His eyes widened. I'd guessed correctly. He shook his head, jaw tight. "You are impossible."

I was, and I refused to break eye contact.

"Fine," he said at last. "I will send for you tomorrow at nine o'clock. Do not go anywhere without me. You must promise to do nothing reckless."

"Says the limping, head-bandaged man pursuing infinitely dangerous people late into the night."

Smiling against his will at that, he held my gaze for a second, hesitating with some unspoken thought behind his eyes. But he sighed and changed tactics.

"Oh, please convey my apologies to Mr. Kent. I was to have nothing further to do with you, and it appears I've completely disregarded that," he said, before leaving the nook.

I followed him out, trying to set aside my roiling frustration. He gave my hand a final squeeze before limping off down the hallway.

When I took my seat again, Laura would not look at me. I whispered to her, "How did the rest of the conversation go?"

"I don't want to talk, ever again," she spat, looking down and contemplating the wonders of her lap.

"Laura," I persisted. "Laura."

Sullen, she turned her whole body away into a very uncomfortable-looking position to make her point.

On my other side, Mr. Kent leaned over and spoke right into my ear in a low voice. "I must say, that was a curious change you made to my sister's plan."

"She was doing perfectly fine without me. She didn't even need my help," I returned, perplexed.

"Then let's remove safety nets under tightrope walkers to boost their confidence," he said with a bitter edge.

Was he really so angry about this? "Sometimes it's more helpful to let someone do it on their own," I replied calmly. "I clearly ruined her evening, and I'm sorry. But I had to talk to Mr. Braddock about finding Dr. Beck."

"Ah, yes, another secret rendezvous at an inconvenient time. Mustn't miss those. Do you think, has he just been keeping Miss Rosamund in his house this whole time?"

So he was jealous, as well. Ridiculous. I tried to keep my voice even, diplomatic. "No, he's trying to help."

"So am I, but I have to do double the work when you keep information from me. Tell me honestly, do you even think you need me to find her?"

"No," I said. "But that's because Mr. Braddock knows them—"

He stood up. "Of course, I quite understand." He turned to the rest of the group and gave a bow. "Good night, all, I'm sorry but I must be off."

"But Mr. Kent, you'll miss the ending," Miss Verinder simpered.

"All the ending does is ruin perfectly good suspense," he said with a wink and headed for the door.

I shot up, squeezed past Miss Verinder, and stopped Mr. Kent by the box door. "Wait!" I whispered. "That does not mean I don't want your help. Please. Stay."

His face softened a bit, but not enough. "Miss Wyndham, a wise girl told me something a long time ago, and it's stuck with me ever since. She said, 'Sometimes it's more helpful to let someone do it on their own.'" And he left me to the box, where no one else seemed to be on speaking terms with me. Delightful.

When the play, the clapping, the curtain call, and the agony finally ended, our party was rightfully exhausted as we passed through the lobby toward the exit. Lady Kent exchanged parting words with Mr. and Mrs. Verinder, Laura sulked over to the side and stared at framed playbills of old productions of *Romeo and Juliet,* and without Mr. Kent to cling to, Miss Verinder fell into step with me.

"Miss Wyndham, I'm sorry I was quite occupied with Mr. Kent tonight. It's a shame we did not have much opportunity to speak," she said, to my silent disagreement. "How did you enjoy the play?"

Without Mr. Kent or his stepmother within earshot, I didn't quite know what she was planning. I hardly knew how to speak to her like a normal person. "It was . . . dreadful," I replied, hesitatingly.

"I agree," she said. "Hero's ending always bothers me."

"Yes, marrying someone as boring as Claudio does seem terrible," I joked, unsure of her intentions.

"Oh, I think she was rather lucky."

"You would be happy to have Claudio?"

"No, Hero was lucky for an entirely different reason. She was the target of a false rumor, saved only because the villains confessed to their lies. Everything turned out perfectly, just because the play happens to be a comedy with a happy ending. Unlike Othello. Poor Desdemona—she was proclaimed innocent far too late, the damage already done. Can you imagine being the target of such a rumor in society now?"

"I can't," I replied coldly, the blood rushing through my veins as the realization of what she was suggesting overtook me. I rubbed my gloved hands together as we stepped outside into the wet London night.

"One would never recover from it. Fortunately for us, it's perhaps harder to lie and make up false stories, at least in London, yes? There always happens to be someone noting where you are at all times, even if you don't see them."

I tried my best to look less rigid. The question of what exactly Miss Verinder knew beat in my head, and I could barely contain the annoyed scream. Did this girl exist just to make provoking remarks? With everything on my mind, I had no patience for these elaborate Shakespearean metaphors she'd undoubtedly spent all day devising.

"Yes," I said. "But it's a shame those people don't have anything better to do with their time."

At that moment, Mr. and Mrs. Verinder voiced their good-byes and called for their frowning daughter. With a swift curtsy, she wished me good-bye—her voice a veritable coo. "It was a pleasure seeing you again, Miss Wyndham."

"*Pleasure* can hardly describe it."

She flashed me a knowing grin, amusement and devilry glinting in her hard green eyes. "I will see you at tomorrow's dinner party, then." She disappeared into the waiting carriage. I hoped it had a loose wheel.

Our ride home was a silent one. Laura closed her eyes and shut herself off from the world. Without anyone to listen to her, Lady Kent lethargically peered out the window and recited her dinner-party guest list for tomorrow, which was, coincidentally, also my list of people I hoped would get horrifically sick. When we returned home, Laura sulked up the stairs, and I had to chase her to provide another apology.

"Laura, I'm sorry," I called after her. She continued to her room, ignoring me.

"I thought you were doing well on your own," I said cheeringly.

With a huff, she spun around at the top of the stairs to face me. "Well, I wasn't!"

And this was somehow my fault? "I just don't understand why you even needed my help."

She blinked back tears and crossed her arms so tight, it looked like she would somehow suffocate herself. "I asked you, Evelyn, and you agreed. Then you deserted me," she said in a tremulous voice.

"It was an urgent matter. I had to speak to Mr. Braddock about Rose!"

Instead of listening to a word I was saying, Laura plowed on, sacrificing coherency for tears and half sobs. "And . . . and then—Mr. Edwards warned me—he said he heard all sorts of awful things about . . . you and what you've been doing . . ."

What could he possibly have heard? "Wonderful, Mr. Edwards has opinions about other topics he knows nothing about. I'm sorry I ruined your chances with such an eligible man. I'll send a letter to Rose asking her to wait until you get married. Or do you somehow have a more selfish goal in mind?"

"I've—been trying . . . to help you!" she said, desperately swiping the tears away to no avail.

"No, you just want a fun adventure."

Laura's voice screeched with desperation and a full-on tantrum. "Miss Verinder says you're simply having fun with all the men in London!"

I could only gape, stung by her accusations. Stonily I climbed the stairs. She stared at me with the hugest eyes anyone had ever had as I stopped on the stair below and spoke ever so gently.

"Is that really what you think of me? I am sorry, truly sorry, that I upset you tonight. But my sister is gone, God knows where. And if you're going to believe Miss Verinder over me, I am not sure what else we can do."

With that, I left a pale Laura on the landing, marched to my room, closed the door, and fell heavily against it. If only I could slam it. Tentative footsteps shuffled outside. A very small knock came, but I was already undressing for bed. It had been too long a day to try and soothe Laura on top of it. The voices of stubbornness and exhaustion proved far more convincing than anything nagging me to her door.

Nineteen

THE NEXT MORNING arrived, but Mr. Braddock never did.

Exhausted as I had been, sleep proved to be impossible. From the moment the sun rose, I waited in the downstairs parlor, reviewing Miss Grey's dream entries and trying to make more sense of the vague, fragmentary clues and images. None of the entries on Dr. Beck, Claude, or Mr. Hale gave a hint of where to go, and there was only one mention of Lord Ridgewood on Dr. Beck's page. It read, "Difficult to contact, Whitechapel, spotted dog." That was all. No description, no history, nothing more.

Tedious hours passed without any sign of Mr. Braddock. Two messages were sent to his home, but no response came back. I peeked out the window. A rare sunny day for London—no rain, snow, or processions delaying traffic. I didn't know whether to be angry or worried (though anger was certainly winning out at the moment). Had he safely returned last night? Did someone discover him? Why could he not send a short message? Would my power keep me from murdering him?

In fact, everyone seemed to have disappeared. Mr. Kent remained silent, and Miss Grey hadn't yet replied to my reminder to meet. Heavens to earth, I couldn't sit here waiting all day. I'd already wasted last night at the Lyceum. At this moment, Dr. Beck could be moving to a new secret laboratory across the world, where we might never find it.

Some twenty-three minutes past noon, I discovered my breaking point. I had come to London to search for Rose. Why couldn't I do it alone? Without Mr. Braddock trying to protect me or Mr. Kent acting jealous. That had been my original plan from the moment I left my parents'. I had to do something, even if I had no idea what that was.

It was in this state of desperation that I found myself skimming through the rest of the diary, reading descriptions of other powered people across the world. The information was fascinating but mostly irrelevant, until I noticed another spotted-dog owner in London. And then a third. Which meant either a citywide conspiracy against solid-colored dogs, or the words *spotted dog* had nothing to do with animals. The dictionaries and encyclopedias in the Kents' library had nothing to say about either of my theories, but a guidebook of London did. The Spotted Dog was a small, unremarkable public house located in Whitechapel. That had to be where they meet.

I stilled my frantic pacing through the library. There was only one problem: I couldn't go there like this. A lone woman in that public house would attract far too much attention, and if Dr. Beck did show up for a meeting, he would immediately recognize me. I shuffled through the cards in my possession, and as I pulled out the last one, a ridiculous plan sprang fully formed into my head.

Thirty minutes later, I stepped out of the cab somewhere in the East End. A derelict building towered in front of me, looking ready to tumble over in exhaustion onto the street. I made my way through the squeaking iron gate, up the dank stairs, and to a half-rotted door. Seconds after I knocked, a strangely exotic woman, draped in shawls and jewelry, greeted me. I promptly decided to go jump off the building.

"I'm sorry, I believe I have the wrong place," I said helplessly.

"Who are you looking for?" the woman asked. It took me a moment to understand that English words had been spoken in the thick accent.

"A Miss . . . Camille," I replied hesitantly.

She smiled and made a floating gesture of welcome. "Come in."

She led me into a luxuriously decorated living room—an incredible change from the rest of the building—and disappeared into a back room while I gazed at my surroundings. She clearly had an odd love for the color violet. Hardly anything in the room was another color. Even lamps and bookshelves and tea things had been repainted with a violet layer.

"I'm sorry to be rude, but does Camille in fact—" I stopped talking as I realized how foolish I really was. There was no Persian woman—she was Camille.

"It is you, is it not?" I asked.

The woman returned with a younger, angular face and greeted me in her French accent. "'Ello."

"I'm terribly sorry, I did not recognize you."

"*Ma fille*, no apologies. It is a compliment." She flashed a devilish smile and reclined on her velvet sofa. The transformation was remarkable. "Did you find your sister?"

"Yes," I said, taking a chair across from her. "But they managed to escape with her. I was hoping you might know where they've gone."

She shook her head. "I only had the one address."

I would have been disappointed, had I not been expecting that already. Dr. Beck wouldn't trust her again.

"But that is not the reason you come here, no?" she asked, brows arching in perfect curves.

"No, I wished to speak to you about a job."

"And who exactly is the job? Before and after, please." She winked and removed her shoes.

"It is me," I said, to her surprise. "And I must look like . . . well, a man."

Camille lit up like a child with a brand-new toy. She shot up in excitement, closely analyzed my face from every possible angle, and murmured "Hmm" and "Ah" continuously, relishing her work. "What sort of man?" she asked, kneeling to view my chin from underneath.

"Young, unrecognizable, unremarkable, the sort who would never receive a second glance," I said. "Can you do that?"

Her lips curled into a creamy smile. "Of course."

"But I must ask you something. You don't simply use makeup, do you? You must have . . . a power, yes?" I asked.

She laughed. "Dress it up and call it whatever you wish."

"Well, what I want just seems quite impossible to ask—"

Camille floated back up like a pleased little snake. "Nothing is impossible for me, I assure you. This is one of my most popular requests. Come with me."

I followed her into another room, where she glided over to her rosewood dresser, opened a drawer full of makeup bottles, and collected a few before progressing to the next drawer. With two armfuls of makeup, she returned to me. "You would make quite a beautiful man, you know," she purred. "But I suppose we must find the beauty in the commonplace. When I am done, nothing of you will be left!"

This woman. Was there anything left of the real her in the

image I saw? I studied her face and wondered about her past, about the faces she uses. "Is this what you truly look like?"

"I don't quite understand you."

"Your real self—without the disguises."

She chuckled to herself and led me to a chair stationed in front of a bright window.

"Miss Wyndham, I have no 'real self,' as you say." I heard the pop of a jar and felt the sting of cold on my head. She kneaded handfuls of a jelly through my hair, and I gasped as I felt the strands shortening.

"What does it feel like? Living that way?"

"You know as well as I," she said opaquely and crossed the room toward a small metal sink, where she wet a thin rag.

"I don't . . . often disguise myself. This is my second time."

She knelt in front of me and vigorously scrubbed my face. "Do you act the same in society as you do in private? Do you speak to everyone the same way?"

"No, not quite," I replied, wincing.

"Of course. No one does. You put on one disguise for society. You put on another for your sister. For your parents. Your costume the other night."

I felt my face warm. "But what about in private? Anyone can be themselves then without—ah! Ow!—without putting on an act."

"We do not remain the same each minute to the next. Every word you hear, every sight you see, every smell, every thought you have, every moment—it all changes you. We keep putting on mask after mask, layers over layers. That's how one grows."

She scooped up a handful of a light cream and massaged it into my skin. My face felt lightened, malleable, fluid. "That sounds dismal. Never truly seeing someone."

"No, the true face is wretchedly simple and empty. The absolute joy in life, in friendship, in love, is learning about a person, deciphering them, taking each and every mask off to find a new one, waiting to be explored and understood." She put some precise, finishing touches on my skin and stepped back to admire her work.

She gave me a sly smile. "I gather it is why you find both your . . . companions so intriguing."

"They are just helping me."

"Do not lie, child. It doesn't suit your features. Now come, we are not close to finished."

An hour later, I stood in front of a looking glass, astonished by the sight.

Good God, who was this stranger? Frowning, smiling, pouting, sneering, yawning—no expression gave me away. Camille had truly done splendid work, and it wasn't simply good makeup and a hair-cropping trick. She had molded my face into something completely different and then, using a combination of her powers and padded underclothing, even rendered my shoulders broader, my body somehow intimidating. As her final touch, Camille slipped a black morning coat over my shoulders, dropped a dashing bowler hat over my short brown hair, and put a thin umbrella in my hand. Had this all come from her imagination? Or was there the slim possibility that I'd find myself in an awkward face-to-face moment with my double?

"Do you want me to change your voice? It only takes a half hour."

"I don't intend to speak very much."

"Then be sure to lower your voice only slightly. Do not attempt to imitate a man's voice. It will sound ridiculous. Choose your words carefully, claim your throat is a bit scratchy, and mutter."

She packed everything back into her dresser, finishing the stream of advice. "Above all, you must be comfortable. If you act as if you are used to looking like this every day of your life, no one else will question you. The moment you doubt your appearance is the moment others will scrutinize your behavior."

I nodded and paid her generously for her work. It was money I could not afford to give away. Sighing, I slipped some coins and Mr. Braddock's card in my pocket in case of emergency and left my dress in the wardrobe. Camille reminded me to return the borrowed costume when I finished. I tipped my hat—a custom I surely looked awkward doing—and dashed down the stairs to head to the tavern.

"The Spotted Dog," my gravelly voice told the cabdriver.

"Yes, sir," he replied, unfazed. A rush of an uncomfortable and deliciously wicked power overcame me. The freedom of an invented reputation lay in my hands—the power to create problems, accumulate enormous debt, commit horrific crimes, and shed all responsibility in an instant. But the sudden euphoria began to ebb as quickly as it came. Of course, I could never do that. The blame would simply be shifted. And there would always be someone suffering the consequences. I wondered if Camille felt freedom or stifling responsibility every time she took on a new identity.

Soon, the cab stopped in front of the establishment, and by habit I waited, wondering what was keeping the driver, while he was probably wondering the same about me.

"Sir?" he called out. "We've arrived."

How foolish. No one would hand me out. "Oh yes, of course, thank you," I yelled back, scrambling to climb out and resisting the urge to smack myself.

Crossing the street, I tried to imagine a bored man doing this every day of his life, but even a distance of fifteen paces presented obstacle after obstacle—climbing up curbs, giving way to passersby on the busy sidewalk, ignoring the requests of a tenacious newspaper boy, dodging the swaying drunkard by the Spotted Dog entrance. I attempted a grunt to greet him, and it came out sounding rather equine, but he did not seem to notice or care in the least.

Inside, a pervading stench of alcohol and smoke filled the air, but it was not nearly as revolting as I expected a public house to be. Everything was just a plain, unadorned brown: the stools, the tables, the bar, the walls. Even the various paintings—portraits of famous London men or landmarks—had lost all their luster. No attempts had been made to dress up the establishment in any way.

Cautiously, I glanced around, fearing every eye was upon me as I approached the bar without an inkling of what to do next. Some faces were lively in conversation, and others were lifelessly sipping their drinks and smoking. There was no sign of Dr. Beck or Claude. Lord Ridgewood's face was a mystery to me, and I knew not how to identify any other members of this secret society. If only there was a butler to announce the arrival of every distinguished guest.

The clinking of glass diverted my attention. The bartender. I caught his eye and made my debut as Unremarkable Public-House Patron Number Eighteen with a couple of grumbled words. "Ale, please."

A dripping-wet glass slammed down in front of me. "Sir," I added before he could run off. "Question, sir."

"Whaddya want?" he grunted. His shirt soiled, he reeked of some sour scent that made me never want to breathe again. I maintained my distance.

"Would you happen to know a Lord Ridgewood? Or Dr. Calvin Beck? Do either of them frequent this place?"

"No sir, but if ya want an introduction to the Queen, I'm your man!" Cackling to himself, he left to serve another customer.

How amusing.

No choice but to wait patiently and watch the door, it seemed. The early afternoon did not attract much of a crowd, which left plenty of empty seats scattered around the room for me. But as I searched for a table in a dark and solitary place, my eyes landed on a man who had fallen into that sorry state instead. "Oh, Rose!" he cried.

What in heaven's name had brought Robert here?

Without realizing it, I had risen from my seat and snatched up my glass, ready to ask him. He rambled to an old man sitting next to him at the bar, who took long swigs of his beer and nodded sympathetically. My feet brought me closer and closer, but restraint or sense prevailed and I continued onward without a word, taking a table along the wall. This was neither the time nor the place to comfort Robert.

"This is a picture of my Rose," he said, holding up a monstrosity he had drawn a couple of years ago.

"A . . . uh, fine-looking girl, sir," his drinking partner replied.

"There's something wrong, I know it," he said, shaking his head. "I just wish I could see for myself that she was well!"

He drained the remains of his beer and was in the process of calling over the bartender for another when my view was entirely blocked.

"Yer sittin' at our table," a rough voice told me.

Peering down at me was a large, bearded man and his stout, short companion not far behind.

"Oh, I'm sorry," I said, leaping up from my seat.

"That ain't our table," the short one corrected. "Ours is outside."

"My 'umblest apologies," the bearded one said. "But seein' as yer up, 'ow'd you like a drink wif us?"

I shook my head. "That's quite all right—"

"We insist," the short one said, giving me a false smile. "Any 'quaintance of Dr. Beck is a 'quaintance of ours."

I picked up my glass, silently cursing to myself. The big one led the way to a wooden back door, and his companion prodded me from behind to follow. It scraped open to a secluded alleyway behind the bar. Sickening smells and foreboding reddish stains assaulted my senses, and my heart went off thumping again. The two men seemed to be quite at home here. What was their connection to Dr. Beck? And where did that short one acquire the long scar along his face?

The tall man rolled up his sleeves and took a swaggering step forward. The false politeness disappeared from his face. "Who are ya?" he growled.

"I—I'm sorry? Ah—uh, James . . . Brick?" I squeaked, backing against the wall.

"No ya ain't—now tell us." He scowled menacingly.

"An' what're ya 'ere for, girl?" the shorter one growled as he reached into his pocket. Another squeak loosed itself from my throat. How did they know?

"I—I was, um—I am looking for my sister, Rose, and—" I started to say.

The two exchanged the same curious glance. Smiles passed across both their faces, and they turned to me with synchronized bows.

"Ah! As we suspected. *Yer* the gal."

"The one Braddock's been tryin' very, very 'ard to 'elp."

"You aren't with Dr. Beck?" I managed.

The two men whispered between each other.

"Course we can trust 'er," the bearded one said encouragingly. "She dunnit sound like she's lying."

"Dunnit look like it, either," the other finished.

"Settled, then." The bearded one turned to me. "Muh name's Arthur, this 'ere's William, and we're with yer friend Braddock. We provide 'im with information on 'ccasion—call us merchants, yeah?"

William sniffed the alley air and wrinkled his nose. "Arthur, we best be back, this ain't no place for a lady."

"And in 'ere is?" Arthur asked, smirking as he pulled the door open for us.

William led the way back into the black void, and the faint outline of his body was the only thing keeping me from crashing into everything as my eyes adjusted.

"Who—how did you see through my disguise in here?"

"We're talented," William said over his shoulder.

"Quite talented," came Arthur's voice from behind.

William stopped at an open table and pulled back a chair for me, which must have looked like strange behavior to anyone sober enough to notice or care.

I sat down, trying to find the right words. "Are you? Do you have? I mean . . ."

Arthur nodded at me. "Yea, we're special-like, just as you are. I could 'ear the strain—in yer voice. Ya shoulda let 'er change it."

"Don't matter," William put in as he sat, "I could see the makeup and the alt'rations. Brushstrokes, yeah? Like you's got a mask. Still, that Camille bird's gotten right good at it, took me 'most two seconds to see ya through it."

"You are acquainted with Camille?" I asked.

"'Ow'd ya think we got these threatenin' faces?" They smiled, teeth glinting in a sharklike way.

"Charged a fortune, though."

Arthur gave a disappointed shake of the head. "Shouldn'ta paid extra for the scar, Willy."

"Scar's the most impor'nt part," William said. He looked to me. "Terrifying, innit?"

"Quite," I said, my pulse finally slowing. "Why did you change your faces?"

"Went into 'iding," they spoke together.

"From?" The two exchanged rapid, hesitant glances before coming to a silent decision, turning back to me.

"The one yer lookin' for. Experimented on me ears."

"An' me eyes."

"We'd rather not dredge up those memories, love."

"Unpleasant, see?"

"Where'd that lass get to?" Arthur asked, twisting around and searching the room.

"There she is," William declared triumphantly, holding up three fingers for a barmaid across the room to see. "Drinks on Arthur 'gain."

Arthur scoffed. "If she were talkin', I'd've won," he said, shaking his head.

"But ya din't."

They looked easy enough, but I could sense an undercurrent of pain that was strikingly similar to Mr. Braddock's. Still, I had to keep on the difficult topic. "So why are you two here?"

"Braddock asked us to keep our ears out for information about Beck," Arthur whispered. "And this 'ere is the top place for 'earing about special-like folk."

"Why this place?"

Arthur shrugged. "Don't know 'ow it started. Maybe's more comfortable drinkin' with your kind?"

"Everyone keeps it quiet, though. You gotta look extra close. See that barmaid?" William asked, nodding toward our server. "Beer comes out warm, but watch 'er hands."

The bartender poured our glasses as he had done mine earlier, but when the barmaid fetched them, she took an extra moment to wrap her hand around each base. Within seconds, each glass fogged up, chilled to its core. After she delivered them to our table, I couldn't help but scrape the frost in amazement.

"Of course," I sighed. "Mr. Braddock doesn't tell me about this place, either."

"That there—wait." William eyed me in a terribly uncomfortable way—it felt as if he were slowly peeling off layers of my skin. "He don't know you're 'ere?"

"He doesn't tell me anything and then goes off searching without me," I complained, my exasperation not particularly well disguised.

"'Haps he's tryin' ta protect you."

"An' we ain't 'elping by keepin' you 'ere. You should return 'ome. We'll keep watch. Better suited for it anyways." William spoke in the soothing tone one uses with an irrational child. Of course, the effect on a rational adult was anything but soothing.

"No. I need to find my sister, and all this 'protection' does is slow the search!" I said, the table rattling as my fist banged down.

A couple of sleeping drunkards at the tables around us jerked their heads up, bewildered. Neither Arthur nor William flinched at my outburst, though. Arthur just gave me a look of pity, which felt rather insulting, considering our pathetic surroundings. "He's got 'is own reasons."

"What on earth is his hold over you? Did he threaten you? Beat you up? You know, I could help if he injured you—"

"Dearie, we owe 'im our lives."

I gaped at them, certain I was mishearing. Perhaps they owed him their wives? Knives? "I'm sorry, what exactly do you mean?"

"He's the reason we ain't dead. Freed us from Dr. Beck," Arthur said. William nodded along enthusiastically.

"I see . . . and this was when he was not testing his power on innocent subjects?" I was rather viciously pleased to see their abashed reactions.

"It's true—'e did that," William said ruefully.

"Yeah but 'e dinnit wanta, did 'e?" Arthur turned back to me, earnest. "Tore 'im right up that 'e couldn't control his power, but he didn't hav'a choice—he was locked up. Dr. Beck'll do anything for his research. It starts out real friendly-like, but then one day 'e locked us up, and 'e would'a cut us open if Braddock hadn't helped us 'scape."

"And if Mr. Braddock hadn't let Dr. Beck go," I said, "you or my sister wouldn't have been locked up in the first place."

They both frowned and exhaled. "That's a messy business, dearie," Arthur said. "You're right 'bout your sister, but Beck 'ad us in another laboratory."

"If Braddock had killed 'em instead of followed 'em, we'd'a never been found."

I stared into my cloudy glass, watching the whirling liquid settle into stillness. So Mr. Braddock had told me the truth. He really hadn't had a choice. And he'd saved Arthur's and William's lives. But the two images—of Mr. Braddock killing an innocent and showing mercy to Dr. Beck—proved impossible to banish with Rose still out there.

The duo seemed to silently communicate again with glances before Arthur cleared his throat, speaking low. "Even if 'e don't tell ya everything, you can trust 'im to 'ave a good reason for it."

"Did he tell you Dr. Beck has an unknown power of his own?" I took a heavy gulp of the ale.

When I set down the glass, I was faced with identical expressions of confusion. "Dr. Beck's special-like?"

"We only learned of it yesterday. We're quite sure he has a power—we just don't know what it may be."

Nauseated, William pushed aside his drink, while Arthur drained half the glass, foam collecting on his beard. Neither reaction was entirely reassuring.

"Then I gather you don't have ideas of what it might be?" I asked. "Did you ever see anything out of the ordinary with him? Anything at all?"

Arthur closed his eyes a little and touched his ears, wincing in pain at my strained tone. "Dinnit think 'e could get scarier, didja, Willy? But that 'bout makes me wanna run ta 'nother country," he said miserably.

"Sorry, can't say I noticed anything," William put in. "Cunning bastard iffin you'll pardon me for sayin' so. Always planned well. Never let it slip. He musta known 'ow to hide the power. Nuthin' ever seemed strangelike." He nodded in his short-necked way.

I took a final sip of the beer. The bitter taste was a bit more tolerable this time, but it was nothing I'd miss. "And do you still mean to keep watch here for Mr. Braddock? You still trust him?"

They both nodded, without the need to look at each other for agreement. Very well. Staunch supporters of the cause.

"Then I will thank you for your help and take my leave. You two are infinitely more suitable for the task, and I've distracted you long enough." I pulled out a scrap of paper and wrote down the Kents' address. "If you discover anything at all, please include me. You can imagine how difficult it is knowing the danger my sister is in and not being able to help."

They stood up with me and Arthur took the address. "We do. And I s'pose that fella there knows a bit about it, too," he said, nodding toward Robert, who by now had buried his face into the crook of his elbow to weep.

"He is a dear friend of mine. Would you make sure he does nothing stupid?"

"If you'll do us a favor in turn."

William gave me an earnest look. "You try ta forgive Braddock. He means ya well."

I pushed in my chair and nodded a clumsy, hesitant good-bye to them. The sticky floor brought me through the smoky haze and out the front door, where I found a sudden, blinding reminder that it was still the middle of the day.

Lost in the bustle of my thoughts, I only realized where I was when my cab came to a jolting stop outside Camille's building. When I knocked on her door, an elderly man poked his head out this time. "Oh, Miss Wyndham, come in."

She led me into the dressing room, where she tilted my chin up, admiring her work one final time. "Did it all go accordingly?" she asked.

"Not quite," I said. "But it was instructive, nonetheless."

"It often is." She soaked a rag in a bucket of water warmed by the sunlight and set to reversing the process, scrubbing off my makeup, massaging a tingling substance into my hair, manipulating my shoulders and chest. As she worked, I could swear my muscles were relaxing and my hair lengthening with her every touch, returning almost imperceptibly to equilibrium. It took only a fraction of the time to undo her work.

When she had finished, she motioned to the large looking glass. "Please tell me if there's anything I've missed. I'll fetch your dress from the other room."

She left me alone with my reflection. My appearance looked as close to normal as I could tell, though it still felt strange with the loose men's clothing I wore. Maybe my dress—wait. I'd left my dress in this wardrobe.

I cracked the dressing-room door open and called out, "Miss Camille, my things are here."

No response. The entire apartment sat silent. She was nowhere to be found in the other two rooms. A chill ran down my spine as I rushed to open the front door and stepped out into the vacant hall. Why had she just left without warning?

"What a pleasant surprise, Miss Wyndham."

Smiling up at me from the lower staircase landing was my answer. Dr. Beck.

Twenty

No. No. No.

Not him. Not now. Not this way.

No one even knew where I was. My breath caught, and I fumbled for words before realizing that I should have been running. I bounded upstairs past the second floor, third, fourth, the clatter of footsteps following from one flight below. My chest heaved and my cravat flapped wildly out of my open waistcoat as I pushed myself forward. My suit was less cumbersome than a dress, but it was of no help to me once I burst through the roof door and stumbled outside. A vacant roof, a single entrance, and a five-story drop. The setting sun over the London skyline pleasantly bade me good-bye.

"Miss Wyndham, please." Dr. Beck and Claude had already caught up, standing by the door. "If you will oblige us for just a few minutes."

"No, I am in a bit of a hurry, thank you," I shouted back.

Camille poked her wrinkled head out the roof door behind them.

"*You* called them?" I shouted at her. "Why?"

She gave me a sort of frowning smile as if I'd asked a stupid question. "I told you. There's no greater pleasure than removing one mask to reveal another." She turned to Dr. Beck. "Are we finished?"

"We are. Go enjoy this beautiful evening," Dr. Beck said with a pleasant smile.

She nodded and shut the door with an aching metal wail.

"You were seconds away from death the other night," Dr. Beck said. "Yet you still persist in chasing us. It seems stubbornness runs in your family."

A strong wind rushed in from the west, sending my hair flailing across my face. My heart thumped for Rose. She was still alive, then. I felt flushed, tense, seething. My mind flashed through hundreds of painful fates for him if only I had Mr. Braddock's abilities.

"Don't you *dare* hurt her!" The empty threat escaped against my better judgment.

Dr. Beck took slow steps forward and shook his head. "You keep insisting one girl's comfort is far more important than millions of other lives. Do you understand how ridiculous you sound?"

He didn't deserve a response.

"You attend church, yes?" he asked. "Of course you do. Why is it acceptable that martyred saints and even 'the Son of God' can sacrifice themselves all for a set of beliefs? The actual results from those sacrifices are still up for debate, while the possibilities that stem from Miss Rosamund's are as clear as day to anyone—and you cannot accept it."

There was nothing else to do, nothing to say. I could hear people from the street below, but could they hear me? Could I call for help without Dr. Beck knowing? Backing up to the edge of the roof, I lashed out the way I knew best. Loudly.

"Even with your power, you're still a terrible scientist! There's a reason your fellow scientists ridicule you," I yelled. "It's because they—"

"—know my work is going to accomplish nothing and *help* no one?" Dr. Beck finished calmly. A look of mild amusement unfurled across his face. "I'm sorry, I took the words out of your mouth. Please, continue."

Oh, God. A frightening revelation struck me. It explained how he could block my attacks, how he responded to unfinished sentences, how Arthur and William saw that he never made mistakes, how he always had a plan. Was it possible? It existed in myths, but . . .

"You—you . . . can see—"

Dr. Beck smiled serenely at me. "The future, yes, Miss Wyndham. I am impressed. Now you know I am not exaggerating when I tell you I am one step ahead of you. I was born to be one step ahead of you. I will know if someone is coming through this door before he himself even knows. And I can assure you with complete confidence, no one noticed your plea for help, no one cares, and no one is coming."

I didn't know how it felt to have the life sucked out of me, but his words managed a close approximation. He could see the future, and he was only admitting everything because he knew I was going to be dead in less than a minute.

Dr. Beck met Claude's eye and nodded in my direction, and the giant stomped closer. Dear God, this was really the end of me. What a stupid way to go. Strangled, stabbed, bones broken, maybe all three at once. I had to do something. Anything. And then I saw it. As I moved toward the corner of the roof, another building came into view. It was right next to us, one story lower, a manageable jump, an actual escape.

"Stop her!" I heard Dr. Beck yell.

I took off in a sprint.

My shoes smacked across the thick stone roof and crinkled over the small gravel pits. The steady rumble of Claude's tread followed me doggedly. I could feel him moments away from grabbing me, but I caught sight of the ledge, a few long strides away, and the simple plan burned into my mind. Just run, jump over it, and live. That's all I had to do.

So I leaped, my glimpse of heavenly freedom on the opposite building moving closer, closer, within reach. My stomach floated up weightlessly as my jump became a drop. My chest hit the edge of the roof hard, knocking out my breath. As I slid back, my hands scrambled to grasp brick, rock, anything, for God's sake, please.

And I fell.

A rush of air and a blurry procession of bricks streamed by me and cut out with empty thuds and cracks of pain spiking through my legs and across my side. I tasted bitter metal, and a sudden numbness took over. Carriages clanked, a baby cried, bells rang, a woman screamed, and then it all quieted down to final thoughts (so this is what dying is?) before even those faded away into a blissful shroud of nothingness.

Twenty-One

A STARK ROOM greeted me when I awoke.

With a groan, I sat up and rubbed the blur out of my eyes—it felt like I had overslept by several years. The glow of gas lamps shone through the room's tiny window, and drops of rain pattered against the pane.

I rolled and twisted off the bed, feeling a shudder when my feet touched the cold floor. Instinctively, I rubbed my leg: no lingering pain, no scar, no mark at all. My last memories were hazy, but I could distinctly recall the falling, the utter fear, and the peculiar understanding of pain. The reality of being fully recovered instead of fully broken sent goose pimples prickling up all over my body.

At the sound of my sheets rustling, a nurse, slumped over in a rickety chair by the corner, stirred and shot straight up. "Miss Bradent, one moment, I'll go fetch him," she said, already half-way out of the room.

Miss Bradent? I glanced around the room, noting the white stone walls and the dreary lights. I wasn't in an asylum, was I? What other place on earth could look this depressing? It was too dark to see out the window and not quite tempting enough a prospect to wait and find out for myself. In a hurry, I slid off the stiff bed and tiptoed to the door. I pulled it open, and there stood Mr. Braddock on the other side of the threshold, his breath drained and his person drenched.

"Miss . . . Wyndham . . ."

"So. You've finally arrived," I managed to mutter, my voice hoarse from disuse.

Only a few inches away, he heard me clearly. His tense hands clutched the doorway, and his eyes dropped downward. "I'm—I'm sorry. How do you feel?"

"Absolutely blissful. Perfect is an understatement," I replied drily, pulling back and widening the gap. "How did you find me?"

"The hospital. They found you in an alleyway with no identification. My card was in your pocket, and they contacted me."

As Mr. Braddock spoke, he raised his head and stared pointedly above my right shoulder, his flushed cheeks growing even redder. I looked down and realized my white hospital gown appeared to be slightly transparent. It was hard to care about covering up my body after it had been through so much, but for the sake of Mr. Braddock (who had retreated into the hallway), I turned around with forced composure, padded back inside the room, and crawled into the bed.

"Mr. Braddock, please come in," I called. "I don't give a fig for propriety at the moment."

His dark head peeped around the corner. He slipped in, closed the door, and leaned against the farthest possible wall.

"Why does the hospital think I am Miss Bradent?" I asked.

"I told them you were my cousin Elizabeth and had you moved to this private room, so I could watch from the street," he said.

"Always a distant cousin," I muttered.

He bit his lip for a moment before giving in to the questions he was holding back. "Tell me. What happened? How did you come to be hurt?"

"I fell off a roof," I said vaguely, clenching my jaw. I wanted him to feel miserable.

Concern and disbelief filled his eyes. "It was true, then," he murmured, unlacing his arms and starting toward me before pulling back, remembering to remain stoic. "By the time the ambulance arrived, your injuries were so minor, they concluded you fainted in the alley. The only witness was a drunkard, and his story about the roof sounded too unbelievable—even to me. Given the circumstances, you were quite—"

"Lucky?" I finished with a bitter laugh.

The silence boiled through the room. If he bit his lower lip any more, it would fall off. "Does anything still hurt?" he finally asked.

"No."

He rubbed the back of his head in distress, stepping forward slightly. "What were you even searching for? What was possibly worth all this?" he asked.

I steadily told him about my encounters with Camille, William, Arthur, and Dr. Beck. When I finished, I found him glaring at me. I was getting particularly tired of that look.

"So it was for nothing," he said, taking another step. "I don't think you fully understand how fortunate you are. We're still figuring out the extent of your powers. You just as easily might not have been protected from such severe injuries. Or if the ambulance had arrived earlier, one of the doctors could have observed your healing ability, and you would be—I don't know—locked up somewhere to be studied! It was pure chance that you're not de—I thought you promised to stop this recklessness."

"And what about your promise? Why did you just disappear . . . ?"

". . . leaving me to that terror and pain?" was the unspoken end to the question, but he heard it nonetheless. A stricken expression crossed his face, making him look younger and gaunter as he grasped the end of the bed. I almost felt delight in his reaction. Then I remembered the mountain of guilt he was already struggling with and simply felt wretched for us both.

"I was following Lord Ridgewood," he said.

"And lied to me about searching together," I said dully.

"I specifically chose not to inform you, because I worried something dangerous might happen," he said, angrily grabbing the bedsheets. "And I stand by that. This afternoon, Lord Ridgewood realized I was following him and paid three men to attack me."

I stilled, heart hammering, searching him for injury. The menacing black eye and bruise on his face were fading, but they still lingered. "Are you hurt?"

"No. But he disappeared while I was occupied."

Not ready to concede the point, I continued. "It still sounds like I would have been safer with you."

"You would have been even safer remaining at home," he returned sharply, moving himself much closer. My heart quickened, and suddenly he was so close, I could smell leather and mint. "Do you know what it was like? To hear you were in a hospital? I thought you were dead. I thought—" He cut himself off, but by now he was sitting next to me, cradling my face in his hands.

We both seemed to realize his actions at the same time. I couldn't feel anything except the rush of blood that sprang up wherever his fingers touched my skin. I couldn't hear anything except for the rustle of my hair as he brushed a strand behind my ear. I couldn't see anything except his expression, so strange I was sure he was about to kiss me again. But when he leaned forward, lips parted, I found my voice.

"At least *I* found Dr. Beck," I said, choking back this moment we shared, hoping to return us to our natural state: bickering. Slowly, he pulled back, as well. I could almost read disappointment in his eyes before a sneer took over his face.

"Being ambushed hardly qualifies as finding the man." The walls were back up, and I should have felt safe, secure. But somehow, it was only isolating.

"Well, unlike you—"

"Please, stop," he interrupted, backing away to the farthest corner. "It's late. If it's all the same to you, we can continue this argument while we get you home."

"I don't have any proper clothes," I snapped.

"I bought you a dress," he snapped back, gesturing to a simple green gown hanging by the window. "And . . . things. For underneath it."

"What? Wh-where did you even get it?"

"Is it not to your liking? I had to kill two peo—no, that isn't very funny . . ." His attempt at levity only brought more tension to his shoulders and lines to his injured face.

"It's, ah, fine," I said, slightly stunned. "Thank you."

"I'll wait outside. Take your time," he said, closing the door behind him.

That man. I took a deep breath and wiped my face with his handkerchief left by my bedside. I hardly knew if it was my injuries or the conversation or the brief touch, but I felt a rush in my head, as if I were still falling through the air without control of my movements or my thoughts.

I stood and slipped off the hospital gown to assess my body closely for injuries. There was nothing to be found. No one would know what happened to me today, and that was exactly how I wanted it to stay. The green dress fit perfectly, and I could even admire its rich color. Nothing could be done with my wild hair besides running my fingers swiftly through the heavy strands.

When I was ready, Mr. Braddock met me in the corridor and walked me through its twists and turns. He spoke to the woman at the front desk, but she seemed to be distracted by a crisis over a stabbing victim. My sloppy *Elizabeth Bradent* signature was sufficient to sweep our way out of the dingy hospital and into the waiting hansom.

"Now, I believe you were yelling at me?" Mr. Braddock said, once we were on our way.

"Did you learn anything from those men who attacked you?" I asked.

"No," he replied with a grimace. "They'd only met him minutes prior."

"Do you have another plan?"

"Camille's building is the only possibility—though I doubt she would have remained there, considering the recent commotion."

"But there is no reason for her to move. I'm the only one who knew the location, and they didn't expect me to survive that fall. We should go now."

I already knew what he was going to say, but I thought if I slipped in the suggestion quickly and he agreed to it by accident, it would somehow be set in stone.

But he caught it, his brow knitted in frustration. "No. There's no *we* for this search. In fact, there are even more reasons for you to stay away now. If they see you are healed, Dr. Beck will want you for his experiments, too."

"I doubt you will get very far yourself. We clearly need each other's assistance."

He scoffed at that. "*You* need *my* assistance. Your presence only makes it more difficult for me."

"Then you don't need to know what Dr. Beck's power is? Silly me, I thought it might be helpful."

His eyes stopped, dead still, his lips half parted and frozen. I had his full attention. "You learned what it is?"

"He admitted it on the roof. He can see the future, expect things before they happen."

Lines twisted across Mr. Braddock's forehead as he receded from the present, replaying his encounters with the man. "He never did seem surprised or anxious. He always looked bored, like you were speaking too slowly."

"So if it's true, what do we do now?"

For an eternity, he stared out the window at the streaming rain, the muddy streets, the dark shops shuttered and gated, the buildings half hidden in fog. "I don't know," he finally said. "I'm sorry. I need more time to think."

"I have one idea," I lied.

"What is it?"

"You don't need to know that yet. I'm sure you plan to go to Camille's tonight after you take me home. But I won't have you doing everything without me. Tomorrow morning, you will pick me up, along with Miss Grey and Mr. Kent, and we will go together. If not, I shall go out on my own again, and you will have to kidnap me to fully stop me, which in some ways would be considered a strange and criminal turn of events."

He had no response, or—judging by his expression—no polite, gentlemanly one. His eyes flickered as he struggled to determine what clues he had overlooked, what I had solved that he couldn't. After another long, uncomfortable silence, Mr. Braddock filled it with a half-grunted, half-muttered something that sounded like "As you wish."

The victory felt hollow this time. "Well, I *wish* I knew what the right choice was."

He looked at me steadily, perhaps trying to determine if I was being sarcastic. "What do you mean?"

"If Dr. Beck can see the future, then he knows what actions he must take to realize it, no matter how vicious they may be. But all we can do is make a decision and pray it's the right one. None of them have been so far, though."

He turned away in contemplation. With every movement of the cab, the glare of the reading lamp washed over his cheek, the moonlight glimmered in his green eyes, and the gas lanterns flickered around his straight nose. The hues mingled together, floating over his face, exchanging caresses with the shadows.

"I don't believe there's ever a right choice," he said finally. "No matter how much you plan, there's always something unexpected, something unaccounted for that goes wrong."

"That . . . is a terrible answer," I said, shaking my head.

"I suspected you would say that."

"Because it was terrible."

"Because of who you are. When we first met, I thought you angry, stubborn, and infuriatingly willful."

"And now?" Even as I spoke the words, I wondered why I cared so much.

He blinked. "I still think you're angry, stubborn, and infuriatingly willful. But I've come to rather like it, especially when it's directed at someone who isn't me. You simply refuse to settle. You keep pushing forward to get what you want, no matter what gets in your way, no matter what hurts you. It's most admirable."

I found his admiration made my head spin slightly and had to have a quick, firm talk with myself before I could meet his eyes again. The carriage stopped outside the Kents', and Mr. Braddock climbed out, circled around, and helped me down. My fingers prickled from his touch, which seemed to last an age.

"Tomorrow, then," he said, letting go of my hand.

"Tomorrow," I repeated, swells of my breath mingling with the frigid air. The fog had risen out of the streets, kissing the rooftops of buildings, and the rain had stopped, leaving the city slick, shiny, and vivid. "If I can trust you'll come this time."

"You can." Mr. Braddock hesitated at the cab and half turned, looking unconvinced himself. He came back to me, taking off his hat and speaking hurriedly. "But I know my word isn't quite enough for you now. All I have left to offer you is my name, so that you may curse it if necessary."

"I've already done that a great deal, Mr. Braddock."

His fingers tapped on the hat. "Well, I—I was hoping my given name had a clean slate."

Oh, that's what he was asking. My face warmed as I tested the name in my head.

"I'm sorry," he said after a moment, shaking his head. "That was improper of me to ask. I apologize—"

"No, it's . . . certainly no more improper than seeing me in a hospital gown. I was just seeing how I liked it."

The corner of his lip pulled up slightly. And was that a blush? "Does it meet your approval?"

"Well, Sebastian," I said, feeling the strange sound wash over my tongue like a breaking wave. "It isn't at all good for cursing.

But I suppose we can find another use for it. As you might with mine."

He smiled widely at that and opened the cab door.

"I look forward to it, Evelyn," he replied, and the way my name left his lips and drifted into the air sent a peculiar glow through me, not unlike his touch did.

Except this lingered long after he rolled away.

Twenty-Two

Tuffins opened the door with a bleak expression. The lights were bright, and the muffled sounds of a chattering crowd floated downstairs. The dinner party.

"Lady Kent wishes to see you in the drawing room," he said, almost timidly.

My stomach roiled as he marched through the portrait-plastered hallway, up the stairs, and past the music room, where all the guests seemed to be gathered. I desperately clung to the hope that all this fuss was to offer me a fresh raspberry tart to try before the others, but Tuffins's manner made me feel more like a prisoner being led to the gallows.

"Do I get any last words?" I asked.

A smile almost broke on his reserved expression. He let me into the room. "She will be here in a moment," he said, shutting the door gently behind me.

As usual, the stuffy room was filled with the waft of perfume and smoke. I stood in the center, unsure what my strategy should be. This was about my absence, surely. I needed a good excuse. I cautiously huddled into a side chair by the fireplace, preparing profuse apologies and innocent gazes.

The door flew open, and in hobbled Lady Kent, who greeted me with a glare.

"Miss Wyndham," she said before stiffly lowering herself into an uncomfortably close seat, only a low tea table separating us. She took a sip from her wineglass and twisted her mouth sourly. "Absent all day again."

"I'm so terribly sorry," I said with such remorse, one would have thought I burned down a schoolhouse full of sick children. "I did not mean to return so late. I was at the Cages' in the afternoon, and they insisted I stay longer, and I was such a poor judge of time. Between listening to Eliza play the pianoforte and hearing John tell stories of his travels, I completely lost track of the evening! Oh heavens, I feel so very awful for not being here. Is Laura cross with me?"

"Did you say the Cages?" Lady Kent asked, leaning forward with a piercing look.

"Oh, they are lovely—dear old friends from Melchester," I said, praying I wasn't describing real people. "It's a rare occurrence to find them in town, so I do hope to get the chance to introduce you if there is to be a party."

"I don't believe I know of them," Lady Kent said, folding her hands on her lap. "Chiefly because I don't believe they exist."

I barely knew how to respond to that. "I . . . uh, I'm sorry, did—"

"This morning," she continued, her words stampeding over mine, "I heard some distressing news about your recent . . . activities at the Argyll Rooms."

Hang it. Sebastian and Mr. Kent had warned me. My mind cycled through hundreds of potential excuses: I had a twin; another Evelyn Wyndham was attempting to ruin my name; I had mistaken the place for a dressmaker's shop; I had visited multiple rooms of a church on Argyll Road, which must be the source of all the confusion. Dear God, nothing would work.

"Perhaps their vision—"

"Spare me the excuses and pretenses," Lady Kent replied with infuriating certainty. "I don't have the time for a story about another delightful family. I knew it was a mistake to let my daughter near you, but still, I was persuaded to invite you for dinners, even let you stay as a guest, and *this* is how you repay a kindness? You stay in *my* home while you visit brothels, travel unaccompanied with unmarried ruffians, and even . . . attend to them privately at their home! I knew you had come for some man, but I hadn't anticipated even *your* behavior could be so wanton and disgusting!"

A gust of wind noisily rattled the windows and whistled through the cracks. Bloody hell. How did she know all of it? I stared down at the ugly brown rug, urging my mind to think of something. There was nothing I could say on such short notice, except the truth. I prayed that Lady Kent could remain discreet for once.

"My sister has been kidnapped," I confessed. "I came to London to try to find her. We've avoided telling—"

"After countless lies, you try to feed me another?"

"It's the truth. Laura will tell you."

"Laura can barely tell her life apart from a novel." Lady Kent raised her head authoritatively. "Now, was this, as you say, 'kidnapping' before or after your sister started working at the brothel, as well?"

"That wasn't her—"

"You admit it, then. You visited the vile place."

"It was a dancing room, and I know it may look indecent, but I had no other choice. Everything I did was to find my sister," I replied, wincing at how bad it really did sound.

A terrible silence fell upon the room. Lady Kent shifted her gaze to the window as she gathered her thoughts. The firelight flickered across her face, and it seemed to soften, relax.

But then she spoke: "You will pack up your belongings and leave immediately. We can no longer have you as our guest."

I waited for the clacking laugh. It was a horrible, ill-spirited joke, surely. But no amusement broke through those cracked lips. She wanted to throw me out in the middle of the night because the truth was too unbelievable? I hadn't even mentioned the powers.

"You—you must believe me," I pleaded. "I need to find Rose."

"That should be quite easy if you get your story straight. She's with your aunt and uncle or at this brothel. A number of people have identified her without a doubt," Lady Kent spat out.

"I *wish* that was my sister, but it was someone acting in her stead. I have no idea where she is! That is why I need your help," I pleaded, rising to my feet in desperation before plopping back down in the chair in the same movement, so I wouldn't seem threatening.

She grimaced and rubbed hard at her knees. "You've involved us in your disgusting scandal, and you have the nerve to ask for help? All of London is already talking about it—heaven knows how much damage you've caused to Laura's marriage prospects by staying in this house. The sooner you leave, the sooner this can be undone."

"It would be just as easy for you to explain the truth—"

Against all odds, Lady Kent's stern face managed even less sympathy than ever. "Miss Wyndham, I've seen girls like you and your sister for years—it never changes. You all think yourselves so clever, so pretty, and so entitled that you believe the rules of society don't apply to you. That you're free to do whatever you wish while the rest of us have to struggle and suffer and sacrifice to get what we want the right way!"

I barely had it within me to argue. It would only further hurt my chances of staying.

"No one cares to ever look beyond appearances. Society prefers it to be simple. And you spend years reaping the benefits, and suddenly, when it no longer works for you, everyone must change then, is that right?"

Meekly, I shook my head and took the abuse, resisting the burning desire to shove the woman into the fire.

She readjusted her position, gritting her teeth and giving a firm nod. "Of course not. Now, ask Tuffins to send someone for your trunk, and leave quietly. I must see to my guests."

"I don't have anywhere to go . . ." I said.

Her veiny hand gave me a dismissive wave. "I'm sure your parents will take you. Or some convent."

". . . or anyone to help me."

"Your sister will keep you comp—company," she said, her speech veering off as she strained to keep the pain down.

As I stood up, though, a wild, desperate idea came to me at the sight of her grimace. The answer. I'd cure her illness in an instant, and there'd be no way she could refute that evidence.

Hurrying around the low table, I reached over the arm of the settee and grasped Lady Kent's wrist.

"What in—what are you doing? Get off!" she gasped.

Just five minutes. It's all I needed to convince her of everything. To convince her to let me stay. "Relax, Lady Kent, please. I can heal you and remove the pain, just—just give me a few minutes."

She wouldn't stop feebly squirming and shoving as she attempted to wriggle across the cushions, away from me. "Don't touch me!" she wailed. "Get your hands off—"

I stretched out farther, struggling to keep balance. "I can help you! Sto—"

"Tuffins!" she screeched like a banshee. "Help me! Someone! She's gone mad!"

"I'll fix everything—it'll be all ri—"

And a stinging blow tore across my cheek. The unexpected welt sent me recoiling, and I let go of her as she nearly collapsed out of her seat.

While I stood, still frozen in shock, she staggered up and managed to make it to the door, where Tuffins appeared with a concerned footman and Mr. Kent.

"I was under the impression the party was in the other room," Mr. Kent joked. His smile vanished the moment he saw his disheveled stepmother and me.

"S-see that Miss Wyndham is gone immediately," Lady Kent choked out to Tuffins, before turning to Mr. Kent. "And you! I have had enough of this silly infatuation you seem to entertain. If you speak one more word to that wicked girl, consider yourself cut off from this family!"

She disappeared down the hall and up the stairs. It took seven uncomfortable steps to leave the drawing room and three more to reach Mr. Kent in the hall. Behind him, guests spilled out of the music room to see the commotion.

As I passed him, I urged him silently: *Tell her the truth. Say anything. Please.*

But his head stayed down, and he refused to meet my eyes. I could swear that I heard a slight murmur of my name, but then he mustered up a polite smile for Tuffins, gave him a curt nod, and retreated to the music room, steering the crowd back in with him.

"Where was I? I was just starting or finishing my list of France's virtues . . . oh well, either way, we've come to the end," he said, the door shutting behind him.

Tuffins gave me a look of sympathy, told the footman to fetch a cab, and led me up the stairs. My knees followed, but my mind was entirely blank, shocked, and unable to make any plans. How could everything fall apart in a matter of minutes?

Slumped against what used to be my bedroom door, Laura waited for me, her face red and raw from crying.

"Oh, Evelyn! I'm so sorry!" she cried, clasping on with a hug. "I tried to explain it to her, but she wouldn't listen! She never listens to me."

"She didn't believe me, either," I said, managing to unlatch her person from mine.

She shuffled into the room behind me. "She—she said it was not possible. Someone in Mrs. Verinder's house staff said they saw everything you did. And your sister."

I pulled out my trunk from a closet and stuffed my clothes inside. No point in folding them. "Oh, for God's sake, it's Miss Verinder, of course. She set this all up! Why—how could this even happen? We've told the truth, and they believe her fabricated tale!" I exclaimed.

Laura shook her head, fresh tears streaming down her face. "Even Nick won't try to convince Mama! I refuse to talk to him."

I shook my head, trying to shut my trunk. Overloaded, it wouldn't close. "Don't do that—he's your brother."

"And I hate him. I hate everyone! I just want to run away from home . . . or set it on fire. Or set Miss Verinder's house on fire! Oooh, we should do that, Evelyn!"

"No, you must stay here, and I will leave. It's too late. There's nothing left to do but hope the damage will not be so bad." Bless her little heart. The longer I drew this out, the more upset she was going to get.

I knelt down, pushed all my weight onto the trunk, and secured the rusted clasps. Then I gave Laura one last hug. "Thank you, Laura. Just listen to your brother, and everything will be well here. And I'm truly sorry about last night with Mr. Edwards."

She sniffled. "Hang Mr. Edwards. After what he said yesterday, I've already added his to the lists of houses to be set ablaze."

As the footman dragged my trunk down the stairs, I told him to keep an eye on the house's supply of matches.

I half regretted that warning, though, on my way out. There was no alternative but to pass by the music room, which I could swear hushed to a painful silence as I hurried past. All of Lady Kent's perfect guests were undoubtedly aware of all my dalliances and crazed assaults on defenseless, kindhearted hosts.

Downstairs, the only other person in that house I wanted to wish good-bye to waited for me. "Thank you, Tuffins," I said when my cab was loaded. "Thank you for being so eternally efficient and pleasant and gracious. If you ever want to work for a human being, instead of a machine, please find me."

His lips made the smallest quiver as he bowed, and I turned to head out the open door when *her* twitter came down the hallway after me. "Miss Wyndham!"

Miss Verinder glided in front of me with a beaming smile. "Leaving so soon?" It took everything within me to refrain from dragging her out the door by that blond hair of hers and hurling her down the stairs.

"So you really did have nothing better to do with your time than to have me spied on?" I said.

"Actually, every little piece of evidence miraculously happened to fall into place right before my eyes," she calmly rejoined. "And

I would have been just as guilty of indecency if I had allowed it to continue. I had a moral responsibility, a duty. It's what society demands."

"No, all of this was your doing."

"Most definitely not." Her countenance turned deathly serious. "You and your sister are the ones to blame. You did this to yourselves, and, in the process, you almost dragged the Kents down with you."

"Then your aim in all of this was what? To render yourself irresistible to Mr. Kent by comparison?"

She laughed. "You do have quite the talent for making anything sound petty and frivolous. Even when we were first introduced, all you did was complain about the season, make snap judgments, and act like you were better than it all. Better than me."

"Anybody is better than you."

She laughed and seemed to savor her words as they dripped off her tongue. "And now you are a nobody. You never deserved a single glance from Mr. Kent. You'll be lucky if a street sweeper deigns to look at you."

Her arms wound around me before I could move, enveloping me in thick, cloying perfume and the world's worst hug. "Goodbye, Miss Wyndham. There's no need to thank me. You made your disdain for society very clear, and I simply thought to liberate you, so that you might pursue those lofty and thrilling goals of yours."

With a giggle, she flounced away and disappeared back up the stairs toward the warmth and the laughter.

I went the other way.

Twenty-Three

My cab rumbled forward, though I barely cared where it was taking me.

How pathetic. I shouldn't have cared about my reputation or society—my sister was missing! But the crawling snakes in my stomach were impossible to ignore as I thought about the choices left to me. I may not have known what I wanted to do with my life, but I had always pleasantly assumed that I could make my way. Tonight would hardly be the worst of it. Now our friends would avoid us. Society would slam every door in my face. Even if I rescued Rose, we could never return to our normal lives.

I stared out the fogged window, watching the desolate street and the glowing houses. All I wanted was to find a comfortable bed and end this horrible day. No choice now but to steel my skin and become that improper single woman wandering London for lodgings late at night.

I slid open the cab's rear hatch. "Where are the closest lodgings?" I asked.

At that moment, the driver stopped. "Right here, miss. This was the address your footman gave." He hopped down, let me out onto the unfamiliar street, and handed me a small envelope. "He also asked I deliver this upon your arrival."

Inside was a short note from Mr. Kent:

The old bat said nothing about writing you another word. Please wait for me, I'll be home shortly. Feel free to save Robert's life if you're bored.—Nicholas Kent

Sure enough, when I knocked on the door to Mr. Kent's home, his maid, Miss Gates, welcomed me into an entrance hall that surprised me as much as his invitation. Anytime Mr. Kent had mentioned his own home, I had imagined it a sprawling mansion filled with ornate decorations and hundreds of portraits of himself covering the walls, eyeing guests wherever they went. Instead, this home was small (nowhere near the size of his parents'), well kept, and modestly furnished for comfort rather than show. Miss Gates led the way upstairs into a cozy bedroom with not a thing out of place, save for Robert's unconscious body sprawled across the bed.

"When did Mr. Elliot . . . arrive?" I asked.

"Before Mr. Kent left for his dinner. Not two hours ago," she said. "He appeared at the door quite out of sorts."

"And he's been sleeping since then?"

"We tried to feed him, but he would not eat a single morsel. And he . . . he purged himself twice."

"I see. Thank you," I said, and she gladly left me to him.

I pulled a chair by the bedside and seized the damn fool's hand. He doesn't hear from Rose for a few days, and he drinks and cries himself into a stupor? Perhaps I should have told him everything. But if this ridiculous behavior was his reaction to vague suspicions and anxiety about Rose's well-being, I shuddered to imagine what the truth would do to his delicate constitution.

For ten minutes, I sat with him, listening to his snoring,

healing his sickness, wondering if I could replenish the Wyndham fortune by restoring drunks to full health the morning after.

The bedroom door creaked open behind me.

"Will he live?" Mr. Kent asked, leaning against the doorjamb.

"Yes," I replied. "Very fortunate, saved from the brink of death."

"Was he awake? Did he explain anything?"

"No, he still seems to need rest," I said, setting Robert's hand back on the bed. "Did you speak to him when he arrived?"

"Unless you count his melancholy mutterings about your sister a conversation, no, I have not."

"I presume he knows something is wrong with Rose. I just don't know what to tell him when he wakes."

"It may as well be the truth. It will be better than any rumors he hears."

"Ah, yes, the truth. The strategy that worked so well on your stepmother."

"Please forgive me . . . or, well . . . please forgive me twice—no—three times. First because I must be serious for a moment, and I know how unsettling that may be, second, regarding what happened with the old bat . . . I must apologize—"

"There's no need," I interrupted. "I'm surprised you even invited me here after her threat."

"I don't care one whit about her threat. We will keep this a secret and deny it. Heaven knows she's done enough of that."

A breeze drifted in through an open window, and I shivered. "What do you mean?"

"I find it amusing when the most ardent and vocal defenders of propriety and morality are often the ones who've most heinously transgressed those values. Maybe they're atoning for their behavior, trying to keep others from making the same mistakes. Or they're scrutinizing and accusing others simply to divert suspicion from themselves. Do you think one needs to cross the line to be able to properly understand and defend it?"

"No," I found myself answering. "That sounds like an excuse."

"And excuses are nothing more than . . . neatly packaged reports on the messy, unknowable truth. My father had plenty of them. That he and the old bat had suffered and struggled with their forbidden love for years. That my birth mother was mad, mercurial. That everything was done for the good of the families.

"But the story I saw was of two selfish people carrying on a secret affair, while my sick mother languished in Ireland until she learned the truth and lost the will to live."

I sat there in disbelief. Mr. Kent had never discussed such personal matters with me before.

"You knew this was happening?" I asked.

"I only found out a few years later. After the funeral, the mourning period, the wedding, and living with them."

My rage grew as tall as the Tower of London, and I was tempted to start the beheadings. Knowing that this was the real reason for Mr. Kent's trouble with his parents, I found myself impressed that he could even stand being in the same room as them. "Why does no one else know of this? Was it not a big scandal?"

"Only my mother's maid knew. Otherwise, it was kept secret."

"And you've said nothing?"

"Believe me, I wanted to. I don't think anything would ever give me more pleasure than to make it known to all of London. But I couldn't say anything for the same reason I can't with your unfortunate scandal."

When I saw the tension in his expression, my brain made the connection. "Laura . . ."

"She's done nothing, yet she's the one who'd suffer most."

He was right. If Mr. Kent defended me and continued to associate with me in society, he wouldn't be lifting me up so much as I would be pulling his family down. It wasn't simply about Lady Kent's threat to take away his money.

"You're a good brother," I finally said.

He held his head up proudly. "It's been said that I'm actually the best in the world."

"An honor to match your greatest-detective medal."

"Yes, well, about that. I have another terrible confession to make. I know this may come as a shock to you, but I'm not actually a detective. It was all a lie."

"My God, fetch the smelling salts."

"But I had intended to atone for that lie tonight. It was the only reason I showed up to that dreadful dinner party in the first place, and you weren't even there. Laura said you had been gone all day. Did something happen?"

"Something did," I said, and it was my turn to let everything out. The impatient morning hours, the disguise, the visit to the public house, the encounter on the roof, and the hospital.

When I had finished, silence settled between us, a rare moment when Mr. Kent found himself at a loss for words. He had a troubled look on his face that very much resembled Sebastian's at the hospital.

"I don't need another lecture," I warned him.

"I wasn't going to give you one. You can make your own decisions. I only regret storming off last night and abandoning you when I could have helped."

"You had good reason to."

"No, I only had this grand plan of disappearing into the perilous London night, and just as you feared I was dead, I'd dramatically return to you with the case solved."

A bit of hope rushed through me. "And is it?"

"Not quite anymore. I can't account for Dr. Beck's power. He'll always be expecting us. I'll have to think on it. And you still must fear I'm dead at some point."

I slumped back into my seat. It took a staggering amount of willpower to keep from continuing to the floor and melting through it.

"I'll send for your trunk," Mr. Kent said, rising and clasping his hands. "It's been a long day—you should rest. I'll have an idea in the morning."

My discomfort shocked me to my feet, and I headed for the door. "No, I can't possibly stay here. I must find another place to sleep."

"What if I were to put a sign out front that declared you were not staying here?" he asked with a winning smile.

"As convincing as that sounds," I said, making my way downstairs, "I must decline."

"You'll be back here when we meet tomorrow morning. And honestly, this wouldn't be any more scandalous than the old bat's accusations."

"Ah, yes, since my reputation took a hit, I might as well just clobber it to death with a cane."

He stopped me at the front door. "I would not be a hospitable host if I threw you out on the streets at this hour."

I stared at him silently.

"You will thank me tomorrow morning—"

More staring.

"My God! Fine. You've made your point," he said, opening the door in defeat.

He walked me outside, helped me fetch a cab, and handed me into the ride. "I highly recommend the Drumswell Inn. It's close, and you are far less likely to run into someone who knows you. Its . . . comforts will take some getting used to, but by morning you'll feel right at home."

"Anything should feel like home after your stepmother's welcome."

Within ten minutes, though, I found myself taking that claim back as I inexpertly asked for an empty room at the inn. I ignored the stares and murmurs, paid for the night, and followed the inn-keeper upstairs with a scruffy young footman in tow. The room boasted many luxurious perks: a narrow bed, a rotted writing table, a stained wall, and a warped looking glass dangling on a rusty hook. I wondered if Mr. Kent recommended this hellish place so I would hurry back to his home.

To make my decision seem final, I plopped onto the bed, which sank disturbingly low under my weight. The footman placed my trunk at the foot of the bed and waited for a tip. Scrounging around my reticule for a coin, I came across Sebastian's crumpled card and remembered how drastically my plans had changed since I last spoke to him or Miss Grey. I had to let them know where I was staying and that we were to meet at Mr. Kent's the next morning. I begged the footman to wait, dashed off two quick notes, and dropped them along with two coins into his hands. He scurried back downstairs.

I leaned back on the bed and suddenly opened my eyes to find the room darker, the candle a mere stub. Must have dozed off. I heaved myself off the sagging mattress and rummaged through my trunk for a clean nightgown, relieved that sleep was actually com-ing to me, even if it was in this Godforsaken place.

Just before I blew out the candle, a solid knock sounded on the door, startling me. I didn't move an inch. Visions of a hulking man who broke doors and bones like twigs clouded my eyes and better judgment. I dove under the bed. It was dusty, the air rank, and the bed's horse hair mattress poked into my back.

Another, louder knock rattled the door and rumbled the room. An eternal silence followed as I dared not breathe. Finally, some rustling, and a slip of paper slid under the door. The footsteps and the orange glow of the lamp slowly faded back down the stairs.

Ashamed, I crept out of my hiding place and snatched up the paper. A note from Miss Lodge? She had been made aware of my situation and was already on her way in a carriage to pick me up. She somehow knew I was here. My note to Sebastian. Damn him.

I pulled off the nightgown and stepped back into my crumpled day dress. Within a half hour, I received another knock, and the overly excited footman from earlier informed me that Miss Lodge was waiting downstairs. Besides a sleepy look in her eyes, she appeared to be in good health again and clasped me to her warmly. "Are your things ready, Miss Wyndham?" she asked.

"I am perfectly settled here. I'm sorry to have inconvenienced you at so late an hour, but truly, it is not necessary that you host me."

Miss Lodge turned to the footman who had followed me downstairs and made some kind of sign to him. He nodded furiously, seemingly awed by the pretty young girl, and brushed by me upstairs.

"What's going on?" I asked, rushing to follow him.

She sedately climbed the stairs behind us. "This is no place for you to stay overnight and unaccompanied. Considering you have restored my health on two separate occasions, I refuse to take no for an answer. If you do not wish this obliging footman to pack your trunk, I suggest you run ahead and do it yourself."

For someone I was so used to seeing sickly, she had a resolve to be reckoned with. She waited on the bed while I managed to snatch an underthing back from the footman and inform him that his assistance would be most unnecessary. After he finally retreated and I squeezed in the few items that had spilled out of the trunk, we were ready to leave. Tom (Miss Lodge had sweetly asked the footman his name and received his entire life story) struggled back down the stairs with my trunk. He assured me he would inform the sleeping innkeeper that I had departed, and happily, if clumsily, handed Miss Lodge and me into the waiting carriage.

She hardly spoke the entire trip, except to make sure I was well. No intrusive questions, demanded explanations, or conditional promises. Given the scrutiny I'd endured from Lady Kent, it was oddly unbearable, and I was forced to break the silence.

"Miss Lodge, are you not curious about the reasons for my strange situation?"

"Only if you wish to share them," she responded politely.

"It's just—I'm not exactly the company anyone would like to keep now."

Her expression was rather calm and businesslike. "No matter how catastrophic the rumor, people always adjust and find it dull in hindsight. Or they forget about it altogether."

"I highly doubt society will forget. There's always someone to keep reminding everyone else. God, I'm so foolish. I brought it all on myself because I didn't care. All society did was irritate me. Now I can't help but wonder, what else is out there?"

"There is plenty out there. You need not worry about London society."

"Do you not care for it?"

"I have neither a low nor high opinion. It seems ideal for those who love doing nothing and keeping things that way. But I think it's best to treat it as one of those disposable matters of life where you learn something and move on."

"Learn what?"

"Who you are, who to marry, who to remain friends with, where to live. But I've had all that settled. When we marry, we shall go back to the country, and it will all be peaceful."

The world went sharp, all colors and sounds heightened, and my tongue dried. "Marry?"

She looked cautiously at me. "You didn't know?"

"I, do you mean, you, you mean Se—Mr. Braddock?" His name came out more breath than sound.

"Yes, we have had an understanding for years."

"And you love him?"

She stared at me with those large gray eyes, seeing everything. "Don't you?"

A whipcord of tension ran between us as I stared into her composed face. "Of course not! Where did you ever get such an idea?"

"Do you have any idea what you were like the night you brought him to me, unconscious?" she asked. "I thought you would go mad with worry."

I could only stare as her words poured out. My head was swimming, sinking, drowning.

"The truth is, I do love him, and he loves me. We've known each other so long, and I'm the last part of home he has. That's a powerful tie for a man who has lost so much family. But there's much more to him that I can't see. I know that he will never fully belong to me—part of him will always be lost in a different world.

"It's the same way I felt when I first saw you," she continued, her eyes huge and shining in streaks of passing streetlights. "The other doctors who came to treat my incurable condition, no matter whether they hopelessly went through the motions or ambitiously failed at a radical approach, all looked at me the same way.

My disease was a means of keeping their livelihood or making a new discovery. They looked at me without really seeing me.

"But you were different. You knew how hopeless the task was, and you didn't put much faith in your skills, but there was still a fire, an ambition, and it was not a selfish one. It was in service of something beyond yourself. You saw my life for what it was and imagined a better one."

She took my hand and gave me a steady smile. "You are so restless, Miss Wyndham! I know that you will be compelled, soul and spirit, to achieve great things and help the world. It will be a beautiful life."

Her eyes probed into mine, and I wanted to look at anything but her. "I truly do like you—you remind me so much of him. But as drawn to Sebastian as you may be, you will both end up heartbroken because of that restlessness, that energy. He may not love me the same way he could you, but neither will I run off at a moment's notice. I will be a home for him, an anchor. With my illness, I didn't know what would happen, but thanks to your cure . . . thanks to you, I will be there for him. Forever."

Her breathing steady, she turned away and sat composed, silently staring back out the window. I lost my tongue along with all my other functions. The air between us felt like a thin pane of glass that would shatter with the slightest movement.

But it was all presumption. It had to be. Miss Lodge barely knew me. Just because I could handle Sebastian's touch, I hadn't expected it to mean anything more. I hadn't even thought about what would happen after he finished helping me. What did I really suppose he would do? Miss Grey was evidence that someone could control their powers if they had motivation, and I could not imagine anyone more motivated to do that than Sebastian. He's been searching for a cure for years, and he's known Miss

Lodge for longer. Pressing my forehead to the cloudy pane, cold sinking into my skin, I watched the city flow and melt by, reminding myself that I should be feeling nothing.

When we entered the darkened Lodge home, I sent two new messages to Mr. Kent and Miss Grey, informing them of my newer lodgings and confirming the next morning's plans. Sebastian needed no such letter.

Miss Lodge showed me to a small, well-appointed room and kindly informed me that I had a place to stay for however long I required. The bed was already turned down, and I climbed onto the firm, nonsagging mattress with a child's lack of coordination and pulled the warm quilts up to my neck. My ears felt hot, and the more I thought about my breathing, the more irregular it became. I fell asleep whispering to that confused, frustrated part of me that had held onto an abstract hope: "You stupid girl, what did you think? Why would you even care? It's fine. It's good, even!"

And though I managed to convince the pillow, I am not sure I managed to convince myself.

Twenty-Four

"I saw Rose ... I—I saw her with Dr. Beck," Miss Grey gasped, clutching me tightly.

I responded with marvelous coherency. "When—how—you—"

She pulled herself away and walked the length of the Lodges' parlor, fingers of early-morning sunlight reflecting off her tearstained face. "In my dreams. Yesterday."

"What did you see? Do you know where she is?" I asked, standing at the edge of the room, both giving her space and fearing to go farther inside.

She tried to steady her breathing by leaning on a chair. "No, no, I'm sorry, Evelyn, I'm so sorry, I only saw a brief glimpse. Dr. Beck, Claude, and Mr. Hale were discussing her and what to do next."

"Was she ... well?"

"I ... I—I don't know. She was weak and injured ... she had cuts and bruises all over. And Dr. Beck was furious. He said she was being stubborn and refusing to heal, and he had no choice but to ... find the organ that does it."

I was wide awake now. My insides wrenched up like never before. This is what Arthur and William had said. He'll do anything for his research.

"They were planning to go to his surgical laboratory," she continued. "All I had to do was keep watching and follow them. But I was too agitated, and I only woke myself up."

I steadied my shaking hand and reminded myself that I would never find her if I kept panicking. It hasn't happened yet. I organized my thoughts piece by piece and finally managed to find my words. "They never said an address?"

She shook her head miserably. "I lost them before they left."

Even with Miss Grey's power, we couldn't do anything, except learn how much more dire the situation was. But it was motivation enough for me. I glanced at the ticking clock on the mantel. "Now we have all the more reason to find her as soon as possible," I said in the strongest voice I could hold. "We must go—it's almost eight o'clock. Let's hope Mr. Kent will have a plan."

Shakily, Miss Grey nodded and followed me to the carriage, and within a minute, we were clattering to our destination.

On the way, I recounted what had happened since we last spoke: the play, the public house, Camille, and Lady Kent. Miss Grey finally explained why she had been unavailable. She had taken laudanum to aid her sleep and spent hours desperately trying to find my sister with another dream. As a result, she missed the entire day, only receiving my messages this morning. As if she hadn't already given me enough apologies, she continued to pour them out for abandoning me and for losing Rose again. Only by the time we arrived at Mr. Kent's had I managed to convince her that all was forgiven and that I healed rather quickly, in both senses.

Miss Gates let us into the bright, empty entrance hall, where Mr. Kent and Robert happened to be making their way downstairs.

"Ah, Miss Wyndham. A lovely day to solve cases, don't you

think? Glorious lamp of heaven and all," Mr. Kent said, peering down from the top of the stairs. Sun streaked across his face as he descended.

"Not exactly," I replied. "We don't have much time left."

"That's what I was saying with my poetic allusions. Carpe diem. Gather our rosebuds as we may."

"I just hope you have a plan."

"Not only do I have a plan, but I have a plan for the picnic we will all surely have time for after," Mr. Kent said, tapping his cane.

Behind the energetic Mr. Kent followed Robert. In contrast, his movements were a bit sluggish, but they were still a dramatic improvement over the collapsed heap he was last night.

"Robert, are you well?" I asked.

"Evelyn, will you please tell me what is going on?" he barked.

I was taken aback by the sudden anger. "I don't know—"

"Oh, don't bother with him," Mr. Kent said as he reached the bottom of the stairs. "I've already tried to explain everything to him, and he refuses to believe me. He's convinced we've concocted this fantastical story to hide the truth that she's run off with Mr. Braddock."

"I don't care about her virtue!" Robert shouted.

Mr. Kent shook his head and closed his eyes, exasperated. "Neither do we, Robert. Neither do we."

Robert crossed his arms and remained halfway up the stairs in a stubborn sulk, his attention on a seascape painting beside him.

"Very well, no time for that, then. Now, introductions," I said, gesturing between him and Miss Grey. "You have both heard of each other. Miss Grey, meet my friend Nicholas Kent. Mr. Kent, my governess, Alice Grey."

Mr. Kent bowed and reached out his hand, and Miss Grey let him take it, though she appeared pained.

"Mr. Kent. Have we—" Miss Grey raised her eyebrows and spoke tautly. "Oh. Yes. Excuse me, *Mr. Kent*. Evelyn, perhaps we might speak in private?"

"At this very moment?" I asked.

"It is urgent."

Mr. Kent nodded politely, retracting his hand to gesture down his narrow hallway. Miss Grey shuffled me into a small parlor, oddly decorated with all sorts of artwork of maritime disasters, before shutting the door behind her.

"How well do you know this man?" she whispered.

"Fairly well . . . I met him during the last season. Why do you ask?"

Her eyes flitted about the room, as if she were checking for eavesdroppers. "I've seen him in my dreams."

"Your dreams? Then . . ."

No. That couldn't be true.

Miss Grey tightened her lips and nodded.

"So . . . he has an ability, too?" I asked in a daze.

"A talent for learning the truth. Any question he asks will receive an honest response. One is simply compelled to answer him. I've never seen anyone resist."

I was thunderstruck. The memories hit me by degrees. The search, the ball, the entire blasted season! I had been candid in every conversation with him, believing I couldn't hold my tongue or that he was trustworthy. But it had been a power—his awful, intrusive power.

I tightened my fists and threw open the door, ready to accuse him. One angry step forward was all I could manage before Miss Grey seized my shoulder. "Evelyn, wait! Now is not the time."

"He manipulated me!" I whispered in a fury. "All of us! With his every word!"

"Yet his assistance is extremely valuable. You can trust his plan if he can retrieve information from anyone who may have clues, whether they want to or not."

She was right. I stepped back into the parlor to quell my anger with distractions. Cracked ships in glass bottles. Broken compasses. A Turner print of a shipwreck on raging seas. I was almost glad it had wrecked.

I couldn't take any more of this. The stories and secrets. The facades and frauds. I missed my life from a week ago, when my biggest complaints were about the poor personalities of Englishmen. At least I knew what they were. I was sick of putting my trust in Mr. Kent and Sebastian and constantly being wrong. Camille was completely mad—there was nothing fun about peeling off layers, constantly finding you believed in someone who did not exist. I wanted to see behind the masks and see their true expressions, their true beliefs, their true selves. Not just endless lies.

"Are you all right?" Miss Grey asked.

"Yes, I just—there have been too many surprises this past week. It all seems so absurd. Do I know anyone who does not have an ability?"

"I have wondered that, too. There must be something that draws us together, an instinctive knowledge—"

The doorbell rang across the house and cut our conversation short. We hurried back to the entrance hall to find Sebastian, Robert, and Mr. Kent locked in an awkward three-way standoff.

"Evelyn, what is the meaning of this?" Robert exclaimed. "Why is he here?"

"A fine welcome, Robert," I said. "As you can see, he hasn't run off with Rose. He's been incredibly helpful with the search."

I turned to Sebastian, and Miss Lodge's words pounded in my head. I had to remain cordial and polite, nothing more. He just wants to settle his debt to me and then go off to be with her.

"I'm sorry for the trouble," I said to him, trying to rest my gaze on his most innocuous part, which seemed to be his left earlobe. "That is the exceedingly polite Robert Elliot, this is my former governess, Miss Alice Grey, and you've already been acquainted with Mr. Kent."

He swiftly bowed to greet them, while Robert persisted. "So she's run off with this Dr. Beck, then? My God!"

"She's run off with no one," I snapped.

Mr. Kent smiled smarmily and crossed his arms with a commanding air. "First, I want to ask Mr. Braddock a few questions. Do you have any good ideas where Dr. Beck might now be?"

"No," he muttered.

"And do you know how we might combat his ability to see the future?"

"No, I'm sorry, I do not."

Mr. Kent looked pleased by Sebastian's shortcomings.

Robert still remained clueless. "This is absurd. I must go to the police. You're all mad!" he exclaimed.

"We can trust Mr. Braddock," Miss Grey replied, looking pointedly at Mr. Kent. "At the very least, you know he is telling the truth."

"Evelyn, was Miss Grey not dismissed from your house hold for losing her wits?" Robert asked.

"Enough!" I yelled. The sound echoed across the room, up the stairs, and through the entire household. Everyone fell silent. "Robert, it might help to actually listen and consider the possibility of these abilities. Otherwise, you will find yourself in the minority."

"Of course. Because it's so easy to believe in something so ridiculous," he said, looking around the room for agreement.

I gave him a glare. "You can either remain quiet and help, or perhaps you might want to just return to that public house, drown your sorrows, and share your drawings with those other useless lumps. Actually, send one of them back here—they will be of far more use to us."

Robert fumed and bit his lip, unable to think of a response. Child.

"Then that settles the matter," Mr. Kent said, putting his hand on Robert's shoulder only to have it shaken off. "She makes a sound point."

Ha! As if he were any better.

"We are here to find Rose," I continued. "Everything else can be argued about later. Mr. Kent, you said you had a grand plan. Please, enlighten us."

He had the answer ready. "We start with the most concrete location. The house where you first found them."

"There is nothing there," Sebastian said. "It's been abandoned."

"Yes, but records are eternal," Mr. Kent shot back. "I have discovered the mysterious and vaguely named company that owns that home and a list of their many other properties. I've eliminated the properties that don't serve Dr. Beck's needs, and I am certain he will be found in one of the ones that remain."

"What about his ability to see the future?" I asked. "How can we ever overcome that?"

"For that, I have a simple solution," Mr. Kent proudly announced, rubbing his palms in anticipation. "Consider that first house. Dr. Beck went through all the trouble to hire Camille to impersonate Miss Rosamund, but Mr. Braddock simply paid her to learn the address. Dr. Beck should have expected her deception and never hired her in the first place, or the house should have been vacated by the time you arrived." Mr. Kent paused, smiled, and tapped his head with his finger, indicating where his brain was.

"Judging by those mistakes, I must conclude that he's short-sighted. He can only see the future to a certain extent or specific elements of it. So he did not know of Camille's nature or your arrival at the apartment until it was too late to alter his plans. If this is true, then we have to move swiftly and seize every opportunity we can. There is no way to ever know the limitations of his power—unless, of course, we ask him. And if I were him, I would maintain this illusion of . . . omniscience . . . simply for the discouraging effect it produces upon those who believe it.

"The problem is, the two times you encountered him did not go well because you were trying to follow him, which put you at a natural disadvantage. He could escape with his head start or turn around and ambush you, depending on his mood. Due to the combination of his power and planning, he's always been better prepared, but now we can best him with this list of his possible locations. Instead of chasing him, which he'll anticipate, we will anticipate his anticipations and, in a way, have him come to us."

He stopped his pacing and held out his palms, as if he had performed a magic trick with flair. Our gasps filled the room. "Impressive, I know," Mr. Kent said, smiling.

"It is . . . if you anticipated *him*," I said, pointing behind him at the pale, thin man who had appeared through a crack in the air.

But judging by Mr. Kent's startled reaction, he hadn't. Mr. Hale's arrival most definitely wasn't a part of his grand plan.

Twenty-Five

MR. HALE HELD up his hand cautiously and spoke in a soft, hoarse voice: "Please, I've come because I need your help."

He looked earnest—and in fact rather desperate. His rumpled clothing barely fit him, his graying hair sat in disarray, and he seemed to lean his thin, gaunt frame entirely too much on his cane. In this light, there was nothing threatening about him.

That only disconcerted me more. "You want *our* help? After what you did?" I asked, convinced that the world had turned inside out.

His eyes widened when he saw me, and he stepped closer. "Miss Wyndham—you are all right—"

Sebastian slid between us, cutting the man off. "Do not come any closer, or I will," he interrupted, anger pitching his voice low and gravelly.

The wooden floorboards creaked uncomfortably as Mr. Hale stopped by the stairs. "Of course," he said. "I am just . . . glad to see she is well after I heard—"

"What your friends did?" Miss Grey spoke up, only wavering a little. "What do you want?"

"I want to help save Miss Rosamund," the man answered.

Silence greeted his appalling statement.

"This is a trick," I gasped, almost ready to laugh.

"A terrible one at that," Mr. Kent added. "But there must be a reason Dr. Beck is doing this. Perhaps he anticipated our anticipation of his anticipation . . ."

"This is no trick, I promise you," Mr. Hale pleaded. "If I was your enemy, I could have opened doors under your feet and dropped you all into the ocean without stepping in here."

"How reassuring," Mr. Kent said.

"You could have also saved Rose without stepping in here," I returned. "But you've persisted in helping Dr. Beck."

Mr. Hale's eyes went wide at the accusation. "I only learned of his terrible plans for Miss Rosamund yesterday. And when I tried to free her, Dr. Beck was already there, waiting for me. I couldn't fight him. He was too fast with his knife." He clutched his stomach in pain. "He would have killed me had Miss Rosamund not distracted him. I barely escaped to a hospital."

"What happened to Rose?" I asked.

"They were all gone by this morning. They must have taken her elsewhere. He has laboratories all over the city."

"And you cannot open a door directly to them now?" Sebastian asked.

He shifted and winced again. "No. I can only create doors to places I've seen."

"I can't recall ever inviting you in here for tea," Mr. Kent said.

Mr. Hale reached into his coat and revealed a small telescope. "In which case, I rely on this tool."

"How clever," muttered Mr. Kent. "But this has still been a waste of time. We already have a list of locations."

Mr. Hale shook his head urgently. "If you follow that, it'll be too late by the time you find them. I know how we may find him before he starts her . . . surgery." We all fell silent. Even the city streets outside seemed to hush at those words.

"How?" Mr. Kent finally asked for us.

Mr. Hale's hand tightened around the wooden banister. "He requires a sedative for the procedure. It is a unique substance— one more controllable than any other and without side effects. And it is made with a newly discovered chemical from Germany called barbital. His servant purchases directly from the merchant, and this afternoon, he will be at the Royal Docks. A man named Mr. Greene who owns a ship called the *Aurora*."

Sebastian shook his head doubtfully. "Dr. Beck will not send someone there now. He knows you escaped."

"You could be right," Mr. Hale admitted, staring at a narrow panel of stained glass above the entryway. "But he does not know that I know of this chemical. And there is no one else in the city he can purchase it from. The next shipment won't come for weeks."

"Will we truly be able to find the location this way?" Mr. Kent asked, smoothly testing Mr. Hale.

"Yes, I am sure of it," he replied truthfully.

This seemed to be all Mr. Kent needed. "Then I think it's best we go to the docks now. Dr. Beck, in a way, will be coming to us— just as I suggested."

"No. We aren't doing that yet," I replied, feeling uneasy. "I don't trust him. Miss Grey has seen this man do horrible things, but now he suddenly has a crisis of conscience?"

I caught Sebastian's eye, but he quickly looked away, jaw clenched. Pushing the heels of my hands into my eyes, I considered my choices. Trusting Mr. Hale could well be the best decision we make, or the worst. I had to be sure.

"Miss Grey, do you know anything else to give us reason to trust him?" I asked.

She shook her head. She seemed to still have trouble even looking at the man.

It must be borne, then. "Mr. Kent, Miss Grey has recently informed me that you have an ability to obtain the truth. Is that true?"

Sebastian, Robert, and Mr. Hale looked at him in utter astonishment, while Mr. Kent, without breaking his gaze, nodded slowly to me. "It is."

"Then I have questions I want you to ask him."

"As you wish."

I turned from the door back to the stairs. "Mr. Hale, have you conspired with Dr. Beck or Claude to lead us into a trap at the docks or another location?"

"No, I have—"

Mr. Kent interrupted. "You must wait for me to ask the question."

Mr. Hale nodded and bit his lip nervously.

"Have you conspired with Dr. Beck or Claude to lead us into a trap at the docks or another location?" Mr. Kent asked.

"No, I have not," he said, his eyes widening at his own openness.

"Is it truly your aim to see that Rose is rescued, safely and unharmed?"

Mr. Kent repeated the question.

"Yes," Mr. Hale said.

"Do you have any ulterior motives for that, Mr. Hale?" I asked, and Mr. Kent repeated after me.

"Yes," Mr. Hale said immediately. A look of shock came over him when he realized his admission. His guilty eyes locked on mine, and he blanched. "It's nothing like that!"

"What is it, then?" Mr. Kent and I spoke together.

"I—I love Miss Rosamund," he choked out. "I want to protect her."

"What!" Robert exclaimed, eyes wild. "I knew what this was all about. You don't think you're going to win her over like this, do you, sir?"

"It's not like that, young man! She's like a, a daughter—"

"Robert," Mr. Kent cut in. "As amusing as it would be for you to duel a world-jumping man for Miss Rosamund's hand, now is not the time." He turned back to me. "Do you have more to ask?"

"I do," I said, still uneasy. "But it can wait."

Mr. Kent nodded and opened his front door, ushering us all out. "To the Royal Docks then, Mr. Hale."

Mr. Hale shook his head fervently as he limped toward the doorway. His nervous behavior somehow grew worse. "No, I cannot come with you any farther."

The lot of us stopped and looked at him in surprise.

"I—I'm s-sorry," he stammered softly. "I want Miss Rosamund saved. That's why I came here to help you. But I won't be caught by them."

"You're scared of Dr. Beck?" Mr. Kent asked. "Even when there's six of us?"

"No—no, not Dr. Beck," Mr. Hale replied.

"Then who?" Mr. Kent asked.

"The Society. Of Aberrations. They assigned me to watch over Dr. Beck. When they learn of this . . . you don't know what they are capable of."

"I think I have some idea," I replied, a shudder running through my bones at the thought of more scientists.

"No. You don't," Mr. Hale said, deathly serious. "Pray they never learn of your powers."

Before we got in another word, a door crackled open behind

him, and he vanished into thin air. Desperate, I dashed outside after him down the stone pathway, past the squealing gates, and along the narrow sidewalk, scanning the bustling London crowds, the countless windows, the rooftops. He was nowhere to be seen. Given his terror, he was probably halfway across the world by now.

I spun around to find everyone waiting by the gate, hopelessly searching for the briefest sign of the man.

"Terrible manners. He didn't even offer us a ride," Mr. Kent said, looking as crestfallen as the rest of us. But in a moment, he managed to cheer himself up as usual. He fetched a passing hackney and opened the door.

"Well, when one door closes, another slightly more inconvenient, out-of-the-way one opens. Let's be off, shall we?"

Twenty-Six

E VEN FOR A Londoner thoroughly acquainted with the crowds of the city, the hubbub of the Royal Docks is nothing short of overwhelming. Chaos finds its form in burly sailors in all sorts of sunbaked hues wandering about; porters wheeling tall stacks, sacks, and crates to warehouses; customs officers and clerks analyzing the goods in front of them, noses deep in their books; small groups of passengers skeptically eyeing the ships for an upcoming voyage; weathered hands maneuvering chained sets of boxes from the ship to the quay; and, of course, the backdrop of ironclad hulls, towering spars, complicated rigging, and puffs of smoke from inbound ships.

After passing through the front gates, we threaded our way through the mess, attempting to fathom the disorganized layout. It seemed impossible to find one ship stationed among one hundred in all this madness, but somehow Mr. Kent managed without even inquiring for directions. He wove through the maze with purpose, and the rest of us struggled to keep pace, putting our trust in him. My only sense of our progress came from the waves of odors that consistently alternated between carcasses, spices, tobacco, and brine.

After some minutes, the trust proved to be well placed. We found ourselves looking up at the three tall masts of the fully rigged *Aurora*, fittingly reaching for the sun. Mr. Kent turned to us, his countenance showing some reservations. "Miss Wyndham, Miss Grey, perhaps it would be best for you to wait down here, and we will return shortly," he said.

"I highly doubt a docked ship can be so offensive to our sensibilities after this past week," I replied. "I'm coming."

He said nothing, studying me closely.

"It's no use—she will," Sebastian added, scuffing his heel along the hard ground. Robert snorted as an addendum.

"Ah, well," Mr. Kent said with a shrug. "If you say so. Up we go."

He led the way, climbing the wood-and-rope platform onto the deck. From the moment we stepped onboard, the loud, vulgar dialogues of the workers and sailors were rather audible and unavoidable, though I must own that I scarcely understood their meanings. Only Sebastian's raised eyebrows and reddened cheeks gave me some indication of the subjects of their discussion. As we made our way along the balustrade, most of the men gave us strange glances and I soon felt out of place in my fashion.

Mr. Kent sent me a teasing smirk. "I warned you."

"Yes, I cannot stand it any longer. Lead me to the bow of the ship, where I may toss myself into the Thames out of despair."

"Surely you can find your own way. I have pressing business to see to right now," he replied.

He stopped in front of a luxurious captain's quarters on the main deck, where two finely dressed men stared at us curiously. One of them—a tall, bespectacled man—lurched forward and spoke briskly: "Excuse me, but we don't take passengers on this ship! She's purely a merchant vess—"

"We are not looking for passage," Mr. Kent interrupted. "We're looking for Mr. Greene."

"Who wants to know?" he seemed to grunt rather than ask.

"My name is Nicholas Kent. I'm a detective." I groaned silently at the brazen lie. The tall man's eyes involuntarily bulged for the briefest moment before he composed himself.

Mr. Kent noticed. "I simply must ask a few questions related to your cargo. Are you the owner of this ship?"

"I am, but I'm busy!" Mr. Greene declared, waving his cane and stepping back toward the cabin.

"Are you really?" Kent asked, staring closely at him.

"No." Mr. Greene frowned, confused by his honesty.

Mr. Kent slipped the merchant some money. "If we may speak in private for a moment."

Mr. Greene turned to the other man. "Captain, one minute!" he said, and the captain disappeared into his cabin with a tip of his hat.

Mr. Greene led us to an empty part of the ship and made no effort to hide his irritation. "Now, what do you want?"

"I wish to know if you import and sell a rare chemical called barbital."

"You want to buy it?"

"No, but is there someone who has purchased it recently or is due to purchase it in the next day or two?"

"Yes," the merchant said, his eyes looking increasingly frustrated with his mouth's poor decisions. "But Mr. Kent! I don't discuss my customers!"

"I understand and admire that," Mr. Kent replied, "but this is a matter of life and death. Who do you sell to?"

"The boy."

"The boy? Who might he be?"

"A servant, I don't know for who."

"And why is his name preceded with *the*?"

"He's a frequent customer, goes to all the docks, pays more than the asking price for these rare chemicals from anyone selling. He arranges with the customs men and dockers to take it straight from the warehouse."

Mr. Kent glanced back at us with a cocked eyebrow. He was on the right path. This had to be Dr. Beck's servant.

"Where can I find him?"

"I don't know."

"When is he coming back here?"

"Always in the afternoon."

"What does he look like?"

"He's a boy," the merchant replied bluntly. He held out his hand to denote height. "Like a man, but smaller."

A long pause followed. Mr. Kent's power could do nothing to improve Mr. Greene's power of description.

Mr. Kent stretched over the railing, eyeing the docks. "Can you point out the boy to us when he returns?" he asked.

"Yes." Mr. Greene straightened and puffed his chest out, to make himself appear more intimidating. "But I won't! I've already told you, I respect my customers' privacy."

Mr. Kent tried to hand him more money, but Mr. Greene slapped the coins away. "Who do you think you are, Mr. Kent?"

"I believe you just answered your own question," Mr. Kent replied winningly.

The joke only angered the merchant further. "I refuse! You can't just—" He squinted closely at Mr. Kent.

"Kent!" he exclaimed with an uproarious laugh. "I knew I recognized the name. You're Sir Peter Kent's boy, that damned rotten thief and vile human being!"

Mr. Kent put on an easy smile. "Besides the human being part, I wholeheartedly agree. I cannot stand my father."

"No, that won't work! You dandy detectives with your tricks!"

"I can honestly assure you, this is no trick," Mr. Kent replied.

"Honesty! From a Kent? Ha! We're done here, my boy. Get off my ship. And don't expect to find that servant boy! He'll be warned before you ever spot him." Mr. Greene struck the ship's steel railing with his cane as an exclamation point and stomped back toward the captain's cabin.

Mr. Kent stiffened and clenched the railing. I had never before seen him frustrated, but I knew what he was feeling. Mr. Greene's grudge against the Kent name left us in an even worse place than before. The boy would be warned off the minute he passed through the dock gates, and we'd never find him.

"What do we do now?" Robert muttered. No one had a response. Even Mr. Kent was uncharacteristically quiet as he watched Mr. Greene's departure.

Then, snapping into motion, he slammed his own cane down onto the deck with a heavy thump and set out after the merchant, leaving us no choice but to follow.

"We're not finished!" Mr. Kent yelled out, a newfound charge to his movements.

Mr. Greene twisted around and shot him a menacing look. "Must I have you lot escorted off this ship, Kent?"

"What is your deepest secret, Mr. Greene?"

Mr. Greene replied without hesitation. "I have stolen £40,000 from the company for my personal use." After finishing, his face contorted into one of sheer horror.

"And where might I find evidence proving it?"

"A safe in my office," answered Mr. Greene, clamping a hand to his mouth and endeavoring to escape.

Mr. Kent pulled the merchant's arm away. "What is the combination?"

"Sixteen, thirty-six, four! Stop it! What in heaven's name are you doing?" Mr. Greene yelled desperately.

"And just to be safe, what is your next most damaging secret?"

Sebastian took several uneasy steps toward them. "Perhaps . . . we're finished," he said.

"I have been unfaithful to my wife," Mr. Greene said, furiously struggling out of Mr. Kent's grip.

"How many times?" There was a cruel pleasure in Mr. Kent's voice. It was going too far.

"Twenty-seven."

In a rage, the merchant broke free and swung his fist straight at Mr. Kent, striking him on the left cheek and sending his hat flying off. Mr. Greene followed with another punch, but a hand stopped the attack inches away from Mr. Kent's face.

Mr. Kent stumbled away while Mr. Greene, dumbfounded, stared at Sebastian's grip on his fist and fell to his knees, coughing and gasping for breath until Sebastian released him. I kept my distance but remained on the threshold in case anything else went wrong.

"Yes, well. Ahem, thank you, Mr. Braddock," Mr. Kent said, brushing off his suit. "But that was going quite according to the plan."

"Then let's hope we never see you forced to improvise," Sebastian replied, slipping his glove back on.

"Wha—who—who are you people?" Mr. Greene managed to choke out.

Mr. Kent, now with a little gloat to his step, hopped back toward the merchant. "Sir, I am an honest man who simply wanted to make an honest deal. I'm sorry you have no faith in my honesty, but there's no need to blame or attack me because of yours. So please, before you act rashly again, keep in mind that it is entirely within my means to destroy your life."

He let that friendly threat sink in and then continued with a big smile. "Now, with that unpleasantness out of the way, perhaps we can finally return to the subject at hand—the boy!"

Twenty-Seven

THE DEAL BROKERED was an exceedingly simple one. Mr. Greene generously cleared his busy afternoon schedule to wait with us on the docks and point out Dr. Beck's errand boy. In return, Mr. Kent promised not to reveal Mr. Greene's dark secrets and wreak havoc on the merchant's life. Then we could all happily go our separate ways.

The sun was in its slow decline by the time we had spread out along the dock. Robert waited near the front gate, Miss Grey in the middle beside a customs office, and Sebastian on the roof of a storage warehouse, where there was no one he could hurt. My lucky spot was on a berth right next to the *Zephyr*, which happened to be unloading twenty nauseating tons of fish at the moment. We all stood within sight of the *Aurora*, where Mr. Kent provided pleasant company for Mr. Greene, who kept watch from his vantage point, ready to signal the boy's arrival.

The detective work might have sounded exciting when proposed, but in reality, the wait was dreadful. It was not quite as bad as a ball, but it was exhausting and demoralizing to scan through the crowds, spot hundreds of young servants, and turn to see Mr. Greene shaking his head *no* like some sort of malfunctioning

automaton. I couldn't bear to imagine the pain Rose was enduring every extra second this took.

Meanwhile, Mr. Kent's waves, smiles, and attempts to amuse
me bounced off the side of my head for hours. I looked up only for
Mr. Greene's signals and ignored everything else. I paced and
searched and paced and searched until I noticed the empty space
by the customs office. Where did Miss Grey go? Had she found
the boy? My eyes darted up to the *Aurora* and there she stood,
having taken the spot near Mr. Greene. And behind me, uncomfortably close, stood Mr. Kent, trapping me between himself and
the water.

"A word please, Miss Wyndham," he said.

"No, thank you," I replied, refusing to look at him directly. His
image, wavering and undefined, reflected back at me in the water
along the edge of the dock.

"Right, I clearly don't need to ask you if you're angry."

"Your detective skills continue to impress."

He clasped my hands, pivoting my body toward him, and spoke
with complete sincerity. "I—I want to apologize for not telling you
earlier. But if you consider the time we've known each other—"

I pulled away. "I knew something was wrong. I felt it that night
at the brothel—"

"Dancing room."

"Wherever it was that you were shamelessly flirting! Did you
honestly know it was me?"

He frowned. "No, but it was to gain access to your sister. I just
didn't want to offend you about your . . . appearance."

"That sounds like an excuse you came up with later. And you
can't very well ask yourself for the truth—"

"No, see, I can." He walked over to the edge, perilously close, and waved to his reflection in the water. "Nicholas, were your intentions honest at the Argyll?"

"Why, yes! Of course they were, Nicholas," he replied to himself. "How silly of you to ask. Nothing could distract me from serving Miss Wyndham. Except perhaps *you*, you dashing fellow—"

"Fine! Forget the Argyll! You still have no excuse for the way you abused your powers!" I insisted.

"I know, but please consider this from my perspective," he said, staring off beyond the *Zephyr*, straight at the horizon. "We both are of a rare breed already with these abilities, but you are blessed even further. Your power to heal cannot be inconvenient or detrimental to any situation you may be in, except . . . perhaps if you were attempting to kill a man on a cliff, and he was horribly injured and clutching the rocks on the very edge, clinging for dear life, when by chance, he grabs your arm and restores himself back to health, but now . . . how often are you in that sort of situation—"

"Mr. Kent, I believe you were attempting to make a point."

"Ah, yes, well, what I meant was that I cannot switch my ability off. I have to hear the truth from every person I speak to, and if you heard some of the things I've been privy to, your opinion of the people in this world would not be . . ."

I snorted. "What? That sunny, optimistic opinion I have of society now?"

"You would think *even worse* of it, which I know is saying a great deal." The sun glinted hard off the bay, covering his face in slants of light and making it impossible to read.

"I'd prefer if everyone were not so deceitful and hypocritical," I said. "And this diatribe of yours against the truth isn't changing that."

"That's simply because you have not had to suffer it. Consider yourself fortunate. I'd much rather have false civility and feigned politeness."

"Very well, your life is pure misery. You would have had my sympathy if you'd told me about your powers instead of constantly using them on me the whole time we've known each other!"

His eyebrow twisted upwards. "*Constantly* is a bit of an exaggeration—"

"It doesn't matter! You—I thought we were friends, and I was comfortable being candid with you, but now I don't even know if it was all against my will—and—and if you were . . . taking liberties."

He set his hand over his heart, wounded by the accusation. "I don't know when I could have told you. Whether I did it on the day we first met, after a few months of hiding it, or yesterday, it wouldn't have mattered—you would have had as little trust for me then as you seem to have now. You would have put your guard up or simply never spoken to me, out of fear for what I could ask. And I never would have gotten to know you."

He stepped closer and tried to catch my gaze while I fixated on a muddy coil of rope. "You're the only one I've ever wanted the truth from, Miss Wyndham. But I wanted you *to want* to tell me everything. There was just no way I could accomplish that if I told you about this stupid mouth of mine. The best I could do was take the utmost care to ask you only of inconsequential matters, and, besides that unforeseeable accident at Sir Winston's ball, it worked flawlessly.

"Beyond that, I never asked you any significant question: no deep inquiries about your life, your fears, your secrets, or your affections." He tilted his head and continued to stare at me, waiting for approval.

I met his brown eyes, strangely still and direct. "That is . . . true, I guess," I admitted. "Thank you."

"But seeing that there's no other way of getting around it, I must ask you, do you love Mr. Braddock?"

"I—I don't know," I sputtered out, even as rage overtook my entire body. "You complete ass!"

"You don't know? What sort of answer is—"

I was raising my hand to slap him across the face when he looked over my shoulder and shouted, "Look!"

Up on the *Aurora*, Mr. Greene was frantically waving and pointing down into the massive crowd on the dock. He mimed the gesture of putting on a hat, and we spotted our target. The boy, wearing a scruffy gray cap and loose, tattered clothing, squeezed through the crowds and constantly checked in every possible direction where danger might lurk. He clearly understood the secrecy needed for his pickups. Unfortunately, this meant he easily saw Mr. Greene's crazed jumping and waving and then just as easily noticed us. He started in a panic and bolted back whence he came.

"We will continue this later," Mr. Kent spit out, racing to catch up to Robert.

In a flash, the boy wove through the hordes, hopped atop crates, and slipped under railings. He made fast progress and reached the streets while Mr. Kent and Robert, both lacking the boy's agility, trailed by several yards.

Meanwhile, Miss Grey, Sebastian, and I were blocked by the crowd and pushed too far away to keep pace. I desperately tried to keep hold of my breath as I dodged wagons and squeezed between massive displays of barrels. By the time I raced out past the dock gates and stopped onto the street, the crowds had folded back in, eliminating all evidence of the chase. There seemed to be no way to follow until Sebastian shouted from an alleyway entrance, holding Mr. Kent's hat.

"Get to a hackney! Perhaps we might overtake them!"

Within a minute, our carriage was careening down the vacant street parallel to the alleyway, buildings streaming by and debris flying up from under our wheels. I almost believed we would cut the boy off, at least until the driver swerved around a corner and abruptly brought the vehicle to a stop. Stalled traffic filled the street. From behind, more horses and carriages boxed us in before we even had a chance to react.

"Sorry, sir!" the driver yelled down an apology. "Can't turn the horses 'round here!"

So we lost him. Our one link—a little boy—outran five of us, beating two grown men on foot and a two-horse carriage. I curled my hand around the metal railing, experiencing a frustration nearly strong enough to bend the iron. Now the boy knew we were waiting. Dr. Beck would soon be told. The plans would change, and the trail to Rose would be gone yet again.

"Keep watch for Mr. Kent and Mr. Elliot," Sebastian said, breaking the dismal silence.

Miss Grey and I peered around the curtains, searching the sidewalks for a miracle. The miles of congested carriages slowly lurched forward, and Sebastian guided our driver toward an emptier side street. We took a complicated route, turn after turn hoping to happen upon Robert, Mr. Kent, or the boy, but it was all for naught.

"We should return to the docks," Miss Grey suggested. "Perhaps they will be waiting there."

Sure enough, she was correct—or at least, half correct. Mr. Kent was leaning on a splintery post by the *Aurora,* shaking his head as we approached. "It took you three far too long to return here," he said. "Did you not learn that universal tenet as a child? If you ever lose track of your mother, go back to the last place you shared, no other. It's not terribly complicated."

"No, I never read the rule book," I replied.

"Perhaps you should get started on that. And on finding Dr. Beck," he said, checking his pocket watch. "The race started a half hour ago."

"Excuse me?"

"We caught the boy and got the address. And because you took your time, Robert—in his infinite wisdom—went on ahead."

"He did *what*?"

"He wanted to enlist the police's assistance and go immediately to arrest Dr. Beck."

"And you let the fool go?"

Mr. Kent gave an exhausted sigh. "I've never met anyone so impossible to persuade. And it's not as if I can knock him unconscious with my touch."

"He just thinks he's playing hero," I said.

"I thought that's what every girl wants from a gentleman," he said, wedging his cane into gaps in the planks and giving Sebastian a pointed look.

Surprise and confusion momentarily crossed Sebastian's face. He regained himself and turned to make his way out of the docks. "We must go now," he said. "If Mr. Elliot went to the police first, we can still catch up."

"There's no chance," Mr. Kent said. "We need to go to the police, as well."

"They're in league with Dr. Beck," I reminded him. "It'll only make matters more difficult."

"I doubt he's spoken to every single policeman. All I need to do is ask each of them whether they plan to betray us, and we'll have fifty trustworthy men at Dr. Beck's door in two hours."

"In two hours, Robert will be dead and Dr. Beck will be gone," I corrected and whirled around to follow Sebastian.

"Please remind me why we're friends with Robert again," Mr. Kent said, following me past the busy ships, the salty odors, the endless warehouses, and the rusty front gates. Once we reached the muddy street, he bowed and tipped his hat. "Well, good luck to you, then."

"What? You aren't coming?" I asked, appalled.

"If you're truly going through with this foolhardy plan. And I don't think you need my help for it anyway," he said, glancing at Sebastian crossing the road to find a hackney.

"I can't tell if you are joking, Mr. Kent."

"I'm not. In fact, I've been so sincere lately that I wouldn't be surprised if my name has magically changed to Frank."

"Excuse me, Evelyn." Miss Grey tapped my shoulder from the side. "May I come along?"

"Yes, of course. I just worry it might be dangerous," I said, glaring at Mr. Kent as I spoke. He pretended to be enthralled by some seagull settling on a warehouse roof.

"I know, but I must help in any way I can."

"Thank you," I said, my heart thawing a bit.

Mr. Kent seized my hand. "Excuse us a moment, my dearest, selfless Miss Grey," he said and pulled me aside, next to a shoe-shining stand, to speak privately.

"Miss Wyndham, I know you're not pleased with the shocking things you've discovered lately, and I know you'll think even worse of me when I tell you of the things I did before we met. But everything I—"

"Sir, you are a liar and a cheat!" a customer bellowed at the shiner behind us.

Mr. Kent glanced over his shoulder and attempted to ignore the yells. "Everything I do is to—"

"These shoes are still soiled! The mud is right there! Return my money, sir!" the customer yelled again.

Mr. Kent bristled and spun around to the shoe shiner. "Sir, are you wrong in this matter?"

"N-no," the shoe shiner stammered. "I'm trying to be fair."

Mr. Kent turned to the customer. "Are you wrong?"

"Yes, of course I am," he said, his face flushing.

"Then avoid stepping in the mud, shut up, and be on your way! I am trying to convince a girl to love me!"

Stunned into silence, the customer grumbled and stormed off. The shoe shiner profusely thanked Mr. Kent, who waved him off and turned his attention back to me.

"Now, where was I? Oh, yes, as I so perfectly proved right there, everything I do is to be the good man that you deserve, and I want you to understand the effect you have had on me."

I gave him a sharp look. "Is this *really* the appropriate time to be discussing this?"

"It's essential we do this now, with all the heroics that'll be going on and the emotions running wild and the hasty decisions being made. I want you to know that you are the perspective I was talking about at the Argyll. You are what makes everything else melt away."

"Yet you won't help me right now."

"Must I really die to prove it to you? I know my limitations, and I'm wise enough to accept them. Miss Rosamund may need a hero, and she has plenty of qualified individuals to handle the matter. But you . . . you don't need one. You need me, just as I need you."

He stepped closer and put out a hand to my cheek, forcing me to look right at him. "Miss Wyndham, when I first met you in London, I thought you the most intelligent and the strongest girl I had ever had the pleasure of meeting. She would never moon after some mopey, dark boy. She would look for the man that challenged her, amused her, and made her sparkle and enjoy life."

I sucked in air, trying to understand and sort out all the stirrings, the pressure, the knowledge, the trust I felt. But could I? Could I ever love this man, who'd only care for comfort, who'd skate on the surface with wit alone, who'd refuse to let us confront anything deeper, who'd ask me this question at a time like this?

Miss Grey rolled up with the carriage, Sebastian jogging behind. If Mr. Kent would not join me, I could waste no more time.

"You are right about one thing, Mr. Kent. I don't need a hero," I said in a firm, even voice. "But I could never love a man who would not be my ally."

His confident smile faltered. I took Sebastian's outstretched hand, and he helped me into the carriage, following right after. I refused to look back. But just as Sebastian pulled the door shut, Mr. Kent's figure appeared on the other side of the carriage with a reluctant smile.

"Then if that's what it takes, by all means, let's get ourselves killed."

Twenty-Eight

THE CARRIAGE FLEW north at breakneck speed. Pedestrians dove onto sidewalks, and the occasional constable would blow his whistle, chase us on foot, and finally abandon the futile task in exhaustion.

Soon, we reached the outskirts of London, where the smog, bustle, and gray of the city opened up to the verdant, hilly scenery and quiet of Hampstead. The driver slowed his pace, bending around corners and rolling past languid Heath Street lamplighters making their evening rounds. Despite the tranquil setting, I still felt bilious, in part from the turns, but mostly from our impending task. Mr. Kent had kept up a stream of babble, presumably to keep our minds off the upcoming fight, but I don't think anyone had listened to a word. We were all busy trying to form plans without knowing what to expect upon our arrival. There was only one matter of which I was certain: Sebastian and I could not go together to get Rose, unless I wanted things to end as badly as last time.

Once the driver veered onto the right road, Dr. Beck's large corner house was not hard to find among the scattered buildings; the two unconscious policemen on the side lawn served as a rather helpful signpost. Several yards away stood Robert, the last man standing, cornered by Claude against the side of the house. My stomach flipped furiously at the sight. We were too far, and Claude only needed a few seconds to do his worst. Frantically, I banged at the carriage roof and turned to the men and Miss Grey. Sebastian opened his mouth to speak, but Mr. Kent's mouth, with its vast experience, proved quicker.

"Allow me."

He leaped out of the slowing carriage and reached into his coat, brandishing his silver pistol, which glinted impressively in the late sun. My body flinched as he fired a shot into the air to draw Claude's attention away from Robert, then hurdled a fence, and ripped across the vast lawn with unexpected speed. Looking taller and fully the hero, he took aim directly at a charging Claude, sending my heart into my throat, and fired.

And then somehow Claude had taken the bullet in his arm and taken the pistol away. We heard the distinct snapping of bone, and Mr. Kent was on the ground, cradling a broken arm, while the other man in my carriage was already racing to stop Claude from breaking anything more. I dithered between the awful uncertainty of the fight and the certainty I'd weaken Sebastian by going any closer. My heavy knock at the roof sent our carriage forward with a start.

As we rumbled away, the house slowly blocked our view of the fight. Mr. Kent climbed to his feet, as if to give us one final reassurance and persuade my heart to climb down from my throat. His words floated back to us on the wind: "Blast it all, you overgrown oaf! What are your weaknesses, besides, of course, the obvious *French* qualities?"

The last we saw was the start of Claude's answer and Sebastian's fierce leap at the giant. And the three were out of sight.

"They will be all right, Evelyn," Miss Grey said weakly. "Mr. Kent's injuries can wait."

"I hope so."

The carriage slowed to a pitiful stop in front of the unimposing house. It took everything within me to remain on our side of it as we held our breath, listening for any sound, any sign from the fight. There was only dead silence, broken by the heavy huffs of our horses and the distant smacks and clatter of the street traffic.

What now?

I had two choices: wait for Sebastian to handle everything or stupidly charge in and get myself captured or all of us killed. There had to be a better alternative.

Unfortunately, Robert, staggering from around the side of the house, seemed to disagree. Unperturbed by his brush with death, he headed straight for the front door. Miss Grey and I were barely able to clamber out of the carriage and block his idiotic path in time.

"Robert, stop!" I whispered sharply, grabbing his arm. "We must wait."

He pulled it away. "I *don't* need to wait for Mr. Braddock's help. I can handle this so-called doctor with his cheap tricks myself."

"Don't be foolish," I said to his back. Ignoring me, he grumbled, rattled the locked door, and finally, as if it had made a personal affront upon his character, he resorted to kicking it in with surprising strength. We watched helplessly as the splintery door cracked open, and Robert disappeared inside.

Miss Grey gave me an anxious look. "He cannot do it alone," she said.

Most definitely not. I forced my mind to move, plan, solve. If Robert could distract Dr. Beck for long enough, perhaps I could get Rose. Would he see it coming?

"Go with Robert," I ordered. "Keep him from doing anything stupid. And delay Dr. Beck as much as you can. Perhaps I can retrieve Rose without him noticing."

Miss Grey hesitated, not wanting to split up. But I was already making my way inside, down a dim, dusty corridor, passing windows that had all been boarded shut and doors into empty parlors containing the same strange domestic niceties of Dr. Beck's last house. Eventually, I found myself lingering at a staircase, not knowing whether Rose would be upstairs, downstairs, or around the bend in the hallway. A crackle and creaking snapped my head upward, but when I was mere inches away from the steps, my legs stalled at the sound of a loud, distressing crash echoing from deeper within the house.

That decided it. My new course led me farther down the curving hallway to a half-open door at the end. It provided a second entry into the laboratory—the massive space, packed with tables, shelves, and boxes, seemed to take up half of the house. A path of destruction marked by broken bottles, retorts, jars, and other unidentifiable apparatuses led to the center of the room, where Robert painfully stood up and wiped his coat free of the debris from a freshly destroyed table. Well, that was a poor job of delaying. In fact, where had Miss Grey gone—

I spotted a foot. I tasted blood as I bit my knuckles, holding back unhelpful yelps of panic. On my knees, peering between the table legs and equipment, I could see just a sliver of her body lying still by the sink. Instinctively, I was across the room and by her side.

Dear God. Please be all right. Please.

My fingers felt for her pulse and found it—slow but still beating. My stifled sigh of relief came out quivering. Staying low in my crouched position, I struggled to pull her out quietly while a wild and furious Robert occupied Dr. Beck with his unceasing shouts.

"*Where* is she?" Robert yelled.

"That's none of your concern," Dr. Beck coolly replied as he dodged the many flailing attacks. Finally deciding he'd had enough, the scientist plucked Robert's swinging fist straight out of the air, and with his other hand he seized a nearby glass rod. He smashed it across Robert's head and let him drop to the floor.

The glass tinkled to the ground like rain, joining the thunderous thud of Robert's body. Then complete silence, except for my quiet panting and a startling burst of laughter. Dr. Beck already knew I was here.

"Miss Wyndham, no need to worry about your friend there. She's just been sedated." Smiling and snaking around tables, he wandered toward me. "My congratulations on your speedy recovery."

His face showed no surprise at the sight of me, but I better understood Mr. Kent's theory. Dr. Beck had only recently discovered that I had these powers and that I had survived. It left me with one last question: How recently?

"And you claim to know everything?" I snapped. He ignored me, but I persisted. "If you knew everything I was going to do—"

"I quite understand your point. There is no need to repeat it. Perhaps there are some things that I did not know. You may call them faults, but I prefer to see them as progress. The entire basis of science is founded upon making mistakes," he said, shoving something into his pocket as he approached. He pointed to the ceiling. "Your sister was one such example. There have been some fascinating developments since you and I last spoke."

I stood up and drew back from him, but there was only so far I could retreat. I considered running, but no. I could not leave them. For lack of a better plan, I continued to back away from the short, slim, and terrifying man.

Then my back hit the wall. He stopped directly in front of me. I endeavored to dash to the left, to the right, but he was always blocking the way. His abilities were all too apparent. He predicted my exact movements and in an instant grasped my face, holding it as tight as a vise. "I'm sure you'll be as surprised as us to know that your sister was never the healer we believed her to be."

I tried to slap him, but his other hand seized my arm before I even raised it. He shoved me down, and my shoulder struck the floor hard. Wincing, I forced the pain away.

"Y-you're lying," I managed.

"No. I am not. Miss Rosamund has an entirely different ability. It's not so obvious, which is why it took so long for anyone to discover, but that makes it no less intriguing. You see, the girl can charm the breeches right off of you!" He laughed heartily at himself.

"As her sister, you know her far better than me. In the past two years, has there been a single person carrying the slightest bit of ill will toward her?"

He knelt over me, pulling a syringe from his pocket, and I lost my breath. I thrashed my arms to strike him, but he caught one while dodging the other. My legs rose up to kick him and hit only air as he twisted around my limbs before I could process what happened. The needle pierced my arm, and he pushed the plunger and emptied the contents. He grinned as he stood back up, leaving me prostrate on the floor.

I staggered back to my feet, trying not to vomit.

"Miss Rosamund's gift has always been to charm. I gather it was why she was able to earn her reputation for *your* healing. Her voice—even her quiet presence—has a captivating effect, and anyone around your sister will, in simple terms, love her. How that love manifests itself varies from person to person, but in every case, it compels everyone to act with her best interests in mind."

Was that why Mr. Hale helped us? No, no, Dr. Beck was lying. Trying to distract me. There was no way we were all so mistaken.

"You would never have been able to kidnap and hold her if that was true," I replied.

"Ah, a clever point. But that's because she did not train and develop her power. It was not as strong as it could potentially be, and we were able to resist. Granted, I'd never felt more abominable about myself than when I was testing her healing abilities and putting her through all that pain. At the time, I even believed I was growing weak and sentimental, but now I know that it was actually my strong will and determination that made the difference.

"Even Claude, loyal as he is, tried to convince me to let her go. That's how I first made the discovery. And then I tested my hypothesis on Mr. Hale by telling him about the surgery I planned to perform. That very evening, I caught him attempting to help her escape." He laughed shortly—staccato, mad. "I feel so foolish for thinking she was holding back her healing out of stubbornness."

Something felt strange. The room blurred. My legs went limp and gave out, sending me toppling to the floor like a rag doll. Dr. Beck's voice still resonated in my aching head.

"But we had a new problem this morning: We were left without a healer. Then you arrive here and brighten up my day, Miss Wyndham. If I were a religious man, I would thank someone for guiding you to me."

My mind begged my body to move, but my numb limbs refused.

"Don't worry, you should be feeling tired," he said. "It's entirely natural. Just dream of the good you will do."

Dr. Beck circled me, his boots sweeping inches from my face. The sedative worked on my blood. My eyes closed, and it took everything within me to fight back. I seemed to lift the entire world with my eyelids.

I had to stay conscious. Keep them open. Otherwise, I would not wake up anywhere pleasant, and Rose might not wake up at all. I twisted my head upward. A prickle passed along my left arm. It had regained feeling. I strained to move my hand inch by inch across the dusty floor.

"Of course," Dr. Beck softly muttered. He knelt down and reverently touched my cheek. "Remarkable. Your body can fight it off. We'll just have to increase the dosage." He rose and crossed the room toward his supply cabinet.

Rose. I had to take Rose home. I had to help Robert. Miss Grey. Sebastian. Mr. Kent. Everyone. Pushing my tingling fingers on the ground, I lifted myself up an inch, two, hearing Dr. Beck's whistling in one ear, a distant crackle in the other, before falling to the floor again.

"Hel—" My mouth could barely call for help. Useless. The haze was too much. It muddled every thread I tried to grasp, shrouded everything around me.

Except for that damnable whistling.

My right arm returned, and I dragged it up next to my face in an effort to rise. With a desperate push, I managed to slide up onto my knees. My legs struggled to exert control.

Get up. I had to get up. I panted, coughed, strained. Dr. Beck examined his syringe against the light and missed the movement behind him as Robert climbed back to his feet. Clutching a glass bottle, he noiselessly crept behind the scientist, wound his arm back, and lunged with the weapon.

And Dr. Beck caught it with ease. He thrust the bottle straight into Robert's teeth and knocked him back. I clambered up, crying out, pushing weight into my calves, my legs wobbling as I began to rise. Stand, stand, stand.

Somewhere in my clouded head, an answer struck me. Dr. Beck did not foresee even a minute into the future that he would need a higher dosage for me. And he had only reacted seconds before he was attacked. His foresight was severely limited. I had to tell Robert. But at that very moment, Dr. Beck struck him again with the bottle and then reached out across a counter to pick up a knife.

My mouth felt like a rusted door. "Ro'ert," I barely moaned. No feeling in my tongue. My body refused to comply. Locking my knees, I stood fully erect, afraid to move lest I collapse again.

Robert backed away from Dr. Beck, throwing every jar and beaker he could find between them. Dr. Beck yelled at him, "Stop, you'll—"

Chemicals exploded in flames all along the wooden floors and gas-lit walls. Robert continued throwing in his rage until he ran out of nearby ammunition and found his back against an empty shelf. His hand desperately searched for more, then gripped something tightly and swung at Dr. Beck's forehead. Dr. Beck caught the fist yet again. With his other arm, he raised the knife. The blade sliced into Robert's jacket, shirt, and stomach.

Dr. Beck jerked the blood-soaked knife out and plunged it back in without hesitation. At that very moment, Robert's fist, still held by Dr. Beck, loosened above the scientist's face. A glass bottle. Red liquid poured out, and as tangled with Robert as he was, even Dr. Beck only had time to partially avoid it. The substance splashed into his eyes, and he screamed, dropping Robert to the floor as the air filled with an acrid stench.

Robert, that brilliant fool. Step by step, I staggered toward him. Slowly, my vision cleared. The world returned, sharp and ablaze. Robert lay on the floor in front of me, bleeding. I dropped down and placed my hands over his wound, begging it to close. "Keep breathing. Just a few minutes."

His short, labored breaths persevered. By the sink, Dr. Beck seethed and washed his eyes with a dirty towel.

Faster. Dammit, heal faster, Robert.

I pushed harder. I only had a minute at best for a severe wound that needed at least ten. Dr. Beck blinked his eyes furiously, reassessed his vision, and dabbed away the last of the chemical.

"Robert," I whispered, praying he was still conscious. He groaned in response. "He is too fast for you. We have to overwhelm him at the same time—he can't anticipate both of us. Just keep attacking."

His eyes drifted upward and back. "No, Robert, stay awake," I pleaded with him, along with my healing.

Dr. Beck, eyes red with irritation, stalked to the knife on the floor while Robert coughed and rose to his knee. I pulled him up and leaned his body over my shoulder.

"We both know how this is going to end, Miss Wyndham," Dr. Beck said, blade in hand. "Just accept your role. It will be far more comfortable."

Robert shoved me behind him and swung at Dr. Beck with great pains. Dr. Beck swiped at Robert with the knife after every dodged punch and sent him stumbling back with more shallow cuts.

Futilely, I searched along the massive tables for an available weapon. The gas jets couldn't be moved. Scalpels, bottles, books. No, too small, too fragile, too weak. Hurry, dammit. No choice. This had to do.

I lifted a heavy microscope and gripped its neck tightly. There was no time to feel ridiculous.

A deep smack wrenched my attention back to the fight. Dr. Beck kicked Robert in his stomach, striking the stab wound and knocking him down hard. He slid toward the fireplace, a streak of blood marking his path, and stopped just short of the flames. Dr. Beck turned his attention to me, and any courage I had seconds ago vanished.

He charged with the knife, and I staggered backward. Dear God, I could not survive this. I couldn't even see the blur of his arm as he swiped, much less predict where he would attack. I wielded the microscope with its base facing out, hoping to block and divert his attacks. Rapid surges of pain cut across my hand and arm, and my grip on the weapon started to slip.

But Robert had stubbornly risen again from the fireplace, clutching a burning log with one hand and his wounded stomach with the other. He marched behind my attacker, and Dr. Beck turned, again anticipating him at the last second. Robert took a heavy, obvious swing and aimed the log at Dr. Beck's head, while I found a burst of energy and leaped forward.

I swung the microscope into an empty space to the left of Dr. Beck's head. He dodged the log flying at him but moved just where I had hoped. His eyes registered the mistake for the briefest moment before the base struck him square in the head with a crack. He fell back, dazed and bruised, and I swung again and again until he collapsed on the floor, nearly unconscious.

A sob escaped my throat, but I choked it down.

My hands shook ferociously, rifling through Dr. Beck's front pockets as he struggled to breathe and clutched his bleeding head. "Miss . . . Wyndham . . . p-please don't . . . I . . . just want to . . . help."

My fingers found what I needed. As I pulled it out into his half-dazed view, a whimper even escaped his lips. "Please," he whispered.

My grip tightened around the glass syringe—the syringe filled with a sedative meant for torturing me, torturing countless others, torturing Rose. I couldn't let him get up again. He was far too dangerous. My sister's face slid into my mind as easily as the needle slid into his arm. My thumb pushed the plunger, injecting the full contents into his bloodstream, and I couldn't help but wonder if this was the first time he'd ever feared his uncertain future.

Twenty-Nine

PIECE BY PIECE, the burning house fell apart around us.

Robert exhausted his last reserves of strength to remain upright until I was close enough for him to collapse on. My shoulder took most of his weight as I guided him around a blazing table and stepped over shards of glass soaking in strange, discolored liquids ready to ignite.

Panic erupted inside me as my thoughts moved too quickly. I had to get him out. And Miss Grey. And Rose. It was too much. Smoke had already started to collect in the laboratory, leaving me choking and gasping for fresh air as the chemically fueled fire spread. Flames cracked overhead, and a wooden beam dislodged from the ceiling, swinging inches in front of my face. A mere pause and glance at Miss Grey's unconscious body saved me.

I silently begged her: *Please be safe. Just one minute and I'll be back.*

Robert and I dodged, staggered, and prayed along the edge of the room, passing everything of Dr. Beck's going up in flames—his equipment, cabinets, samples, chemicals, and hundreds of pages of notes.

When we finally turned into the main hallway, a voice reached us from outside. "Evelyn!"

The hazy shape of Sebastian emerged out of the smoke by the front door, his face bloodied and begrimed. He fought his way to us and lightened my load, supporting Robert from the other side. "Are you all right?" he asked.

I nodded fervently and hurried my pace. "Yes, but Rose is still upstairs and Miss Grey is in the laboratory and I don't know how much time—"

"Take him somewhere safe. I'll get Miss Rosamund and come back to help with Miss Grey." He bounded down the hallway.

"Sebastian! Wait!" I screamed at the top of my lungs. The roar of flames swallowed my words.

Chunks of falling bricks and crumbling plaster rained down upon us. I had to get Robert out now. I half-dragged him down the hallway, one heavy step after another. Acrid gases and smoke stung my eyes, rendering my vision a blurred mess of orange globules. My legs felt like lead, and Robert slipped down my shoulder, inch by inch. I reached to pull him closer, and a flame flared out, searing my hand. I nearly dropped him.

Ignore it. Keep going. It'll heal.

Digging into his coat with my nails, I wrenched his body back up with aching fingers and forgot the pain. Through the entrance hall, out the front door, down the steps toward indistinct green masses. The crisp, cool air, fleeting heavenly relief. Robert collapsed down onto the grass, his body streaking my dress with bloodstains.

"Will you be all right?" I asked.

He mumbled something incomprehensible, and I hoped our contact had healed him enough for the time being. I sucked in a huge breath of air and rushed back inside, dodging floating flecks of fire and draperies burning to ash. Back down the hallway and into the laboratory, where the ceiling continued to collapse above me. Narrowly missing showers of debris, I threaded around tables, flew past the furnace, and skidded to a stop by the sink—where Miss Grey should have been lying.

A massive pile of fallen rocks and wood sat in her place, burying her underneath.

No, no, no. On my hands and knees, I dug furiously through the rubble. Burning wood and scorched stones piled on endlessly, the heat scalding my hands. Then I jumped at the sight of a boot—not under the debris, but to the side of it.

"I'm like a moth to the flame, Miss Wyndham!" a voice yelled.

I clambered to my feet and gazed through the stifling smog into the straining eyes of Mr. Kent—with Miss Grey hanging over his good shoulder, broken arm cradled against his chest. "It's time we go," he said.

Without the time or air for even a gasp of relief, I led the way back out of the laboratory with a hunched Mr. Kent in tow. We made our way down the hallway to the exit, but my feet stopped, immovable, when I peered outside. Rose and Sebastian hadn't come out yet. Could he not find her? Were they trapped? Had they—

"I need to get Rose!" I shouted, ignoring Mr. Kent's protests. "Get yourself to safety and make sure Robert is well enough!" I flew back down the hallway, made a jump over a burning rug on the first stair, and gasped when my skirt caught flame. I ripped frantically at the fabric before it could spread, leaving the tatters of outer skirts smoldering on the floor, while only my petticoat remained intact.

With each step up, the fumes flared in my nose and my head felt lighter, my neck becoming rubber. A tumbling portrait nearly struck my head as I ducked and crawled up to the top, lungs heavy, heat coursing through my skin.

Ignore it. Keep going. It'll heal.

A tight, smoke-filled hallway met me at the top. Three open doors and a narrow servant staircase at the end. Had they taken that route? Wiping my eyes, I hobbled down the corridor, past blazing wall hangings and embers searing my cheek. I poked my head into the first room. Empty. Second room, empty again. Around the corner to the third room, when an earth-shattering explosion from below—the laboratory—shook the house violently. I stumbled forward into the vacant room and heard a strained creaking before a series of awful snaps. With a violent lurch, I collapsed, along with the rest of the floor.

A blistering pain pulsed through my entire body as I hit the hard ground with a thud, while the house seemed to crash down around me. The back of my head pounded from the barrage of falling rubble that seemed to last forever. When the pain was somewhat manageable, I opened my eyes and found myself buried in a pile of stone and splintered wood. My hands and knees felt damp, sticky. Blood. Somehow I was still alive, but barely mobile. I managed to turn my head up and crawl out of the dusty mess to find I was no longer on the second floor.

It was a cramped storage room. No windows, one door, and two walls engulfed in the fire spreading from the laboratory. My body felt broken, my arms unable to even handle the rest of my weight. I wheezed and choked and gagged on the cloud of smoke, hoping my power could keep me going without air. Up I climbed, wobbling on my weak legs and balancing myself against a box. I limped the few painful steps to the exit and twisted the metal knob, gasping at the searing heat, and pulled. It rattled and stopped with a click. Locked. The blasted door was locked.

My legs wavered, and I caught myself on the wall. The ceiling was now a massive hole, but it was too high to reach—even with the boxes. And I could barely stand, barely breathe, much less pull myself up one story.

Ignore it. Keep going. Dear God, I was going to die here.

I charged at the door. A stabbing pain surged through my shoulder with each push. My fist pounded against the wood in a futile attempt to burst through. My arms ached. I made one more pathetic attack and found myself blocked by hard indifference. My head felt light, my body heavy, my legs numb. I crashed and slumped against the door, which somehow moved it and sent me falling. For a moment I was pure nothingness. But before I hit the floor, hands seized me at the waist. Sebastian flew into my veins as I was pulled out of the room.

"Evelyn—"

"Wait—ple—where's Rose?" I interrupted.

Sebastian helped me through a doorway. "She's outside!" he said with a smile. "She's safe."

He had gotten her out already. Sebastian had saved her. Thank heavens. I clutched his shoulder and he lifted me into his arms, carrying me through a hallway, out the side, and into a small garden, where he set me down on the lawn. He knelt down, holding me against his chest, as I let my eyes close in exhaustion. Beneath the smoke and chemicals, he still smelled like leather and mint.

"That was foolish," he said, the slightest quiver in his voice. "There was no need for you to come back in."

Behind him, the full devastation of the inferno made his point. It was less of a house on fire now than it was a fire using a house for fuel. I gorged myself on the fresh air, unable to say a word. Everything felt clean again, pure, safe. I never knew how good it felt to breathe—to truly breathe.

"You've been burned," he said. He kissed my forehead, then my hand, and the sting of pain was enveloped and overwhelmed by the touch of his lips.

"It—it'll heal," I said. "Thank you."

Lying in his arms, I felt a heavy sort of contentment and relief roll through me. A reluctant moment of ease, where I knew everything was all right, but my body seemed to forget what it was like to relax. I opened my eyes and looked for my sister. "Where's Rose? Why isn't she here?" I asked.

"She's by the back of the house. She was sedated when I found her."

A cold shiver tore through my bones. Sedated. Unconscious. No. I . . . I had misheard him. That could not be right. It would mean—

"Then she—did—did you carry her out?" I asked desperately, gagging on the words.

His face was all confusion. "Yes . . ."

My heart pounded furiously. I leaped up without a word, ignoring the ache in my limbs, and sped around the back of the house. She lay still in the grass. I dropped to my knees by her side and shook her. "Rose," I sputtered out. I lifted her angelic face in my hand and ran my finger across her neck.

Nothing.

I checked with my other hand to make sure I was not mad. I ran them both over her chest. No heartbeat. The same lingering nothing. I grasped her hand and squeezed hard. "Rose," I whispered in her ear. No response. Her hand fell limply by her side.

"Sebastian, she—she—" I could not get the words out.

"What is it? What's wrong?"

"She cannot heal!" I cried. "She does not have th-that ability! Dr. Beck said it was a mistake." I looked to him for a counter, a retort to prove me wrong, to solve everything.

But he only stared down at Rose, examined his gloved hands and stood up, a sickening look of horror and realization paling his face. His deep green eyes sank into mine.

"I—I only held her for a—it was—I thought I felt—" He moved to grab my shoulders, but I flinched at the suddenness. He put his hands down and stumbled back. "Please heal her." His voice faltered as he turned. Twigs cracked. Grass crushed beneath his boot.

And he ran.

He ran until he was out of sight.

I kept my hands on Rose, pushing against her skin, trying to revive her, heal her wounds, bring her back, do one goddamn single useful thing in my pathetic existence.

"Rose, I can heal you. It'll be fine." I held her hands in my own, shutting my eyes, waiting for a sudden revival, a rapid pulse, a steady heartbeat. She couldn't die here. No one ever died. The patient always recovered. That was how it worked every single time.

Police whistles rang from the streets, onlookers yelled, and carriages bustled, rushing to the building to help or crowd or simply gawk at something much greater than them. I hauled my sister into my arms and peered at Dr. Beck's laboratory, overcome with rage. It was him. He did this, not Sebastian. He deserved to burn forever. My sister was supposed to be alive, smiling and relieved to go home. We were supposed to laugh about our adventure, go on walks, heal the sick, and figure out our lives. She wasn't supposed to be lying here, withered in my arms.

I pressed my cheek to Rose's, my hands down over her heart, refusing to let go. *For God's sake, why won't it start beating?*

But wait. My healing always took a few minutes to take effect. This was perfectly natural. Sebastian was far enough away now. This was how it worked with Miss Lodge. Patience and faith:

That's all I needed. The minutes rolled by slowly, achingly, as I endeavored to pour my own life into Rose. Whatever would keep her alive, I had to give to her. All of it. I shut my eyes tight and prepared to be pleasantly surprised when I opened them. Rose would be alive and well and smiling that reassuring grin.

Nothing happened. Everything was still except for the faint rustling of her golden hair and the stray ashes settling on her face. She refused to stir. It was no longer Rose, just an abandoned body.

"Come back," I whimpered, shaking her slightly, then harder and harder, a strange hollow pain settling through my body. "Please. You can't leave. Rose. Rose. Rose, please, I need you to come back."

But all that came was the storm. Torrents mercilessly poured down, extinguishing the fire, depositing rivulets of chemicals into the dirt, and washing everything else into the gutter. The rain made no exceptions, sweeping away every lingering remnant of hope, and I was left alone.

Thirty

THEY TOOK ROSE away.

The police always took her away in my dreams. No matter how much I pleaded with them, they wouldn't listen. Even after I'd explain I only needed ten minutes more, that serious illnesses and injuries always required more time, they'd pry my fingers, my arms, my entire body off, load her in the police carriage, and take her to a cold, white room somewhere to be declared dead.

But this time, this dream, as they were carrying her away, something finally stopped them.

She woke up.

Like an angel, she rose from the stretcher and seemed to float past everyone, their faces frozen in awe. The storm left her untouched, and sunlight spilled through the clouds as if the heavens were parting solely for her. She stopped in front of my mud-covered person and her warm voice drifted through the rain shower.

"Oh, Ev, don't look so surprised," she said with a smile. "Isn't this what you were waiting for?"

In a daze, I climbed to my feet on the unsteady ground. It was true. I'd been waiting for this for weeks, and now that she stood before me, there was so much to say that barely anything made it out.

"I'm sorry."

She shook her head, refusing my apology. "You musn't keep doing this."

"Doing what?"

She raised her eyebrows and gave me that look reserved for my most ridiculous comments. "Trying to bring me back as you sleep. The constant dreaming."

The rain only fell harder. She stood mere inches away from me. I dared not hug her or touch her or even move for that matter, afraid of making her vanish. I struggled to keep my words coherent, my voice steady. "Then . . . what should I be doing?"

Her eyes practically glowed, excited by the possibilities. It was as if we were back in our library. "If I were you, I'd be running around London healing everyone, whether they liked it or not."

"Oh, so now I have to take on your responsibility of healing all of England, then?"

"To start, yes," she said with a giggle.

"They'd all just eventually fall sick from something else."

Her eyes narrowed. "And I would have died eventually, so what does it matter that it happened here?"

The question hung in the air with the ash and the dust. Of course it mattered. Most days, it felt like the only thing that ever mattered.

"How can you expect me to even go back to . . . anything?" I asked, numb and useless. "Without it feeling wrong?"

She cocked her head. "And locking yourself away from the world will give you more reasons to come back?"

"Where would I go?"

"Where do you want to go?"

It was unsettling and familiar, the way she answered my questions with more questions. It reminded me of my childhood . . . and suddenly, it was very clear and very infuriating: This was not my sister. Not even in my dream.

"Get out! Miss Grey, get out."

In a blink, my governess had taken my sister's place, and my stomach lurched as if I were losing Rose all over again.

"Would she have said anything different?" Miss Grey asked after a moment.

"It doesn't matter. You have no right to enter my dreams and do that!"

"It's the only way I can contact you when you refuse all visitors. I've been worried," she said. "But I am sorry."

I fumed in silence, and she waited. She could always outwait me. Behind her, the fire that had consumed Dr. Beck's house was all smoke. The noxious stench of chemicals filled the air.

"So, is that everything you came to say?" I finally asked.

"No . . . I hoped you might meet me in Bloomsbury Square in an hour."

"You can't tell me here?"

"It requires your healing, so I'm afraid you'll have to wake up."

I did. Jolting awake in a tangle of blankets and bedsheets, I nearly knocked over the empty laudanum bottles and wine decanters that filled my bedside table. Enough to kill a normal person, yet unable to grant me more than five minutes of sleep before my power washed the effects away. Useless.

I lay prone for a long while, in a sort of limbo, barely registering my dim surroundings. The Lodges' guest room still felt strange, despite Mae's insistence that I make myself at home here. But I didn't exactly want to make myself at home anywhere. Strange seemed more bearable. Even when my parents tried to take me back to Bramhurst after the funeral, I'd refused and they didn't press me. Mae must have made some strong arguments against the constant reminders of Rose. She knew that pain all too well herself.

But nothing could be done about that vexing worry for Miss Grey. It forced me up and into the hallway, where Cushing froze in surprise at seeing me outside the bedroom. He then proceeded to do an admirable job of masking his disbelief when I asked him for a maid to help me dress and a hansom to take me to Bloomsbury Square.

The weather outside was cool. A brisk chill cut through the streets and offered unpleasant confirmation you were still alive, able to feel shivers on your skin or the warm pulse in your arm. The city flowed like it always had, the indifferent traffic and pedestrians carrying on with their business. I couldn't help but take it as an insult, as if London had forgotten Rose and simply filled in the empty space she'd left.

Miss Grey was already waiting at a bench by the time I alighted from the cab. Like me, she cared not for the attention from mourning dress and wore a plain blue frock instead. She looked far better rested than the last time we had seen each other, but she still had that air of fragility about her.

"Thank you for coming, Evelyn," she said. "I know this is difficult."

I frowned doubtfully. "I did not have much choice. Where are you injured?"

She tilted her head, then nodded in understanding. "Oh no, it isn't me. There's a poor boy with several broken bones at the hospital nearby," she said, gesturing down the street.

"A boy you know?"

"He revealed himself in one of my dreams."

Another one of us. "What sort of ability does he have?"

"That is what I hoped to discover today."

"And you've come to explain everything to him?"

"In part," she said, turning to lead the way at a fast clip, pointedly looking nowhere but straight ahead. "But it's also because I've found myself rather afraid lately."

"Afraid of what?" I asked, trying to keep up.

"The disturbing way Mr. Hale talked about that Society of Aberrations. We don't know why they supported Dr. Beck's research. We don't know what others might do to continue his work. And we don't know anything about them, which terrifies me most of all. Part of me wants to run away like—"

She stopped herself before saying Sebastian's name, but it didn't matter. In fact, it felt more appropriate that it was missing. He'd barely given any indication of where he was going when he ran away. Just a letter delivered to Mae the next day, apologizing for another abrupt departure with the excuse that he needed to take control of some of his family's land.

I sucked in a breath of bracing air before asking the question I both had and hadn't wanted to ask for weeks. "Have you seen Mr. Braddock in your dreams?"

"Once," she said, tightly. "He seemed to be traveling through France, but I couldn't learn his destination."

"Was he—how was he?"

"He—he had his health," Miss Grey said, grasping at straws and her purse. "And he seemed to be very much alone."

"A consequence of running away," I said evenly, choosing bitterness over anything else that was potentially embarrassing for the London streets. It was safer than wondering if that day had driven him to isolate himself from the rest of the world. Or if he thought I blamed him for Rose. Or whether he knew that I often found myself on the verge of hysterics when I saw that Lord Byron book in the bedroom.

"What about Mr. Kent? Have you heard from him?" She ushered me past a flower seller, trying hard to be cheerful.

"Yes, he's well . . . and that's why I can't involve him." After I'd helped heal his injuries, Mr. Kent had sent flowers and letters, but I was in no state to respond to them, and he was in no position to receive replies. Any further contact would only cause more trouble within his difficult family.

Miss Grey nodded firmly and surveyed the street as we rounded a corner. "All the more reason why you and I cannot sit idle. I think there is a particular role we must each play. A purpose. Our abilities are too unique and too specific to have emerged entirely by chance, as the saltation theory suggests. I believe I am the one meant to find others like us. I ignored it for long enough, and I . . . I wonder how things might be different had I taken up the responsibility earlier."

"But what are you supposed to do when you find others?" I asked.

"Gather and connect us all, teach them what we are, offer protection. Anything to keep what happened with Dr. Beck from happening again. As far as we know, I am the only one who can locate other extraordinary individuals, and it feels as if it would be a waste of a gift to not use it."

We found ourselves on Great Ormond Street, standing before the hospital entrance. An unhelpful fairy that sounded very much like Rose seemed to whisper in my ear, nudging me to answer my own unspoken question: Would it be a waste if I didn't try to heal every sick and injured person in the world?

As we entered the three-story building and claimed to be visitors on behalf of some fictitious Christian children's rescue society,

I couldn't help but wish someone would see through the lie and send me back to my bed, away from Miss Grey and her ideas of responsibility and purpose. Could I not sleep away the rest of my life? Could I not let others hold the world on their back?

But the busy woman at the front waved us in when Miss Grey pulled out her Bible as irrefutable proof, and I found my feet following her. A nurse asked us the patient's name and led us down a clean, gaslit hallway, passing room after room until she veered into a boy's ward at the end. About twenty beds filled the room, all occupied by ill and injured boys between the ages of five and fourteen. Some of them had a doting mother or father by their side, some had a concerned nurse, and a few had only a book or a toy to keep them company. One of those few, in the far corner of the room, was Oliver Myles, though it seemed like a mistake. Such a young boy couldn't have a power yet.

But after the nurse made the introductions and left to help another patient, I saw from closer inspection of his thin face that he was probably fourteen years old—just sadly undersized from malnourishment. We found two chairs and took our places at his bedside.

"I ain't working in a factory," the boy said defensively, eyes dull and determined, hidden beneath his fair hair. It sounded as if he'd had this conversation before.

"Don't worry. We aren't that sort of rescue society," Miss Grey said soothingly. "We haven't come to force you into a job."

She looked to me, but I glared back. This was her insane idea. She should handle it. With thinned lips, Miss Grey continued. "We just want to help you if you need it. Is any of your family here?"

He frowned, looking suspicious. "I've got friends who'll take care of me till I'm on my feet again."

"But do your friends know about your extraordinary gift?" she asked, leaning in confidentially.

His eyes widened, and he suddenly sank and vanished into his sheets. A thud and a yelp of pain came from below, and I found him on the floor underneath the bed, wincing and holding his leg. Some of the boys around us noticed the commotion as Miss Grey and I scrambled to lift him back up to his bed. Fortunately, the nurses were too busy to notice.

"Here, this will help," I said, relenting and grasping the knee of his injured leg. "Just don't slip away again."

"I can't help it," he said. "Sometimes I lose my hold and fall through walls or floors."

"Is that how you got these injuries?" Miss Grey asked.

He nodded. "It was the stairs that time. But no one believes me. When I try and prove it, it don't work. How did you two know about me?" He lowered his voice and raised his head closer. "Can you do it, too?"

Miss Grey shook her head. "We have our own gifts. When I sleep, I can dream of anyone else with a special gift—that is how we found you. And Miss Wyndham here can heal others. With her hand on your leg, in a few minutes, it'll be as if you never got hurt."

He looked at my hand in disbelief, then back up to me. "Will you visit me every time I get hurt?"

My lips twitched against my will, and in a room with a healer, a dreamer, and a ghost, this moment of happiness felt like the strangest thing there. I tried to stifle it back, waging a silent war within myself between the manageable numbness and the overwhelming pain, thinking the choice was obvious. But I watched as Miss Grey told Oliver all about the powers, teaching him with the same comforting authority I remembered as a girl. I watched as Oliver gasped in wonder and excitement, the world finally making a little more sense. And I watched as Oliver's broken arm and leg were restored to full health, a miracle I could never imagine feeling commonplace. There were countless others out there who needed the same help, but strangely, now it didn't feel quite so daunting and futile. It felt almost comforting, the fact that there would always be more. For the first time in a while, I had that excited rush of a new idea, a new plan unfurling in my head.

"Instead of a visit every time you are hurt, how would you like to accompany us and rescue some new friends?" I asked.

Oliver's eyes danced with excitement. "Really?"

I nodded. "Miss Grey, where did you say that asylum was?"

Her head snapped up at that, though I could not tell if it was in excitement, trepidation, or both. "B-Belgium. In the south."

Well, I had always wanted to see the Continent. I turned to Miss Grey and Oliver. The muscles of my mouth contorted to a smile for the first time in a month.

"All right. I have no other plans. Let's go save a life."

Acknowledgments

Fɪʀsᴛ ᴀɴᴅ ꜰᴏʀᴇᴍᴏsᴛ: to the Swoon Reads team, thank you. This process has been a dream, and we are still pinching ourselves to make sure it's . . . *not* a dream, actually. Jean, thank you for believing in us. Lauren, thank you for all your cheerleading, late hours, and answers to our silliest questions. Emily, you're such a delight and we know this book wouldn't be what it is without you. Rich and KB, thank you for our cover. It's better than we could have ever imagined. And finally, Holly: What would we do without you? Thank you so much for picking up *These Vicious Masks* and for the handholding and hours of editing since. We are a little in awe of you, and eternally grateful. To the rest of the stunning Swoon Reads team, thank you so much for all your efforts on our behalf. We appreciate it more than we can say here.

But before our manuscript ever reached the Swoon Reads site, we had many wonderful readers and cheerleaders. First, Laura Gillis who spent hours championing us and helping us rewrite. Thank you, Laura, for all your time and support. Kyra Nelson, thank you for your notes and advice and for being Mr. Braddock's earliest fan. Elliot Handler, thank you for answering our endless medical questions and for being the first person to read that messy first draft, making us believe it really could someday be a book. To our other friends and family who read this book at various stages and gave us hope, ideas, and enthusiasm when we were lagging: Beth Latz, Peter Richman, Alex Ricciardi, Zelda Knapp, Eric

Messinger, Calaine Schafer, Frederika and Isabella Reinhardt, Vanessa Santos, Erin Keskeny, the Floe family, Dayle Towarnicky, Cayla O'Connell, Katie Owen and, surely more. We love you guys a lot.

To the creative, hungry, funny, and kind people we have met on Swoon Reads, we are so thankful for your feedback and comments and ratings. It's been an absolute pleasure to be a part of this community and 100 percent impossible to do this without you. Thank you.

To Lee Jackson, Judith Flanders, and the person at Google Books who scanned all the nineteenth-century texts, thank you for creating amazing and accessible Victorian resources. We don't know how we could have dealt with the historical research if you didn't exist.

To Jude Morgan, Kelly would be an entirely different person if it weren't for your writing. Thank you for inspiring her with every book you write.

Finally, to our ever-patient, ever-supportive, and number one fans: our parents. Thank you. We love you. Having a writer for a child must be deeply nerve-wracking, but thank you for never giving up on us—or letting us give up on ourselves.

For anyone we forgot, it's because we hate you.

No, no—kidding! We're saving you for book two. Hope you understand.

Lots of love,
Tarun and Kelly

Turn the page for some

Sw♥♥nworthy

Extras....

From the diary of
Miss Laura Kent, soon to be
Mrs. Laura Edwards

Friday, 2.00 p.m.:

    This is it! This is the week my life will change, irrevocably! (Nick taught me that word last month. He was feeling not quite the thing one morning and said he has made some choices the evening before that would change him, "irrevocably"!)

    You see, my dearest diary, this is the week that Mr. Edwards will finally notice me, at the play on Thursday! I will be everything he could ever want in a wife!

Mrs. Laura Edwards.

Mrs. Laura Edwards.   Mrs. Laura Edwards.

Saturday, 10.00 a.m.:

    I have it! The red dress! Or no, that should be for the dinner on Monday.

    Mrs. Laura Edwards. Mrs. Laura Edwards. Mrs. Laura Edwards.

Sunday, 4.00 p.m.:

    <u>Evelyn Wyndham is here!</u> This is truly, the most absolutely perfect and wonderful week.

Swoon Reads

Sunday, 9:00 p.m.:

Dearest Diary, it is my greatest suspicion that Evelyn and Nick are in love! How wonderful would that be! We can have a double wedding! After Evelyn finds her sister, that is.

Mrs. Laura Edwards. Mrs. Laura Edwards. Mrs. Laura Edwards.

Monday, 7:00 p.m.:

Dearest Diary, I accompanied Evelyn and Nick today in their search of her sister, who is missing, and I have not told a soul, no not one! Even though it is a very large secret and I am quite desperate to speak of it. I feel rather like a spy! I wonder if Mr. Edwards will notice how mature I have become this week.

Thursday, 8:00 a.m.:

Tis Thursday! Tis the most glorious day of the week! I have <u>nothing to wear</u>!!

Thursday, 2:00 p.m.:

Have tried on every dress I own. Narrowed down to a favorite fifteen.

Thursday, 4:00 p.m.:

Favorite five, though it was extremely difficult.

Thursday, 6:30 p.m.:

Evelyn will help me woo Mr. Edwards!!

Swoon Reads

Friday, 2.00 a.m.:

Evelyn did <u>not help me with him.</u> she is quite dead to me.

Friday 3.00 p.m.:

I am feeling very badly about saying Evelyn is dead to me.

Friday, 9.00 p.m.:

Mother wants to kick Evelyn out of the house! It is dreadfully unfair as she is not really a loose lady! Mother just doesn't know about her Sensitive and Secret Mission! This is absolutely and most positively the worst thing that has ever happened to me. I shall burn the house to the ground!

Friday, 11.00 p.m.:

Nick found me out with the matches. He was terribly stern but also seemed somewhat amused. I don't believe he thinks me serious at all. Little does he realize I can simply use the fireplace!

From the household notes of Edmund Tuffins

Saturday

During teatime today, Mrs. Hobson barely managed to ask me, through her stifled giggles, if I had any muffins. I spent the night preparing my letter of resignation.

Sunday

An unnecessary set of calling cards arrived for Miss Kent this morning. She had ordered them to be printed with the name "Mrs. Laura Edwards." I do hope Miss Wyndham proves to be an edifying influence on the young girl.

Monday

Miss Wyndham feigned an illness, sneaked out of the house, and walked the London streets unaccompanied for most of the night. At the very least, I'd say she's a better influence on Miss Kent than Lady Kent is.

Tuesday

Between her excursion last night and her "cousin's" visit this morning, Miss Wyndham has been the subject of a great deal of gossip among the housestaff. But when I joined in with a rumor about how anyone unable to hold their tongues would be unable to keep hold of their jobs, the conversation died rather quickly.

Swoon Reads

Wednesday

Miss Wyndham returned very late last night, covered in blood. I still believe she's a better influence than my mistress.

Thursday

Everyone has gone to the theater tonight, so perhaps I will do something fun myself. I might even polish the silver.

Friday

While overseeing tonight's dinner party, I finally found myself in the presence of Mr. Edwards's famed wit when he asked me whether I had visited the zoo to see the puffins. Somehow Miss Wyndham was the one forced to leave the house.

Saturday

Miss Kent is still quite distraught from last night. She claims to have no desire for the matches since the last incident, but we are being cautious. Perhaps I'll hold on to that letter of resignation.

A Coffee Date

with authors Tarun Shanker and Kelly Zekas
and their editor, Holly West

"About the Authors"

Holly West (HW): What was the first romance novel you ever read?
Kelly Zekas (KZ): I was thinking about this and I realized it's kind of crazy. You know the Berenstain Bears books? There was one about Brother Bear being in a *Romeo and Juliet* play with a girl bear whose family was feuding with his father. And I was *obsessed* with this book. I read it, like, twenty times. I have no idea. I don't remember anything about it except that they were in *Romeo and Juliet* and they had to kiss and he would blush every time. So I'm pretty sure that was the first romance novel I ever read.
Tarun Shanker (TS): Is that where you started liking Shakespeare from?
KZ: I think I already liked Shakespeare, so that it was even more amazing.
TS: I don't have as good a story as that. I can't even remember. I just read weird-ass books as a kid. So I think the first romance was probably *Jane Eyre* in high school, and I didn't even like it, and now it's one of my favorite books, weirdly.

HW: Do you have an OTP (One True Pairing)? Like your favorite fictional couple?
TS: Yes. I don't know if this is going to last for a while, but this happened while we were in between edits. Have you ever read Sarah Waters? She wrote *Fingersmith* and *Tipping the Velvet*. She writes lesbian Victorian fiction. I read *Fingersmith* and the two girls in that, Sue and Maud . . . I had to put the book down because they're amazing. Hopefully in a year I'll still like them just as much. I don't know if it's because I just read it. The other one is probably Anne Elliot and Captain Wentworth in *Persuasion*. That stands the test of time.
KZ: I have both fiction in general and young adult. Fiction in general: Beatrice and Benedick from *Much Ado About Nothing*. They are my heart and soul. And at least for right now I'd say Eleanor and Park. I love them

Swoon Reads

so much. They're so great and they make me so happy. That book ruined me for weeks. I'm not the same person I was before I read it.

HW: This one is one of my favorite questions and is also very valid for *These Vicious Masks*. If you were a superhero, what would your superpower be?
TS: Telekinesis, just because I've thought about this way too much and I can do so many things with it. I can make myself fly or freak people out, or, if I really wanted to throw fire at people, I could just carry fire around, too. It's all-encompassing.
KZ: I took this one a little differently. Like, not which one would I want, but which one would I have. I think my superpower would be matchmaking. Being able to see who someone's soul mate is. I have paired so many people together. I feel like it's my secret talent. I kind of want to be a matchmaker for a living.
TS: That sounds like a good novel idea. A superhero with that ability.
KZ: Right?! Spinoff.

HW: Do you have any hobbies other than writing? Because writing no longer counts as a hobby. Once you're being paid for it, it doesn't count.
KZ: Well, I act as well as write. So I work in New York in a bunch of theater companies. And no one really pays me, so I think it could still be called a hobby. Also I'm the world's worst crocheter. Like, truly, truly bad.
TS: You made a scarf. You made lots of scarves.
KZ: I did. And they were very, very bad.

"The Writing Life"

HW: When did you first realize you wanted to be a writer?
TS: Probably tenth grade when I took a film class in high school. I was always movie-obsessed, but it kind of made me think, "Oh, I can actually do this seriously. And people will actually take me seriously." So I was reviewing movies, and then when that got annoying, I realized I should try writing myself, and that's just kind of turned from screenplays to novels.
KZ: Mine was much, much later. Tarun and I went to school together and we were in college, and he was talking to me about writing a young adult

novel because he knew I loved young adult novels, and it was something he thought he might want to try his hand at. And I did not consider myself a writer of any kind, but I was a voracious reader and definitely knew the YA world and markets and things like that, so I said I would totally help. At first it was more like he would write, or we came up with the concepts together, but then he was writing and I was kind of more editing. And then somewhere along the way it just started kind of evolving into us both writing and kind of writing over each other and over each other so we don't even know who wrote what. Although we do like to argue about who wrote what sometimes.

TS: Yeah, because I like to keep in my head what amazing lines I came up with.

KZ: The other day I said, "This sounds like a great line that I wrote," and he said, "No, that was me."

HW: What's it like working so closely with each other writing the same book?
KZ: Great.

TS: When I write by myself now it feels like something's missing. Every time I write something it's like Kelly isn't here to tell me this is stupid or that this is a good idea. So just having the extra support is really good.

KZ: We both trust each other as writers, so it's not like you hate everything the other person's doing and just can't say it.

HW: So what's your process? Do you outline things or start at the beginning and make it up as you go bouncing back and forth?
KZ: Well, we did just start a new document in Google Docs right now entitled "These Vicious Masks Book 2 Very Stupid Ideas." So we outline, because Tarun makes us outline, and we should.

TS: Yeah, I kind of go crazy.

HW: Do you have any writing rituals, like a certain place you are when you write, or anything like that?
TS: I'm literally sitting in the place that I write. It's just my dining table, and I always have tea or coffee. Actually, half the time that I'm writing, I'm not even

sitting in front of the keyboard, I'm just pacing around my apartment thinking up how to phrase the sentences, and then I just stop off at my keyboard and put it down and then start walking around again. It's weird, but it works.

KZ: I write everywhere. This last round of edits, Tarun would be finishing something on L.A. time, and then the next morning on the subway I would edit it. So I'll write anywhere, anytime, any place that I have a moment to.

TS: Yeah, I don't know how you do that. I can only write at home now.

KZ: I'm very impressive is how.

HW: So how does the revision process work?

TS: I feel like we had to go through this process a couple times before Swoon Reads, because when we were querying, a couple times they gave us a big structural change or a few smaller changes, and I think we figured out a pattern at that point. We always just focus on the biggest issues we have in the back of our mind, and even if we can't solve it, we're thinking about it while we jump around and deal with other things. And I guess it's assigning specific subjects, like you handle all the Mr. Kent stuff, or anything thematically related.

KZ: Or chapters. It's like picking a dodgeball team with that stuff. We each get to pick favorites until we're down to whatever one we don't want to do, but someone has to. Also, I write faster and worse, and Tarun writes more detailed and better, so sometimes depending on how many changes we need, if it's a lot of things, I might do the first draft of that and then he'll go in and make it better. Sometimes we do it that way, too. Especially if there's a time crunch.

HW: One last question: What's the best writing advice you've ever heard?

KZ: This is from an author, Chuck Wendig, and he says, "Writing is when we make the words. Editing is when we make the words not shitty." And that's my favorite thing I've ever heard.

TS: For me, I don't think it was as much advice as process. I took a screenwriting course at NYU where I had this teacher who his way of giving feedback was just like, after the kids talk about your script, he just bombards you with questions. Like, what-ifs. What if this happens? What if that happens? And they don't all go together at all. He doesn't have a cohesive vision. He's just throwing so many questions at you. It changed my way of thinking in terms of I shouldn't be so beholden to anything I have in my script. You can always think of some what-if that makes it better. It just made me think of feedback differently. You just kind of accept everything for a little while and see how it makes you feel. Then you just go with the suggestions you like or not.

These Vicious Masks
Discussion Questions

1. The title of the book is *These Vicious Masks*. Why do you think the authors chose that title? What roles do masks play in the novel?

2. At the beginning of the book, Evelyn would much rather be traveling in Europe with her friend than attending a ball so her mother can play matchmaker. Do you agree with her decision to be deliberately miserable? Have you ever been forced to do something with your parents instead of hanging out with your friends?

3. When Rose goes missing, Evelyn's parents, believing she has shamefully run away, do nothing. Given how important reputation was in that time period, do you think that their reaction was understandable? Or were they simply wrong?

4. When Sebastian first tells Evelyn about having special powers, she thinks he's out of his mind. How do you think you would react if someone told you the same thing?

5. Mr. Kent's power forces everyone to answer his questions honestly. Would you want this power? Why or why not?

6. Sebastian can't be too close to anyone for an extended period of time or else his power will kill them. What do you think this means for his future? Could he ever possibly have a normal life with a family?

7. Which gentleman would you rather see Evelyn end up with: Sebastian or Mr. Kent? Explain.

8. If you had Camille's power to change your appearance however you would like, who would you choose to look like and why?

9. At one point in the book, Sebastian is chastised for choosing to let Dr. Beck live. Do you think Dr. Beck deserved to die for his actions?

10. *These Vicious Masks* takes place in Victorian England. How important is the setting to the novel? How would the story have been different if it had been set in the modern day?

SwoonReads

Plans for a season without romance are unapologetically foiled . . .

In which plans for a season without romance are unapologetically foiled.

LOVE,
LIES *and*
SPIES

Cindy Anstey

in this hilarious homage to Jane Austen, when a lady with a penchant for
trouble finds a handsome spy much more than merely tolerable.

APRIL 2016

CHAPTER

1

*In which a young lady clinging to a cliff
will eventually accept anyone's help*

"OH MY, this is embarrassing," Miss Juliana Telford said aloud. There was no reason to keep her thoughts to herself, as she was alone, completely alone. In fact, that was half of the problem. The other half was, of course, that she was hanging off the side of a cliff with the inability to climb either up or down and in dire need of rescue.

"Another scrape. This will definitely give Aunt apoplexy."

Juliana hugged the cliff ever closer and tipped her head slightly so that she could glance over her shoulder. Her high-waisted ivory dress was deeply soiled across her right hip, where she had slid across the earth as she dropped over the edge.

Juliana shifted slowly and glanced over her other shoulder. Fortunately, the left side showed no signs of distress, and her lilac sarcenet spencer could be brushed off easily. She would do it now were it not for the fact that her hands were engaged, holding tightly to the tangle of roots that kept her from falling off the tiny ledge.

Juliana continued to scrutinize the damage to her wardrobe with regret, not for herself so much as for her aunt, who seemed to deem such matters of great importance. Unfortunately, her eyes wandered down to her shoes. Just beyond them yawned an abyss. It was all too apparent how far above the crashing waves of the English Channel she was—and how very small the ledge.

Despite squishing her toes into the rock face as tightly as possible, Juliana's heels were only just barely accommodated by the jutting amalgamate. The occasional skitter and plop of eroding rocks diving into the depths of the brackish water did nothing to calm her racing heart.

Juliana swallowed convulsively. "Most embarrassing." She shivered despite a warm April breeze. "I shall be considered completely beyond the pale if I am dashed upon the rocks. Aunt will be so uncomfortable. Most inconsiderate of me."

A small shower of sandy pebbles rained down on Juliana's flowery bonnet. She shook the dust from her eyes and listened. She thought she had heard a voice.

Please, she prayed, let it be a farmer or a tradesman, someone not of the gentry. No one who would feel obligated to report back to Grays Hill Park. No gentlemen, please.

"Hello?" she called out. Juliana craned her neck upward,

trying to see beyond the roots and accumulated thatch at the cliff's edge.

A head appeared. A rather handsome head. He had dark, almost black, hair and clear blue eyes and, if one were to notice such things at a time like this, a friendly, lopsided smile.

"Need some assistance?" the head asked with a hint of sarcasm and the tone of a . . .

"Are you a gentleman?" Juliana inquired politely.

The head looked startled, frowned slightly, and then raised an eyebrow before answering. "Yes, indeed, I am—"

"Please, I do not wish to be rescued by a gentleman. Could you find a farmer or a shopkeep—anyone not of the gentry— and then do me the great favor of forgetting you saw me?"

Mild-mannered assistant by day, milder-mannered writer by night, **TARUN SHANKER** is a New York University graduate currently living in Los Angeles. His idea of paradise is a place where kung fu movies are projected on clouds, David Bowie's music fills the air, and chai tea flows freely from fountains.

tarunshanker.com

Tim Goodwin Photography

KELLY ZEKAS, a New York University graduate, writes, acts, and reads in New York City. YA is her absolute favorite thing on earth (other than cupcakes), and she has spent many hours crying over fictional deaths. She also started reading Harlequin romances at a possibly too-early age (twelve?) and still loves a good historical romance.

kellyzekas.com

These Vicious Masks is their first novel.